Insatiable

Cloverleigh Farms
Series

Melanie Harlow

Cover Photography: Regina Wamba
Cover Design: Hang Le
Editing: Evident Ink
Paperback Formatting: Champagne Book Design
Promotions: Social Butterfly PR

For my Family

The richest love is that which submits to the arbitration of time.
Lawrence Durrell

One

Noah

HER NAME WAS DOTTIE, HER AGE WAS SOMEWHERE north of ninety, and she was what we at the sheriff's department called a "frequent flyer."

It was nearly seven P.M. on Friday night as I pulled up in front of her house. It had been a slow shift so far, mostly routine traffic stops and a few non-emergency calls, but in a small town like Hadley Harbor, that was the norm.

Dottie was definitely a non-emergency.

She'd called 911—this time—because she was positive someone had broken into her home this afternoon while she was grocery shopping, and while the intruder hadn't stolen anything, he *had* switched her living room furniture around. I hadn't even bothered with the lights on my vehicle.

"Be right back, Renzo." Leaving my faithful Belgian Malinois in the back of the Explorer—and the expression on his face told me he wasn't happy about that—I got out from behind the wheel and headed up the walk. From the window, Renzo watched me like a hawk, as he always did, but there was nothing dangerous about this call.

Still, it was good to know he had my back, no matter what.

I knocked on the front door of the traditional, two-story brick home, and less than ten seconds later, Dottie Jensen opened it and beamed at me, her dentures on full display. She'd probably been peeking out the window. "Oh, hello, Deputy McCormick. I was hoping it would be you."

"Hello, Mrs. Jensen. It's me."

She looked over my shoulder toward the street, where my K-9 unit was parked. "Didn't you bring your doggy with you?"

The same questions every time. I took a breath for patience and answered them. Again. "Yes, he's always with me. But he's in the car."

"Won't it be too warm for him in the car?"

"It's a cool evening, and we have temperature control in the unit."

"Wouldn't he like to come inside?"

"Why don't I come in and look around, and then once you've told me what happened and I have all the info, I'll let him out so you can say hello."

"That sounds lovely," she said eagerly. "Please come in."

"Thank you."

She pulled the door open wider and stood aside as I entered the front hallway. The house was silent and smelled like a combination of furniture polish and whatever she'd made for dinner.

"Can I get you anything?" she asked. "A lemonade? Some cookies? Or how about dinner? I got some beautiful pork chops at the butcher this afternoon and fried them up for supper. Do you like them with applesauce?"

"No thank you, ma'am." Although hunger was gnawing

at my belly, I had to stick to routine. Lonely old Mrs. Jensen would keep me here for hours if I let her. I felt sorry for her—her husband of sixty-plus years had died only a few months ago—and I always gave her a little extra time if I could, but I was off duty in about twenty minutes and wanted to get home in time to watch game three of the World Series.

From the front entryway, I glanced into the living room on my right, then the dining room on my left. Each room looked *exactly* the same as it had the last time I'd been there. "I understand you believe someone broke in?"

"Oh, yes. I'm just sure of it." Mrs. Jensen clasped her gnarled fingers together and opened her eyes wide. Her forehead wrinkles multiplied.

"Want to tell me what happened?"

She nodded and smiled as if I'd just crowned her Queen of England. "Yes. You see, I was in town shopping for groceries—I was picking up a roast because my son George is coming to visit, and his wife, Sue, never did learn to cook a pot roast like I taught her, but Sue was one of those career girls, you know, and I don't think she cared much about what sort of meals she put on the table at night." She lowered her voice and spoke conspiratorially behind the back of one hand. "Sue wasn't much of a housekeeper either, truth be told, but there isn't much we can do about the people our children choose. Do you have children, dear?"

"No, ma'am." I braced myself for the inevitable follow-up.

"Why not? Doesn't your wife want any?"

"I don't have a wife, either, Mrs. Jensen." Which I'd told her at least fifty times, and *every single time*, she reacted the same way.

"No wife?" She recoiled. "Why, you must be close to thirty already, Deputy McCormick."

"Thirty-three, ma'am."

"Thirty-three! Mr. Jensen and I had already been married twelve years by the time he was thirty-three. And had four children. We had six altogether, you know."

"I know." I thought about the cold beer waiting in my fridge and fought the urge to look at my watch.

"And we were married sixty-seven years before he passed. He died last spring. April ninth."

I knew that too, because that's when her calls to the dispatcher had started, with her "emergencies."

Sometimes she heard noises and thought someone was in her house. Sometimes an item was missing that turned up once an officer arrived and helped her find it. Twice, she'd claimed to have fallen and asked for help getting up, but on both occasions, she'd righted herself and answered the door when the officers knocked. On every occasion, she did anything she could to keep the responders in her house as long as possible, which usually involved offering food, telling her life story, nosing into their personal lives, and giving unsolicited advice.

She was a nonagenarian pain in the ass, and I already had a mother around to give me shit about being a perpetual bachelor—and she gave plenty—but I never much minded coming here and making sure everything was okay, even if it was just to make her feel less lonely. It was part of the job. It was what my dad would have done, and he'd been the most beloved sheriff this county ever had. He understood there was more to *serve and protect* than making arrests or preventing crime.

"Yes, ma'am, I was lucky enough to meet Mr. Jensen several times. All of us at the sheriff's office liked him a lot."

She smiled happily. "He was a dear. And so handsome. All the girls were always trying to catch his eye. Now, isn't there anyone who catches yours?"

"Not at the moment, ma'am."

"But don't you want a family?"

"I've got a family. I think you know my mom, Carol McCormick. She's a nurse over at Harbor Family Practice."

"Oh, of course." Mrs. Jensen nodded. "Carol is just lovely. I knew your father too. We just loved Sheriff McCormick. Both Mr. Jensen and I were so sorry when he passed."

"Thank you. I've also got a twin brother, a sister and brother-in-law, two nephews and a niece, and Renzo. Plenty of family around." I smiled at her and tried to move things along. "So when you came home from town, was your door open? Or unlocked?"

She looked confused for a moment. "Why would I leave the door unlocked?" Then she remembered, snapping her fingers. "Oh! Oh, yes. The front door was open just a hair, but I know I closed and locked it before I left. I'm all alone here, and even though it's a small town, you can never be too careful."

I nodded. "But the house was empty when you came in?"

"Yes. The rascal must have left after he rearranged the furniture."

"But nothing is missing?"

"Not that I can tell," she said, almost regretfully, twisting her hands together as she glanced over her shoulder toward the room in question, as if she was sort of bummed the family silver wasn't gone.

"Mind if I take a look around anyway?"

She looked happy at the suggestion and patted my arm. "Of course not. You go right ahead. Take as long as you want. And while you do that, I'll fix you a nice snack. Mr. Jensen always liked a snack about this time of night."

Rather than argue with her, I said okay and moved into the living room while she went in the opposite direction toward the kitchen. She moved slowly, her steps the cautious shuffling of a little old lady, but she hummed a tune as she went, and I knew I'd given her what she wanted—time and attention.

In the living room, there was no sign any furniture had been moved around. But in case my memory was faulty, I picked up one end of the sofa. The deep indentations the feet had left in the carpet told me it had been resting in this spot for quite some time. Possibly since 1951, which was, I'd been told several times, when the newly wedded Jensens had moved in.

It was a nice house on a quiet street in a peaceful town, the perfect place to raise a family. I glanced at all the framed photos crowded on the fireplace mantel, standing in rows on bookshelves, and clustered on end tables. A room-sized shrine to an entire century's worth of one family's life. A black-and-white wedding photo from the 1920s. Another from the fifties. Babies at christenings. Family pictures showcasing five generations of holidays and weddings and birthdays and anniversaries gone by. Children, grandchildren and great-grandchildren.

I thought of my mother's house, also full of family photos. But much to her eternal woe, there were only two wedding photos—her own and my sister Nina's. She did have three grandchildren and one more on the way, courtesy of Nina and my best friend Chris, who'd gotten married right after our first stint in the Army. Despite the fact that we both signed on for four more years after that and did two additional combat tours apiece, he still managed to knock her up twice during that time and twice *more* since we'd come home.

I didn't much like thinking about the logistics of that, but I did love being an uncle to their kids, eight-year-old Harrison, six-year-old Violet, and fourteen-month-old Ethan. Any day now they'd add that fourth to their brood, and my mother was constantly pestering me about catching up, as if we were in some kind of reproductive race.

In fact, she kept one section on her mantel purposefully empty, and she claimed she was waiting for me to get married and have kids so she could put something there. Every so often when I'm at her place, she'll find a moment to stare at it and sigh longingly, or dust it off with a rag. Last Christmas, I gave her a framed photo of Renzo and me and told her that was as good as it was going to get. She harrumphed, but she kept the photo on proud display. She loved that dog almost as much as I did.

"Yoohoo, Deputy McCormick, your snack is ready!" Mrs. Jensen called.

Exhaling heavily, I retraced my steps and headed through the dining room and back to the kitchen. Mrs. Jensen had set out a plate with a sandwich, some potato chips, and a pickle slice on it. Next to the plate was a glass of milk, and she'd pulled out the chair for me.

"It's a BLT on toasted bread, just like Mr. Jensen used to eat." She laughed and shook her head. "God forbid I ever forgot to toast the bread!"

"Thank you so much, ma'am, but I really can't stay. My shift is about to end, and I need to get back to the station and do some paperwork before I take Renzo home for the night." *And you're cutting in to my baseball time, lady.*

"Oh." She looked crestfallen. "Can you come back when you're through?"

Smiling, I shook my head. "I'm afraid not."

"Well, why don't you let me pack this up for you? No sense in letting it go to waste, is there?"

I thought for a moment. "I guess not."

"Wonderful." The smile was back on her face. "You just give me a minute to put everything in a lunch sack for you, and then you can be on your way."

"Thank you. I looked around the living room, but I didn't see anything out of order. However, if something turns up missing, you just let us know."

"Oh, I will," she said, pulling a brown paper bag from a drawer. "I always call the sheriff when I have an emergency."

And when you don't, I thought to myself. But I couldn't bring myself to be angry about it. I knew what it was like to miss somebody. It got to you sometimes.

A few minutes later, I had the lunch sack in my hand and she was following me down the front walk toward my car. Through the window, I could see Renzo's tail wagging in anticipation. I opened the door, and he hopped onto the grass where we stood, excited and happy. He wore a collar that said K-9 Unit, complete with a sheriff's badge.

"Sit," I told him, and he obeyed. "Good boy."

"May I pet him?" asked Mrs. Jensen.

"Sure."

She patted him on the head a few times. "How old is he again?"

"He's five."

"My, such a big dog for only five. He must weigh a hundred pounds!"

"He's about eighty pounds, which is average."

"He seems very sweet."

"He can be." Off-duty, Renzo was energetic and high-spirited and just wanted to play all the time, but when he was working, he was a well-trained, badass machine—fast, agile, aggressive, vicious if necessary, and loyal to me beyond comprehension. I sometimes felt like I had two sides to me as well, so we were a good match. He'd been at my side every day for three years.

"Can he have a little snack?" Mrs. Jensen asked brightly. "I don't have any dog treats, but maybe a cookie? For being so good?"

I shook my head. "Thanks, but working dogs shouldn't be rewarded with food."

"Why not?"

"Well, we often encounter food items during searches and we don't want him to be distracted by wanting to eat instead of wanting to perform."

"Oh, I see." She sighed wistfully. "I suppose I'll say goodnight, then, Deputy McCormick. Thank you very much for coming."

"Goodnight, Mrs. Jensen. Thanks for the sandwich." I held up the bag as Renzo jumped back into the car.

"You're welcome. I put a treat in there for you, too, dear. It's not homemade, but my little grandkids always used to love them, and even though they're mostly grown now and don't come around as much, I can't seem to stop buying them. Silly of me, isn't it?"

"I understand." I still talked to my dad during ball games, as if he was sitting in the recliner just a few feet away instead of buried in the Catholic cemetery up the road.

"You're such a dear." She smiled, as if inspiration just struck her. "You know what? I have a granddaughter almost your age that I think would be perfect for you. Why don't I—"

"Bye, Mrs. Jensen." Cutting her off, I went around the Explorer and got into the driver's seat. The last thing I wanted was to suffer yet another one of this town's wanna-be matchmakers. Seemed like every busybody within fifty miles of here was convinced she had "the perfect girl" for me to "settle down" with. No matter how many times I said I wasn't looking, it never seemed to sink in.

"Aren't you lonely?" they'd ask.

"Not at all," I'd reply, and it was mostly true. There were times when I missed female company, a sympathetic smile at the end of a hard day. A soft, sexy body at night, somebody to please and play with. But my last breakup had soured me for good on relationships, and the few dates I'd gone on with "perfect" girls had only shown me how well some people could hide their crazy. My sex life was a bit depressing, but nobody ever said, *Hey, Noah, I know this completely sane girl with a killer smile and a rockin' bod just passing through town for a night. Can she come over and blow you?*

Until that day, I'd have to deal with a dry spell here and there.

I entered a few notes about the call on my laptop, and then pulled away from the curb. On the road again, I dug out the sandwich and took a bite as I headed for the station. I hadn't had a BLT in forever, and actually, it tasted pretty fucking good.

"She's not so bad, is she?" I asked Renzo. "A little off her rocker, maybe, but I guess she's earned it."

By the time I pulled into the parking lot behind the

sheriff's department, I'd finished the sandwich, the chips, and the pickle. I remembered what she'd said about the little extra treat, and I dug around in the bag with my free hand.

I pulled out a Twinkie and laughed.

It reminded me of someone.

Two

Meg

FOR AS LONG AS I CAN REMEMBER, I HAVE DEALT WITH extreme stress by eating Twinkies.

Like, a ridiculous amount of Twinkies.

It is totally juvenile and absurdly unhealthy and my arteries are probably already clogged beyond repair with delicious golden sponge cake and fluffy sweet cream filling, but I can't help it—there's just something so comforting about them.

However, not even my favorite Hostess snack cakes were going to take the edge off coming home on a Friday night to find my boyfriend of three years packing his bags.

"What do you mean, you're leaving?" I stared at Brooks in disbelief, watching from the bedroom doorway as he methodically stacked neatly folded, pristinely white undershirts in his suitcase.

"I took the job at that firm in Manhattan. My train leaves tonight."

"Tonight!" I moved into the room, my stomach lurching. "You're moving to Manhattan *tonight*?"

"Yes," he said calmly.

"But . . . but what about us?"

"Come on, Meg. You know there's no us anymore." His voice held no emotion whatsoever.

Usually I appreciated his unflappable demeanor—it was a good, calm yin to my more excitable yang—but I couldn't help feeling blindsided by this turn of events and a little annoyed he wasn't displaying any feeling at all. Three years was a long time, even if the last one hadn't been very good. "Can't we talk about this?"

"We *have* talked about this, Meg." Next to the undershirts, he added a pile of navy blue and hunter green boxer briefs—in all the time we'd been together, I'd only ever seen Brooks were underwear in those two colors. "We talked about it during the holidays, we talked about it over the summer, and we talked about it last month, before I interviewed in New York."

"I know, but . . . I guess I didn't think it was a real thing." The panic rose from my stomach to my chest. If Brooks really was leaving, this would be my *third failed relationship* in a row. That wasn't just bad luck. That was a pattern. A cycle. Maybe even a curse.

Brooks stopped halfway between his closet and the bed with a garment bag in his hands and looked at me, a serious expression on his handsome face. "You *chose* not to think of it as a real thing. I told you it was."

I chewed my thumbnail, knowing he was right.

"We've barely even seen each other for weeks." He laid the garment bag out on the bed and went back to the closet.

"Well . . ." I searched frantically for a line of defense. "You're a night owl, and I'm an early bird. I go to bed before you get home, and I'm always up and out in the morning before you. It's hard."

"That is all true." He returned to the bed with an armful of shirts on identical wooden hangers. "But that is not how a relationship should be."

"We've both been really busy with work too." Brooks and I were both attorneys, although he worked for the Department of Justice—last I knew, anyway—and I'd traded practicing law to work as a campaign strategist. Our jobs were demanding and important. There were late night meetings and early morning conference calls, tight deadlines and high stakes. "It's been hard to connect."

"It's more than that." Brooks started slipping shirts into the bag. "There's nothing between us anymore, Meg. We haven't had sex in months."

"That's not entirely true. We tried that one night, but you fell asleep. That wasn't my fault." Although it had sort of *felt* like my fault—Brooks had given it some effort, but had been unable to, ahem, rise to the occasion. Secretly, I'd been kind of relieved, but another part of me wondered why I didn't do it for him anymore.

"I'm not blaming you. I'm just stating the facts," he said. Brooks was always *just stating the facts*. "And be honest. Have you missed it?"

I bit my lip. I hadn't missed sex with Brooks, and he probably hadn't missed it with me. Things in the bedroom had grown staid. Boring. Predictable.

For a while I'd been telling myself to put more effort into it—buy some lingerie, talk dirty, offer to give him a blowjob . . . but I hadn't done anything to turn up the heat. "Maybe we could try harder," I suggested without much feeling.

"No, Meg. We shouldn't have to try so hard. We both deserve a relationship that doesn't feel like another job."

I stared at his shoes, expensive brown leather cap-toe oxfords, perfectly polished, an excellent complement to his navy blue suit. My eyes roamed up the tailored legs of his pants to his starched white dress shirt and tightly knotted striped tie. At six o'clock, his shave was still close, and his dark blond hair looked freshly trimmed—he had a standing appointment every three weeks. He was tall, toned, and handsome—straight out of a men's cologne ad in a magazine.

But looking at him, I felt no stir of physical attraction, no heat pooling inside me, no desire to rip that expensive suit off him and *pounce*. Nor, it was clear, did he feel the urge to pounce on me.

"I'll continue to pay half the rent until the end of the year," he went on. "That gives you time to decide whether you'd like to take over the whole lease, move to a smaller place, or get a roommate."

As the reality of being left alone again sank in, I lowered myself to the bed. "Oh, God."

Brooks finally stopped packing and sat beside me. "I'm not doing this to hurt you."

I took a deep breath and let it out, trying to sift through my complicated feelings. "I'm not hurt, exactly . . . I'm—I don't know what I am. Disappointed. Embarrassed. Angry. And maybe a *little* hurt. Were you just going to leave without even saying goodbye?"

He shrugged. "You know how I am. I didn't want a scene. I assumed you'd be working late as usual, and I could be in and out of here before you got home. I was planning to email you."

"Email me!" I gaped at him. "To end a *three-year* relationship?"

"Or call you," he added quickly. "I hadn't quite decided yet. But to be fair, Meg, our relationship ended a long time ago. We were both just too stubborn—or too busy—to deal with a breakup."

I closed my eyes, fighting tears.

"The last few months only made it clearer to me," he said. "We didn't love each other enough to fight for it."

Deep down, I knew he was right, but even though he'd said *we*, what I heard was *I didn't love you enough to fight for you.*

Maybe it was unfair to twist his words like that, but I couldn't help it. Especially since all my relationships tended to end like this—they just fizzled out. No real drama. No huge scene. No *fight*.

"How come I'm so bad at this?" I heard myself asking.

"Bad at what?"

"Relationships. I mean, I'm thirty-three already. Why can't I get it right?"

"Do you want the truth?"

"I don't know. Do I?"

"It's because you never put your relationships first. You don't even put yourself first. It's always your job. And I'm not saying that to attack you—I'm just stating the facts."

I would not miss Brooks just *stating the facts*.

Not that he was wrong. I'd always been somewhat of a workaholic. A perfectionist. Even as a kid, I did all the extra credit problems. Volunteered to lead the group projects. Read ahead in the book. I stayed up late making sure my homework assignments were perfectly correct and I obsessed over my penmanship. It made me feel *good*. Teachers praised me. My parents bragged about my grades and self-motivation. I won prizes and scholarships and essay contests.

Working hard and being successful was what I did best—and hadn't it gotten me what I had now? A law degree? A great job? A name for myself in a fiercely competitive field?

Of course it had, and I was proud of everything I had accomplished.

But I was beginning to see that it had come with a price.

As soon as Brooks was gone, I traded my work suit and sensible pumps for sweats and fuzzy socks, threw my hair in a messy knot on the top of my head, and headed straight for the pantry, where I kept an emergency stash of booze and Twinkies. Then I made myself a margarita, plunked myself on the living floor, and proceeded to consume a stupid amount of sugar, salt, fat, and alcohol while binge-watching *Law & Order* and trying not to think about the sad state of my personal life.

But two drinks and four Twinkies in, I thought I might need an intervention.

Desperate for someone to tell me I wasn't going to die sad and alone, surrounded by Hostess wrappers, I picked up my cell and tried calling my sister April. I had four sisters, but April was the one I'd been closest to growing up. My sister Chloe was actually nearest to me in age (only fourteen months younger), but she'd been such a handful as a kid, April had often ended up in charge of me. Even though she was only two years older, she was always the caretaker.

Plus, now that Frannie, the baby of the family at twenty-seven, was getting married, and Chloe was recently engaged, that left April and me as the last two single Sawyer sisters. (The oldest, Sylvia, had gotten married right after college.)

We hadn't talked about it much, but I felt like April might be the only one who'd understand me right now. Or at least help me make some sense of what I was feeling—otherwise I saw myself consuming a potentially *lethal* amount of golden sponge cake and fluffy sweet cream filling tonight.

When April didn't answer my call, I texted my friend Noah, a sheriff's deputy in my hometown and one of my closest friends from high school. We hadn't spoken in a couple months, and I hadn't actually *seen* him in a few years, but that's how it was with us. We'd go for long periods of time without talking, but once one of us bothered to pick up the phone or get on a plane, it was like no time had gone by.

Plus, he'd saved my life once. I figured he was kind of responsible for me after that.

Me: Hey.

Noah: Hey. I was just thinking about you.

Me: Have you ever responded to a 911 call that involved death by Twinkies?

Noah: Not specifically.

Me: Good.

Noah: Do you require emergency assistance, Sawyer?

Me: Not yet.

Noah: Ok. If you do, I recommend 911 and not my cell phone. I'm at least 700 miles away. And while Death by Twinkie is likely a slow way to go, I may not arrive in time.

Me: Would you at least try?

Noah: For you, always.

That made me smile.

And then.

Noah: But maybe you should lay off the Twinkies.

Me: FUCK YOU I HAVE TRIED.

Noah: Can't you take up some other bad habit?

Me: Like what?

Noah: I don't know. Something that will do you in faster. How about cliff diving?

Me: No way.

Noah: Playing with matches?

Me: Not interested.

Noah: Sword swallowing?

Me: You wish.

Noah: Hahaha. I was not referring to my sword. Although it could potentially do some damage, I assure you.

Me: You're a pig. I don't know why I texted you. GOODBYE FOREVER.

Noah: That's it? I'm never going to hear from you again?

Me: Would you even care?

It was a childish response, but I was not feeling the love from any direction tonight. I wanted to hear that I mattered to someone.

Noah: Don't be a dickhead, Sawyer. You know I would.

Immediately, I felt better. And a little silly.

Me: Sorry. I had a really bad day.

My phone began buzzing a moment later. *Noah McCormick calling.* "Hello?"

"Hey."

"Are you at work?" I pictured him in his uniform, sitting in his black and white Explorer. Short dark hair. Soft brown eyes with thick lashes. Neatly groomed scruff covering a solid jaw. And big strong arms. I'd always liked his arms.

"I'm home now," he said. "So what's up?"

"My cholesterol. My blood pressure. Possibly my time on earth."

His laughter was deep and resonant. "What's the matter?"

I eyed a fifth golden snack cake. "I'm stress eating Twinkies. But I also have margaritas," I added in an effort to sound more adult.

"Twinkies and tequila. Classy."

I took a big swallow and set the glass down. "I try."

"So what happened?"

"I failed at another relationship."

"With the boyfriend? What the hell was his name again, River?"

"Brooks." I took another sip. "But he's not my boyfriend anymore. He left me."

"Oh yeah? When?"

"Tonight. I came home from work to find him packing his bags." The memory had me grabbing that fifth Twinkie and taking a bite.

"Huh. Out of nowhere?"

"Not really. Things weren't great with us." I chewed and swallowed. "But it's so humiliating. I keep getting dumped. What's wrong with me, Noah?"

"Nothing, other than the fact that you're making me miss the start of the game."

"Maybe that's it. I'm selfish."

He sighed. "Sawyer, you spent all your college summers building houses for Habitat for Humanity. You're not selfish."

Tossing the rest of the uneaten Twinkie aside, I jumped up and began pacing back and forth in front of the couch. "Am I too picky?"

"You should be picky. There's a lot of assholes out there."

"Maybe I'm a terrible fuck."

"Somehow I doubt that."

"But you can't say for sure!"

"That's true," he said, laughing, "so maybe you should come home and let me take you for a test drive. Assess your steering and handling."

That made me smile. "Very funny."

For all his dirty jokes, Noah had never once tried anything with me. I used to wonder why, but eventually assumed I just wasn't his type. He went for hot blondes with at least a C cup. Back then I was a brunette whose bra size matched her math grade: solid A. (Although these days, I am at least a B plus, possibly even a C minus.)

There *was* one time when I was in grad school and he'd come to see me in DC that I'd thought he was about to kiss me. He was in the Army back then, and about to ship out for his second deployment, so our goodbye had felt kind of intense. But the moment lasted for a fraction of a second, and afterward I was sure I'd imagined it.

"Listen, Sawyer. Forget that guy. He's a jackass."

"How do you know? You never even met him."

"I don't need to meet him. He had a chance to be with you and he blew it? Fuck him. He's a jackass."

"Thanks." It made me feel a little better, even if it wasn't true.

"You're welcome. Can I watch the game now?"

"In a minute." I flopped onto the couch and stared at

the ceiling. "Do you think I'm destined to be alone because I keep prioritizing my work over my relationships?"

"I don't know. Maybe."

I frowned. "That's not the right answer."

"What's the right answer?"

"The right answer is, 'When you meet the one perfect love of your life, you'll *want* to put that person first. You won't even have to think about it. You just do it—like a gut instinct."

"There you go."

"But what if it never happens, Noah? What if the guy never shows up? Or," I continued, getting more panicky by the second, "*or*, what if he does show up but I'm too busy and distracted to notice him? What if I'm . . . looking down at my fucking *phone* when he walks by?"

He exhaled heavily. "I think if you truly believe there is one perfect love of your life, your gut is gonna tell you to look up."

I closed my eyes. "You really believe that?"

He hesitated. "At least part of it. I believe in trusting your gut."

"But not one perfect love of your life?"

"That's a fairy tale, Sawyer. But if it makes you happy to believe in it, knock yourself out."

I sighed. That was a good question, actually. *Did* it make me happy to believe in that lightning-bolt kind of love, the once-in-a-lifetime kind that came out of nowhere and knocked you off your feet? Or was I just making an excuse for myself? Maybe I'd been expecting cupid to do all the work, when in reality love required more effort on my part. More lingerie and blowjobs.

I had no idea.

"You still there?" Noah asked.

"Yeah." I sat up, swinging my feet to the floor. "Hey, don't forget I'm coming home for Frannie's wedding next week. Let's hang out, grab a beer."

"I'm around. And I'm always up for a beer."

"How's Thursday?"

"Good. I'm actually off this Thursday."

"OK, I'll call you when I get in. And thanks for listening to me tonight. Sorry I kind of monopolized the conversation."

"I've known you a long time, Sawyer. I'm used to it."

I grinned, realizing how much I missed him. "Asshole. Enjoy the game. See you next week."

"Sounds good. Safe trip home."

We hung up, and I set my phone aside, thinking that it was funny how I still thought of northern Michigan as *home* when I hadn't lived there for fifteen years. I pictured it—Cloverleigh Farms, where I'd grown up; the small nearby town of Hadley Harbor, where Noah lived; the Leelenau peninsula—the pinky finger of Michigan—with its beautiful beaches and deep blue waters and gorgeous rolling hills covered with vineyards and orchards and woods. It had been such an idyllic place to grow up, and yet I'd been desperate to leave it, to get out in the world where important things happened. I couldn't even think of the last time I'd visited for more than a day or so at Christmas or Easter. Maybe Noah's dad's funeral? That had been three years ago.

Guilt tightened my throat.

Work would always be there, but no one lived forever.

Suddenly I was feeling completely homesick, missing everyone I loved. The ticket I'd booked to go home for the wedding had me leaving DC on Thursday morning and returning Sunday, the day after the wedding. But now I wanted more than three days there.

Would taking a full week off anger my boss? Would I miss important meetings and the opportunity to weigh in on critical decisions? We were coming up on an election year, and—

Suddenly I heard Brooks's voice in my head: *You never put your relationships first. You don't even put yourself first. It's always your job.*

He was right. And I could do better.

As for myself, maybe a little downtime was what I needed. A chance to escape the high-pressure hustle of the political world and just relax. Stop trying to *do everything* and just have fun. The world wasn't going to implode if I took a vacation.

Jumping up from the couch, I grabbed my laptop from my shoulder bag, emailed my boss I'd be out of the office longer than originally planned but could work remotely if necessary, and changed my departure to tomorrow morning. I had to pay a hefty fee to the airline, but I didn't care.

Happy with my decision, I went into the bedroom to start packing.

Three

Noah

I WATCHED THE REST OF THE GAME DISTRACTED BY THOUGHTS of Meg Sawyer. (It wasn't really my fault. The hitting sucked, the pitching was even worse. And Renzo could've fielded better, for fuck's sake.)

Plus, Meg had always been distracting to me.

Although we hadn't gone to the same school—she'd gone to public schools while my parents had insisted on Catholic—I'd known who she was. Everybody pretty much knew everybody around here. But we weren't close until the day I pulled her out of the bay at the public beach, barely conscious and white as a sheet, her body frighteningly limp in my arms as I set her on the sand.

Turning off the television, I took Renzo out to the yard one final time and looked up at the stars as I remembered the panic I'd experienced that day.

I was sixteen, barely old enough to be a lifeguard, but I was watching her closely as she tried to swim out to a friend's boat anchored offshore. The current was strong that day, and she hadn't been wearing a life jacket.

I knew instinctively the moment she started

struggling—my chest went tight, my adrenaline spiked—
and I jumped from the chair and took off running.

To this day, my stomach churns when I think about
what might have happened if I hadn't had my eye on her.
Granted, my reasons for watching her go into the water
might have included the tiny blue bikini she was wearing, but
I also believed in gut instincts, and mine were strong that
day.

When it was clear she was okay and able to stand, she
threw her arms around me and sobbed. At that point, I just
hoped I wouldn't spring a boner with her bare, sandy skin
on mine. I didn't hug her back, but she didn't care. That girl
must have clung to me like ivy on bricks for five solid minutes, blubbering her head off.

From that moment on, I felt protective of her. I liked
the feeling it gave me when I thought about how I'd kept
her safe. I'd even call it a turning point in my life—after that,
I knew what I wanted to do. Plus, my dad was a cop and I
idolized him. So it was no surprise to anyone when I joined
the Army right out of high school and later became a police
officer myself.

"Come on, boy. Let's go in." I let Renzo back into the
house, said goodnight several times before he believed me
that more playtime was not happening this evening, and
watched him curl up on his bed in the spare downstairs bedroom. My house wasn't big, but it was plenty of space for
Renzo and me. Downstairs it had two small bedrooms, a full
bath, kitchen and living room. Upstairs was the master bedroom and bath.

Ten minutes later, I lay back in the middle of a bed big
enough for two, but in which I'd slept alone for the last couple years.

She was still in my head.

I hadn't seen her in a while, but she never seemed to change much. Long brown hair with some gold streaks in it during the summer. Gray-blue eyes that could change color depending on the light. Lean, athletic body with long, muscular legs.

I couldn't believe she'd been dumped by yet another DC douchebag—what the fuck was wrong with these guys? At least I'd been able to make her laugh a little. The sound always took me back to the early days of our friendship.

We'd watch TV at my house or hers (she loved true crime and police shows, which I kind of dug at that age too), or we'd call each other late at night and talk for hours. It was crazy, because I was always awkward and tongue-tied around girls, but conversations with Meg were easy—even easier than talking to my guy friends a lot of the time. I knew exactly how to tease her, and she made me laugh without even trying. I could even talk to Meg about girls, and she'd listen and give me advice. Then I'd listen to her complain about all the stupid, immature boys at her school who were only interested in girls who put out.

Of course, I was interested in girls who put out too, but I didn't say so, because I didn't want her to think that's the kind of thing she had to do to get a guy's attention. Because in addition to being beautiful, Meg was fucking amazing at everything she did. Straight-A student. Student council president. Varsity athlete. Sure, she was wound tight and Type A as fuck, but she had the biggest heart of anyone I knew. She was always volunteering for things and dedicating herself to one good cause or another. And it wasn't just for show—she *cared*.

She'd come over to my house and sit with my brother

Asher, who has cerebral palsy and some sensory issues, and talk to him like he was just another one of her friends.

It might not sound like a big deal, but for Asher—and for me—it was huge. My brother was a smart, funny, brave, and interesting kid, but it was the rare person who looked beyond his disability to discover those qualities. And I understood why.

His speech was mostly incomprehensible to anyone outside the family. He used a walker or a wheelchair to get around, and he made a lot of involuntary movements. Sometimes he drooled. Occasionally he had seizures. Add to all this his oversensitivity to light, sounds, and textures, and his inability to express himself, and kids were wary. He was frustrated and anxious a lot, which often resulted in behavioral problems like tantrums or extreme reclusiveness. Needless to say, he struggled to make friends of his own at school and was often bullied and misunderstood. People would call him dumb, which drove him crazy—he wasn't dumb at all. He was perfectly smart. He just couldn't communicate the way people at school expected. And all those stupid IQ tests are geared for kids who *can*.

I'd been ferociously protective of him.

When kids made fun of Asher—and they'd been brutal—I'd snap like a wire in me had been cut. There were countless fights on the playground, in the halls, on the street. The elementary school principal probably had my parents' number on speed dial, I got sent down there so often (she and I have since laughed about my career path in law enforcement). But I just wanted him to be treated like anyone else.

So seeing him interacting at home with Meg, making her laugh, showing her a project he was doing on the computer, talking about a TV show he liked (he shared her interest in true crime) filled me with the best feeling imaginable.

She was way too good for any asshole who just wanted to get a hand down her pants, including me. Not that I ever thought of her that way.

Much.

Sure, there were times when I couldn't stop myself from jerking off to the idea of ripping that bikini off and fucking her expertly as she told me over and over again that I was her hero. Sometimes we were in the shower together. Or the back of my truck. Once, I even imagined us in the barn on her parents' farm. But who can control his fantasies at sixteen?

Or eighteen.

Or twenty-seven.

Or thirty-three, I thought, as my hand wandered down my stomach and slid beneath the waistband of my boxer briefs.

My conscience made a brief but valiant effort to speak up.

Stop it. Think about somebody else this time. The woman at Whole Foods who wears the tight yoga pants. Or the cute librarian with the freckles on her nose. Or, better yet, someone you don't even know—the model on the cover of the Sports Illustrated swimsuit issue!

But it was no use.

Meg was always the best fantasy, because she was both familiar and untouchable. I would never let myself touch her. She had no big brother to look out for her, so she needed me to be that guy. Someone she could trust not to hurt her. Someone she could count on to be a good man in a world full of assholes. Someone she could turn to. I always wanted to be that for her.

She'd certainly been there for me during the tough times in my life. The day after my first dog died, she dragged my sad ass out of the house and took me to the movies. The day before I left for boot camp, she brought me cookies and a letter that she made me promise not to read until I was gone. Of course, I read it that night after she left, and in it she thanked me for saving her life and being such a good friend to her. She told me she loved me like a brother. She called me her hero. It put a lump in my throat the size of a baseball.

And I'd never forget how quickly she jumped on a plane when we lost my Dad. Just dropped everything to come home and be there for me. I even had a girlfriend at the time, but it was Meg's shoulder I cried on the day after the funeral. I'd held my shit together all throughout his illness and the long, agonizing days of hospice, and even during the final, wrenching goodbye. I'd let my mother and sister weep in my arms. I'd stayed solid and strong and took care of everyone and everything, because I knew that's what my dad would have wanted, and because I'd promised him I would.

The next day I'd told everyone, including my girlfriend Holly, that I just wanted to be alone. But when Meg showed up at my door with lasagna, a six-pack of my favorite beer, and open arms, I'd lost it. I wouldn't have dared to let anyone else see my tears, but I held onto Meg and sobbed like a fucking baby for a solid ten minutes.

Best part was, she never made me talk about it. She just let me cry, and after I stopped, we ate lasagna, drank beer, and binge-watched Law & Order. She loved that stupid show, no matter how many times I told her that it was totally unrealistic and predictable.

"I don't care," she'd insist. "I *like* the predictability. They always get the bad guy."

I was glad she'd reached out tonight, and even more glad that she was coming home for a visit. We had a rare and unique friendship that I cherished, and I'd never do anything to jeopardize it.

But if you think that stopped me from getting myself off to the thought of her licking Twinkie filling off my rock-hard cock, you're fucking crazy.

Four

Meg

I ARRIVED AT CHERRY CAPITAL AIRPORT JUST AFTER ELEVEN Saturday morning.

Since I hadn't told anyone I was coming in early and didn't want to ruin the surprise by asking someone to pick me up, I took a cab to Cloverleigh Farms. I couldn't help smiling as the car turned onto the long, winding drive heading for the old farmhouse, which my parents had expanded considerably and turned into a five-star luxury inn.

Beyond the main building, which also included a bar and restaurant, were the familiar red barns and outbuildings that had been there when I was a kid, but there were new structures too: a winery, a tasting room, and a huge new white barn that served as a wedding venue. My sister April was the event planner here, and the weddings she designed had been written up in magazines, photographed for influential lifestyle blogs, and even featured on several episodes of a reality TV show about out-of-the-way spots to tie the knot in style. I had no doubt Frannie's wedding would be beyond Pinterest-worthy, and I couldn't wait to hear about it. I felt bad that I hadn't asked about all the details before.

The driver pulled around the circular drive in front of the inn. "This okay?"

"Sure, thanks," I said. A moment later, I was wheeling my suitcase through the multi-paned glass doors leading to the inn's charming lobby. My mother was at the reception desk, but she was focused on something on her computer screen as I approached.

"Excuse me, can I book a room please?" I asked with a grin.

"I'm so sorry, we're completely—" She looked up, and her expression went from regretful to ecstatic. "Meg?"

"Surprise!"

"I can't believe it!" She came rushing around the desk to throw her arms around me. "Oh honey, it's so good to see you!"

I dropped my shoulder bag and hugged her back, inhaling the familiar scent of her Chanel perfume. There was nothing like a mom's hug to make you feel like everything was going to be okay, no matter what. "It's so good to be home."

She squeezed me hard for several seconds and then let go. "Does anyone know you're here? Why didn't you call? I would have come to get you! I thought you weren't coming in until Thursday!"

I laughed at her rapid-fire speech. "I wasn't going to, but I was feeling kind of homesick, so I thought I'd come in sooner. Spend a little more time here."

My mother cocked her head. "Homesick? You?" She put a hand on my forehead. "Are you feeling okay?"

Swatting her hand away, I rolled my eyes. "I'm feeling great. I just missed everyone, that's all. It's been a while."

"It sure has. Your father is going to be thrilled. So

will your sisters." She looked beyond me into the lobby. "Where's Brooks? Parking the car?"

"Uh, no." I cleared my throat. "Brooks isn't with me."

"He isn't?"

"We broke up, actually."

A small gasp, and she covered her lips with one hand. "Oh, no. I'm so sorry, Meg."

"Don't be. I'm fine, really."

"Are you sure?" Her expression was worried. "You two were together a long time. I thought for sure you'd—"

"Well, things change." I slung my bag over my shoulder again, not really interested in rehashing the breakup. "So where is everybody?"

"Well, Frannie's at the pastry shop, and April hasn't come in yet. She'll have a late night, I'm sure. Big wedding this evening. Chloe's probably in the tasting room, getting ready for the day. The inn is totally booked this weekend, and all the winery tours are sold out." She shook her head and tucked her dark hair behind her ears, which was showing more gray at the root than I remembered. "It's been a madhouse, not to mention all Frannie's wedding preparations."

I held my arms out. "Well, I'm here, and I'm all yours. Put me to work."

She grabbed me in another tight hug. "Oh, it's so good to have you back." When she let me go, her eyes were wet with tears. "I'm so proud of all my daughters, but sometimes I miss those days when you were little and I never thought you'd be out from underfoot. And now I'm a grandmother and my youngest baby is getting married in a week, and I wonder, where on earth does the time go? I mean, look at my hair—gray everywhere!"

"You look great, Mom. Really."

She waved a hand in front of her face. "Well, it's nothing a trip to the salon won't cure. Your sisters and I have appointments Wednesday. We're doing trial hair and makeup for Saturday. Want to join us?"

"Sure. Thanks." I tugged a strand of the hair that had come loose from my ponytail. "I could probably use a trim. Maybe some fresh highlights."

My mother rose on tiptoe, clasping her hands by her heart. "Oh, I just can't wait. When Sylvia gets here on Tuesday, it will be the first time in *years* I'll have all my kids under one roof."

"Has it been that long? Wow."

She nodded. "Want to go surprise your dad? He's back in his office."

"Yes. Let me go say hello to him, drop off my bag at the house, and then I'll come back and help you out at the desk. Or Chloe in the tasting room, whatever you guys need. Sound good?"

"Perfect, darling. I'll grab a shirt for you," she said, gesturing toward her green collared Cloverleigh Farms work shirt.

"Thanks." I followed her around the desk, pulling my suitcase behind me, and slipped through the door leading to the administrative offices. "I'll be right back."

My dad was just as shocked and happy to see me as my mom had been, and he came bounding around his desk to give me one of his giant bear hugs. Wrapped in his familiar arms, I felt my throat get tight. He insisted on walking me over to the house and even took my suitcase upstairs for me.

"Remember which room is mine?" I teased.

"I might be old, but I'm not senile—yet," he replied, heading right at the top of the stairs and opening the door to my old bedroom.

I laughed. "Good thing."

My former room had been painted and re-carpeted since I'd moved out, but my mahogany double bed and dresser was the same, and my desk still sat between two windows overlooking the vineyard and woods beyond it. I'd spent a lot of hours there. "I've missed that view," I said, setting my shoulder bag on the desk and raising the balloon shade up all the way. "I can't wait to take a run out back."

"What are your plans for today?" my dad asked. Like my mom, he wore a green Cloverleigh shirt and khaki pants. Unlike my mom, he was *entirely* gray and paunchy through the middle, and I knew he'd had some heart and blood pressure problems over the last few years. His emails to me were always full of complaints about how my mother was taking all the good things out of his diet. But even though he'd aged since I'd seem him last, he seemed in good spirits.

"Help out around here, wherever I'm needed," I said, giving him another impromptu hug. "I'm so glad to be home, Daddy."

"But you're on vacation! You don't want to spend your time working." His eyes lit up. "Let's go see Frannie at her pastry shop."

I laughed. "Is that going to be okay with Mom? Will we have time?"

"There's always time for pastries," my dad confirmed, rubbing his tummy. "Let's go."

My mother said she could do without me, so my dad and I drove into the city to see Frannie. Her shop was adorable, and she was so excited to see me that she practically vaulted over the counter.

Frannie had always been cute, but today she looked absolutely radiant as she chattered on about the wedding and showed off her sparkling engagement ring. Her fiancé, Mack, a single dad and CFO at Cloverleigh Farms, was at home with his two younger daughters, but the oldest was there working at the shop.

"Meg, have you ever met Mack's daughter Millie?" Frannie asked as the pretty preteen blonde waved at me from behind the register.

"Yes, but she was a lot younger then." I smiled and waved back. "Good to see you, Millie."

"Will you be around later?" Frannie asked. "I'd love to hang out and catch up."

"Definitely." Impulsively, I hugged her again. "I'm so happy for you, Frannie. And so proud—this place is beautiful."

"Want a tour?" she asked, a little nervously. "I don't want to keep you, but—"

"Of course I do!"

She beamed. "I'll make it quick."

After she showed me around, my dad and I had a quick lunch at the counter and then headed back to Cloverleigh. April was there by then, and we had a tearful reunion in the middle of the lobby at the inn. She was crazy busy with the wedding that was taking place that evening, but she said she'd be done by eleven if I was up for a late drink in the bar.

"Sounds great," I said. "I'll text Frannie to come too."

I spent most of the day in the tasting room assisting Chloe, who was short-handed and totally thankful for the help, even though I knew next to nothing about Cloverleigh's wines. But Chloe was an excellent teacher, showing me how to pour, giving me basic info about each bottle to share with customers, and reassuring me that most people wouldn't ask very complicated questions—they just wanted to find something they liked.

We were so slammed we didn't really get a chance to chat, but she said she'd definitely be up for the late night meetup at the bar. "Oliver is in Detroit until Friday, so I'm free all week," she said, setting out new glasses on the counter for my next group of tasters, who were just coming in from a tour.

I smiled, shaking my head. "I still can't believe you're engaged to Oliver. You couldn't stand him growing up!"

She laughed. "Sometimes we can't believe it either. But you know what they say about the line between love and hate." Bringing a hand to her face, she whispered behind it. "Plus the sex is insane."

"Don't tell me. I'm way too jealous."

"I take it things aren't going well with Brooks?" she asked hesitantly.

"Things are over with Brooks." I sighed and put on a smile as several middle-aged couples came in and took the seats across from me. "I'll tell you about it tonight."

I had dinner with my parents at their kitchen table, basking in the familiarity of my mother's cooking as well as the surroundings. My dad told me about all his plans for retirement, which would begin right after Frannie's wedding. "Golf, golf, and more golf," he said.

I laughed. "What about during the winter?"

"Golf in Florida. Your mother and I are considering buying a place down there."

"Really?" I looked back and forth between them. "You'd leave Cloverleigh for that long?"

"Chloe's got an excellent handle on things here, and Mack has assured me he intends to stay on as CFO." My dad put some butter on his roll under the watchful eye of my mother. "I have confidence they can run things as well as we could—maybe even better."

Later, as Chloe poured four glasses of Pinot Noir at a high top table at Cloverleigh's bar, I congratulated her. "So you're going to inherit the farm, huh?"

She laughed. "Not the whole farm. Just the title of CEO."

"Well, that's still awesome. You've worked really hard here, and Mom and Dad can see it. I didn't think Dad would ever retire. He really trusts you."

My sister's cheeks flushed, and her brown eyes shone. Although we didn't exactly look alike, we shared our mother's wavy brown hair, our dad's tenacity, and a tendency to go *all in* when we truly wanted something. "Thanks," she said. "I have worked hard."

"Hey, guys. Sorry I'm late." Frannie breezed up, slipped off her coat, and took the stool between Chloe and me. "I couldn't get out of the house."

"Why was that, sis?" Chloe asked, her voice dripping with feigned innocence.

Frannie giggled and blushed, gathering her long hair over one shoulder. "Well, Mack can't ever get enough. And we have to wait until all the kids are asleep."

"You were having *sex*?" I asked, my mouth hanging open.

"Shhh!" Flapping her hands, Frannie looked around. "Someone might hear."

"Someone definitely heard," said April, coming up behind me and sliding onto the stool to my left. She picked up one of the wine glasses. "God, I need this. Not only was I dealing with a bridezilla tonight, but my baby sisters are all having sex and I'm not."

"I'm not either," I assured her, picking up a glass for myself.

Chloe lifted her glass and tapped it to Frannie's. "Cheers," she whispered.

"No, let's toast to all of us," Frannie insisted.

"I was gonna get there," said Chloe indignantly as she sat down across from me. She raised her glass higher. "To the Sawyer sisters!"

"To the Sawyer sisters!" we chorused.

"I feel bad Sylvia's not here," said Frannie after taking a sip.

"That just means we'll have to do this again after she arrives." April swirled the ruby liquid in her glass. "Lord knows I'm always up for wine."

She said it with a goofy smile, but something in her eyes made me wonder if she was unhappy beneath the cheerful façade. Maybe Chloe's engagement and Frannie's wedding were taking a psychological toll on her too. I'd made up my mind to focus on their happiness and be one hundred percent glad they'd found their soul mates—right under their noses—but I still envied them.

Stop it, said my conscience. *This is not about you.*

I sat up taller. "Okay, you guys. I've heard only the basics, and now I want all the juicy proposal details. Don't leave anything out. Go."

For the next hour, Frannie and Chloe told their engagement stories as we polished off the first bottle of wine and then a second. I heard all about how Mack got down on one knee and popped the question while they were in front of Chateau d'Ussé, the French castle that had inspired Sleeping Beauty and that Frannie had always dreamed about visiting.

"God, I love that story." April sighed. "I'd love to visit that part of France."

"So go," I told her.

"I can't. The wedding schedule here is bananas. We're completely booked up next spring and summer already."

"There's *no one* who can fill in for you?" Chloe asked. "Why don't we find someone? Really, you could use the help, even if it's just part time."

April took another sip of wine. "I might be too much of a control freak. And what if we couldn't find someone who's good enough? Or what if we hire her and I book a trip and she doesn't work out?"

"We can at least try, right?" Frannie asked.

"I agree," I said.

April looked at me in surprise. "The workaholic agrees I should take a vacation?"

"Yes." I spun my wine glass around by the stem, feeling heat in my face. "I do. Being a workaholic is no fun, and I'm going to get better about it. In fact, that's why I came home early."

Frannie put a hand over my wrist. "I'm so glad you did."

I smiled at her, then looked at April. "If *I* can take a vacation, you can."

"I guess," April said, although she didn't look convinced.

"Jeez, have a little faith." Chloe nudged her on the

shoulder. "I know a lot of people. Give me some time to reach out."

"Okay, okay." April held up her hands in surrender. "Let's not talk about me anymore. Tell Meg about your engagement."

From there, Chloe told the story of Oliver's proposal on the barn roof, the same roof they'd jumped off when they were eleven, resulting in one broken leg (Chloe), one broken collarbone (Oliver), and years of getting each other back. But their chemistry had always been fierce and insuppressible. She'd once told me the sex was as volatile as their fights used to be, and I believed her.

Brooks and I never fought.

Suddenly everyone was staring at me, and I realized I'd said it out loud. "Oh, sorry. That probably sounded totally random. But I was just thinking about how different certain relationships are, from start to finish."

"I don't want to pry if it's painful, but I am curious." April tilted her head. "What happened with Brooks? Mom mentioned you guys broke it off."

I tipped up the last of my wine and Frannie moved her glass toward me. It was still half-full. "Here. You can have mine. I have to drive home tonight."

"Thanks." I stared at it as I went on. "There's not much to tell, really. I'm sitting here listening to you two talk about these amazing, romantic, heart-pounding moments and realizing that Brooks and I were actually *really* boring."

"Boring how?" April asked. "Like in bed?"

"I guess, but it was more than that."

"Can you talk about it?" pressed Frannie.

"I guess," I said glumly. "You guys have any Twinkies?"

My sisters burst out laughing, and Frannie reached for

her bag. "Oh, I forgot! It's not Twinkies but I did bring you guys some macarons from the shop. I've got lavender, pistachio, and Fruity Pebbles."

"Fruity Pebbles?" I asked, perking up. That sounded right up my alley. "Like the cereal?"

Frannie set a robin's egg blue box with a clear plastic lid on the table, full of violet and green and pink pastries. "Yes. It was Millie's idea. They're pretty good, actually."

We eagerly dug in, moaning with delight at the sweet almond meringues and delectable fillings. I had to admit they were much better than Twinkies.

"Go on, Meg," urged Frannie. "You were talking about what happened with Brooks."

"Well, when we first met, he seemed so smart and successful and sophisticated. And he was very handsome and definitely interested in me. I was flattered. Then as we got to know each other, we discovered all these similar beliefs and habits and long-term goals. We just *made sense* on every level. So we signed a lease together and started to plan for the future."

Chloe wrinkled her nose. "That's not very sexy."

"No, it really wasn't. I mean, we had sex, at least in the beginning, but it was never at the heart of the relationship. It was never the most exciting thing about us. And eventually, it fell by the wayside."

"You fell out of love?" Frannie asked, as if such a thing had never occurred to her.

I took a sip before going on. "I guess. Although maybe we didn't really *love* each other. At least not enough." Brooks's words came back to me . . . *We didn't love each other enough to fight for it.* "I want someone who will fight for me, you know? Someone who won't give up on me so fast.

Someone who will choose me over anyone or anything else, even if it's not the easy choice."

Chloe reached across the table and put her hand over mine. "You deserve that. So don't stop believing it can happen."

Frannie put her hand on top of Chloe's. "Absolutely. I never thought Mack would look twice at me, let alone fall in love with me enough to get married again. But I never gave up hope."

April reached over and added her hand to the stack. "I have no words of wisdom because I haven't been able to figure my shit out either. But I want a piece of all this positive energy. This is good stuff."

I laughed. "Thanks, you guys. Sometimes it's hard to believe what I'm looking for—whatever it is—is out there. I'm thirty-three already"—thirty-five-year-old April cleared her throat, and I looked at her sympathetically—"and I feel like I've gotten at least *close* to finding the right person but failed at making it work. But you're giving me hope. I won't give up."

"Good." Frannie checked her phone and sighed. "I should probably get going. Mack will worry if I'm out too late. He's overprotective."

"Awww," I said. "So sweet."

"And hot," April added.

"It is." Frannie giggled and lowered her voice. "I'm going to wake him up for round two."

The three of us groaned with envy, hugged her goodbye, and asked one of the bar backs to walk her out to the parking lot. Chloe and April left shortly afterward, and after saying goodnight I headed down the hallway off the lobby that led to our family's private wing.

The house was dark, but my mom had left one light on for me in the upstairs hallway outside my room. There were freshly laundered towels folded on my dresser, an extra blanket at the foot of my bed, and a note on my pillow.

So happy to have one of our little sparrows back in the nest. Love you!

I smiled and set it aside, got ready for bed, and slipped beneath the covers. It felt both odd and comforting to be there alone in the dark in my old room. A thousand memories flashed through my brain—being nervous about an AP exam or a cross country meet the next day, stressing about my campaign for student council president, worrying that my crush on some guy would be forever unrequited.

I turned onto my stomach. I'd gotten up super early and should have been tired, especially given all the wine I'd drunk, but I wasn't. If I'd been seventeen again, I probably would have snuck downstairs and called Noah.

As teenagers, we'd had countless conversations late at night, me usually sitting on the floor of the pantry, where I'd dragged the phone so no one would hear, and Noah on the couch in his parents' basement. No matter how worked up I was about something, his voice would soothe me. Inevitably, I could fall asleep after we hung up.

For a moment, I considered getting out of bed and grabbing my phone, but then I thought better of it. I wasn't sure what his work schedule was, and it was after midnight already—he shouldn't have to lose sleep just because I was feeling anxious. And for all I knew, he was out with someone. It was Saturday night, after all. He hadn't mentioned dating anyone seriously since Holly, but that didn't mean he was celibate.

I recalled his offer last night to take me for a spin and assess my steering and handling, and it made me laugh in my pillow. I couldn't wait to see him. I knew he'd make me smile.

He always did.

Five

Noah

I worked all day Saturday, 7 A.M. to 7 P.M., but I had Sunday off.

After waking around six, as usual, I decided to take advantage of the mild autumn weather by heading out for a run with Renzo on one of my favorite trails. Afterward, we worked on some obedience in a nearby park, which was empty at that early hour—something I insisted on. Renzo was a well-behaved dog (mostly), but he was still an animal, and he was *trained* to bite. I never wanted to take any chances with strangers around.

As the morning wore on, the park got a little busier, and curious onlookers wandered over. I was sweaty and tired and ravenously hungry, but I told Renzo to lie down and let the kids get close enough to pet him and take pictures. This was part of my job too—being part of the community and making people feel welcome and safe.

After leaving the park, I went right to my mom's house for some food. She always made brunch for everybody after she got home from Mass on Sundays. My sister and her family would be there, and Asher, too—he still lived with my mom. Someday he would live with me.

I parked behind my sister's car in front of the house and walked around to the back door, which opened into the big, cluttered kitchen. My mom was flipping eggs on the stove, and my very pregnant sister was sticking bread in the toaster, buttering the slices as they popped up. As usual, the lights were low because of Asher's sensitivity to brightness, but I didn't see him in the room.

Renzo got excited the moment he saw the kids, who were just as thrilled to see him. "Can I take him in the yard to play, Uncle Noah?" asked Harrison.

"Sure, buddy." He looked just like his dad at that age. I ruffled his blond curls and handed him a tennis ball I'd brought. "Here. Hope you've got a lot of energy."

"I do!" he called, running full-speed for the back door, Renzo on his heels.

"Mommy, can I go too?" asked Violet.

"Did you say hello to Uncle Noah?" Nina gave her daughter a Mom look.

Violet, who had her mother's dark hair but Chris's light eyes, gave me a gap-toothed grin. "Hi, Uncle Noah."

"Whoa!" I took her face in my hands and pretended to be shocked. "Is that *another* hole in your smile?"

She nodded happily. "I lotht it yethterday at thcool."

"Wow. I hope you grow another one in its place. You sound a little funny without it."

The grin widened. "I will."

"Good." I gently yanked her by the pigtails. "Go on. Renzo needs at least two of you to wear him out."

She flew out the back door and I went over to little Ethan in the high chair. "High five, dude." I held up my hand, and he hit it and laughed, then threw some blueberries on the floor.

I picked them up, tossed them in the trash, and went over to the stove to kiss my mom's cheek. "Morning, Ma."

"Morning. Didn't see you at Mass this morning."

"Damn, did I forget it was Sunday *again*?"

"Language, please." My sister glanced at her toddler over her shoulder. "Ethan repeats everything these days. And suddenly Violet has discovered cursing. Last week her teacher asked what sound the letter B makes, and she answered, 'B says *buh*, what the hell else would it say?'"

Laughing, I moved over to Nina and poked her side. "Good for her. Morning, Shamu. Where's your good-for-nothing husband?"

"His dad needed him today." Chris's family owned several nurseries and ran a large landscaping business in the area, which Chris oversaw day to day. Asher worked in their admin offices. Nina sniffed at me over her shoulder. "Ew. Couldn't you have at least rinsed off the sweat?"

I held my damp shirt away from my body. "And deprive you ladies of my natural scent? Why would I do that?"

"Gross. No wonder you can't get a date."

"I don't want a date." I grabbed a piece of buttered toast off the plate and took a giant bite.

My sister slapped my hand. "That's for breakfast, jerk."

"Perfect, that's why I came. Got any coffee?"

"It's in the pot," said my mother, sliding fried eggs onto the chipped blue platter she'd put Sunday bacon and eggs on for as long as I could remember. "Could you two please stop bickering? I already have a headache."

"Sorry, Ma." I poured a cup and leaned back against the yellowed Formica. "Where's Ash?"

"Resting."

I nodded. Living with CP meant his body expended

something like five times the energy mine did just doing everyday tasks. Going up a flight of stairs was like a marathon for him. "How was his week? I didn't see him much."

"Okay. He's been having trouble sleeping. Seems agitated about something. And he had a partial seizure yesterday." She shook her head. "I think he's working too much."

My gut clenched. A partial wasn't as bad as the tonic-clonic seizures Asher sometimes had as a child, but they still made me worry. "Is he still taking the muscle relaxant at night?"

"Yes."

"How about exercise? Did he go to swimming last week? Or do his stretches?"

"Swimming, yes. I haven't seen him stretch much lately."

"I'll try to get him out for a walk with Renzo later. Sometimes that helps with the sleep." Asher loved walking Renzo and just being around him in general. I think he enjoyed feeling like a caretaker, since he was always the one being worried about and fussed over, usually by my mom. Despite the fact that she worked full time, she refused to hire any outside help for Asher except for a neighbor lady named Mrs. Reynolds, who drove him to and from work or therapy, and occasionally put together meals for him if my mother had to work late—which she often did. I knew she worried about money, especially with my dad gone, but I'd promised him I wouldn't let her run herself into the ground, and I was always trying to get her to take a vacation.

"You book your ticket yet?" I asked her. For months she'd been hemming and hawing about visiting her two sisters in Florida during the winter, or joining them on a Caribbean cruise. She had terrible arthritis that was always worse during the cold months, and it got pretty fucking cold during Michigan winters. I'd told her a million times to book it—I'd stay with Asher while she was gone, or he could come stay with me. I had a downstairs bedroom all ready for him.

"Not yet. Here. Make yourself useful." My mother handed me the platter of eggs and bacon. "Put this on the table, please. And the orange juice."

I stole a piece of bacon off it first. "Take the trip, Ma. You're not getting any younger."

My mother poured more coffee in her cup. "I'm still thinking about it. But it's difficult to get all the days off at work, and—"

"I specifically remember you and Dad talking about retiring in your sixties so you'd still be young enough to enjoy your life," I said. "You're sixty-two already."

"Thanks for the reminder," she said drily.

"I'm just saying, you need to do these things while you still have the energy. Didn't you two always talk about going to Ireland?"

"You think I want to do that by myself?"

"So get your sisters to go. Ask a friend. Join a tour group. You don't have to go alone if you don't want to."

"He's right, Mom," my sister chimed in. "There are plenty of options. You should do it."

She wiped up some spilled coffee on the counter, her lips pressed together. "It's not just work. It's the expense. And leaving Asher is hard. He needs me. I cook all his meals and do all his laundry. I make sure he's eating and sleeping and not working too much. I make sure his communicator is charged because he often forgets to plug it in. And the disruption to his routine will—"

"I can handle it all, Ma," I assured her. "You don't need to worry about any of that."

"Noah McCormick, you've never cooked a meal in your life."

"But I am excellent at ordering takeout. And I know all his favorite places." I made it a point to take my brother out for dinner at least once or twice a week. He didn't love being out in public because ignorant people often stared, but I knew from experience that letting him stay home all the time just made him depressed. I wished more than anything that he had a wide circle of friends to hang out with on weekends, but as much as we encouraged him to be social, he was more of an introvert. And I felt bad trying to pressure him to be something he wasn't.

"Maybe if you had a wife, someone to help you with the day to day, I wouldn't feel so bad leaving you with so much responsibility," my mother went on, switching tactics like a pro.

Refusing to take the bait, I stole another piece of bacon. "Want me to call the kids in?"

"Yes. And tell them to wash their hands. Nina, will you go get Asher? Everything is ready."

My sister headed down the hallway off the kitchen toward Asher's first floor bedroom. A few minutes later, he followed Nina into the kitchen, carrying his speech-generating device, or SGD. He walked slowly and with a lot of difficulty, but at least he was on his feet without the walker.

For a long time, we weren't sure Asher was going to walk at all. In fact, the doctors told my parents he probably wouldn't. But they refused to believe it and never stopped working with him, even when the poor kid was exhausted and in tears. It used to make me want to cry too. I'd shut myself in my room with my hands over my ears. I felt so bad for him, and so guilty for being able to walk and run and jump without giving it a thought. It wasn't fair.

"Hey, Ash," I said. "How's it going?"

He sat at the table and answered using his device, which looked sort of like a tablet and allowed him to "talk" by tapping on words or phrases or letters. It had made a huge difference in his ability to communicate. I wished he'd had it in elementary school.

"Good," he said. "Did you bring Renzo with you?"

"Yep. He's outside but he's coming in. Want to walk him with me later?"

"Sure," he said.

We weren't identical, but we looked somewhat alike— same brown eyes and dark hair, although his was slightly longer and usually messier because he didn't like combing it. He had learned to use an electric razor, so he was often clean-shaven while I always had some scruff. The biggest differences related to physicality—I was tall and broad, while he was shorter and much thinner. Difficulty swallowing and aversion to certain food textures made eating a chore for him, and he'd never had a big appetite. And where my limbs were long and muscular, his had a thin, twisted appearance due to his body's overexcited nerves.

When we were all seated around the big oval kitchen table, my mother said grace, her eyes closed, her hands folded on the table. "Bless us, O Lord, and these, Thy gifts, which we are about to receive from Thy bounty. Through Christ, our Lord. Amen."

"Amen," I echoed, reaching for the eggs.

"And, dear Lord, if I could just add a prayer for my son,

Noah," my mother went on, a bit louder than before. "I'm so concerned for his sad, lonely heart."

I rolled my eyes, and my sister snickered.

"Dear Lord, *please* let him find someone to settle down with. Someone kind and caring and beautiful. Someone smart. Someone who remembers when it's Sunday. Someone who will tell him to take a shower before coming to his mother's house for a meal. Someone who—"

"Okay, I think that's enough, Ma. God gets your drift."

She opened one eye and looked at me. "But do you?"

"Yes. And I thank you for your concern, but as I've told you before, my heart is just fine." I slid two fried eggs onto my plate and changed the subject. "So how's school going so far, you guys?" I asked my niece and nephew.

Violet sighed dramatically. "Kindergarten was fun, but first grade is a real shit show."

"Violet Marie, you watch your mouth!" my sister snapped. "We don't talk like that."

"Uncle Noah does," my niece insisted. "Last time we were here, I heard him say 'the dispatch desk at the station was a real shit show this week.'"

"Shit show," Ethan piped up.

I burst out laughing as my sister glared at me. Asher laughed too.

"Sorry," I told her, deciding to change the subject. "So guess who's coming to town this week?"

"Who?" My mother poured Asher some orange juice.

"Meg Sawyer."

"Ooooh, the one that got away," Nina teased.

"Got away from what?" Violet asked.

"From Uncle Noah."

"Why'd she want to get away?"

My sister smirked. "Can't you smell him?"

I shoved the rest of my toast in my mouth. "Don't listen to her, Violet. Meg is just a friend of mine. Although I *did* save her life once."

My niece gasped, suitably impressed. "You did?"

"I did," I replied, puffing up my chest and beating one fist on it.

My sister rolled her eyes. "Don't even pretend you weren't in love with her. I used to spy on you guys watching TV in the basement. I was always positive I'd catch you kissing."

"Never," I said, proud of myself all over again. "Because *I* am a gentleman."

"Who'd kiss a girl anyway?" Harrison made a face. "Girls are disgusting."

"Give it a few years, buddy," I said.

My mother sighed loudly. "Such a sweet girl. I just adored her. And from such a nice family. I wish you *would* have been in love with her, even if she's not Catholic. Maybe I'd have your wedding picture on the mantel by now . . ." She glanced into the living room with sad eyes.

"Maybe it's not too late, Mom. If she's still single." Nina wrinkled her nose. "And if Noah buys some good deodorant."

"Okay, enough," I said. "I'm sorry I mentioned her."

"*Is* she single?" my mother asked, her voice full of hope.

"I'm not sure," I lied.

"When's she coming?" Nina asked. "Oh, is it for her sister's wedding?"

I nodded and took a bite of eggs. "Yeah, but I forget which sister."

"Frannie. The youngest." Nina wiped Ethan's mouth

with a napkin. "She's a client at the salon. The wedding is Saturday."

I shrugged. "That sounds right."

"Maybe you could take Meg to the wedding," my mother suggested.

"No," I said emphatically. "We're just going to hang out. Grab a beer or something."

Another long, sad sigh. "Well, don't wear that shirt. And bring her by if you can. I'd love to say hello."

"I'll try," I said, although the last thing I wanted was to bring Meg over here so my mother could ask a bunch of personal questions in order to assess her romantic availability, and then make all kinds of ridiculous comments about my sad, lonely heart. I didn't need to hear it.

My dick might have been a little sad and lonely, but my heart was doing just fine.

After brunch, I hung around a while longer, playing with the kids in the yard, raking the front and back lawn for my mom, and taking a slow walk around the block with Asher and Renzo. He managed it without the walker, which made me happy, and I told him I'd come by this week and we'd do it again. "Sound good?"

"Yes," he said, breathing hard. Then he indicated he wanted me to come to his room. When we got there, he sat on the bed and pulled his SGD onto his lap.

"I remember Meg," he said. "Does she still watch true crime shows?"

I smiled at my brother. "I think she does."

"She was always so nice."

"Maybe I'll bring her by to say hi."

"She was pretty too."

"Yes, she was."

His eyes took on a mischievous look. "I bet she still is."

"Bye, Ash." I punched him gently on the shoulder and walked out.

After leaving my mom's, I headed for home, where I spent the rest of the day painting my garage door while Renzo peed on every tree he could find and tried to get me to play fetch with him.

Eventually he gave up and went inside to sulk, and I finished up the second coat. I was rinsing my hands with the hose when I heard a car door slam behind me. Shutting off the water, I turned around and saw a woman walking up my driveway. I squinted at her as I dried my hands on my shirt. Light brown hair loose around her shoulders. Sunglasses. Medium height. Wearing jeans, sneakers, and a black T-shirt that said *My Favorite Murder* on the front.

"Sawyer?" I said in disbelief.

Breaking into a huge grin, she started to run.

I was still standing there in shock when she barreled into me, throwing her arms around my neck. She smelled fucking fantastic. Feminine, sweet, delectable.

"What are you doing here?" I asked, trying to hug her back without getting sweat or paint on her. "I thought you didn't get in until Thursday."

"I changed my ticket." She let go just enough to smile up at me impishly. "I'm glad to see you too."

I laughed. "I'm glad to see you. You just surprised me is all."

"That was my plan." She stepped back, and I figured my odor was probably repulsing her.

"I stink, sorry. I went for a run earlier and I never showered. Then I painted the garage."

"I never mind the smell of sweat. It means hard work." She brightened. "Will you run tomorrow? I'd love to go with you."

"Sure. We can run tomorrow. I'm off again."

"Great! Although I'm probably way out of shape." She made a face. "My work schedule is so crazy, I don't run as much as I used to."

"You look great," I told her. And it was true—she did look great. Maybe not quite as skinny as the last time I'd seen her, but the added curves looked good on her. My eyes wandered without my brain's permission to her slightly fuller chest and rounder hips. Quickly, I attempted to look at her face again, but then my gaze lingered on her mouth. I remembered what it had looked like the other night in my fantasy as she'd wrapped her lips around my cock and moaned like it was the best thing she'd ever tasted. `

My dick twitched beneath my running shorts, and I cleared my throat. "You've got a favorite murder? Is there something I need to know?"

She glanced down at her shirt and smiled. "It's a podcast about true crime. I'm addicted."

"Never heard of it."

A sound of exasperation escaped her. "You live under a rock! I can't believe you're still not on social media."

"Yes, you can."

"Okay, I *can*, but it makes it really hard to stalk you."

I shook my head. "People like you are exactly why I don't want to be on social media."

She hit me on the shoulder. "I'm kidding! I just want to keep up with your life. I miss you."

"So come home more often. Talk to my face."

She grinned. "I do like seeing your face. Want to go grab a beer? Maybe some food?"

"Sure. Just give me a few minutes to clean up out here and grab a shower."

"Okay. No rush."

"Want to come in and meet Renzo? I don't think you've met him yet."

She clapped her hands and followed me to the back door. "I haven't! I think you got him right after the last time I was home."

I opened the door for her and let her go through. "I got him after my dad died, so that sounds about right."

Renzo came up immediately to assess this new potential friend or enemy, and thankfully obeyed my commands to stay down and be quiet.

"Oh, he's so beautiful," Meg gushed. "Can I pet him?"

"Sure."

She leaned down and gave Renzo all kinds of love and attention, and pretty soon his tail was wagging, his expression was joyful, and I could tell they were going to get along just fine. It made me feel good, seeing Meg with my dog.

"I have to put some shit away out there. Do you want to wait in here or come outside?" I asked her.

"I'll come out," she said, straightening up. "I'll play with Renzo while you finish up."

"He'll love you forever."

She sighed as we went back outside. "At least someone will."

After I was done in the yard, Meg waited in my living room and played with Renzo while I headed up to shower and change. "He does love you," I told her. "Usually I have to shut him in his bedroom while I shower, or else he follows me into the bathroom."

"Maybe I just smell better right now," she teased.

"That's a given," I said, heading up the stairs.

An hour later, we were sitting across the table from each other at Hop Lot Brewing Co., one of my favorite local spots to grab an IPA and some ribs off the smoker. Meg ordered a blonde ale, and we decided to share a full rack and a basket of fries.

Since Hadley Harbor was such a small town, I was pretty recognizable and a lot of people came by our table to say hello. Many of them asked where Renzo was, and a couple of them knew Meg as well. If they didn't, I introduced her, and we ended up talking about Cloverleigh Farms. By the time she and I were left by ourselves, our beers and food had arrived.

"I brought you some extra napkins," said the server as she set them down. Then she smiled at Meg. "And by the way, I love your shirt. I'm totally a murderino."

Meg gave me a smug look. "Thanks."

I shook my head as the server walked away. "Women scare me."

"Oh, stop. Nothing scares you."

It wasn't true, but I liked that she thought it. I reached for a rib. My mouth was watering.

"You're so popular," Meg teased, spreading her napkin on her lap. "At least ten people are staring over here right now."

"That means there will be gossip." I frowned as I chewed and swallowed. "And this is a small town, so it'll travel fast. By tomorrow, we'll be married."

She giggled. "With a couple of kids on the way."

I picked up a second rib and started gnawing on it. "A couple?"

"Twins."

"Twins. Right."

She popped a French fry in her mouth. "How's Asher doing?"

"Good. He's got a new communication device, which was ridiculously expensive yet worth every penny, that has helped his confidence a lot. And he finally got a job, which is great, but he tires easily."

"Where does he work?"

"For Logan's, in the executive offices."

"Cool. That's Chris's family's business, right?"

"Yeah. He was applying for jobs and not having much luck, because people are assholes and don't look beyond the disability. Asher was really frustrated, because he'd worked so long and hard for his IT degree and he's really good with computers."

"That sucks. Poor Asher."

"But Chris's entire family has been awesome."

"What does he do there?"

"Computer work. Inventory, payroll, website management, communications. He started an email newsletter for them too."

"That's awesome. Is he still living with your mom?"

"Yep."

"Is he okay with that?"

"As far as I know. Back when I was still in the Army, they tried a kind of group home for him, but he *and* my mother hated it. I think he was back home within two weeks."

"Why did Asher hate it?"

I tried to think back. "Asher's anxiety was a lot worse back then. I think that had a lot to do with it. He's come a long way with different kinds of therapy and the new speech device, and his doctor recently prescribed an antidepressant too. That's helped him a lot."

She took a rib from the plate between us and sank her teeth into the meat. "Does he have friends or a social life?"

"Not really." I frowned. "I try to get him out some, but it's hard. On top of having CP and anxiety about the way people see him, he's just shy. And between us, I think my mother feeds that anxiety sometimes. Not on purpose, exactly, but it's as if she feels like she's protecting him by discouraging his independence."

"Or it's just how she shows love, by being the caretaker," Meg suggested. "She's still working at the clinic?"

"Yeah. And helping my sister with her gigantic brood."

Meg laughed. "How many kids does Nina have?"

"Three, and another one about to pop out."

"Wow. Full house. That's impressive."

"And loud. But the kids are awesome."

"You like being an uncle?"

"I love it." But what I really loved was the way she was sucking on the rib bone now that she'd eaten off all the meat. And licking her fingers. It was turning me on. How come I'd never noticed what a great mouth she had? Or how sexy it was watching her eat and enjoy her food? Or how one of her eyebrows arched up higher than the other one, as if she knew what I was thinking and liked it?

Jesus, I really needed to stop fantasizing about her.

It was starting to mess with my head.

Six

Meg

BEING WITH NOAH WAS SO *EASY*. I'D ALMOST FORGOTTEN how easy. And he looked so good in his blue T-shirt. It was tight on his chest and biceps, showing off his muscles. His butt looked nice in his jeans too.

He'd been cute as a teenage lifeguard, a total stud in his military days, but now—as a grown man and a cop? Hot as hell. And clearly everyone in town liked him. How the hell was he still single? I mean, good with kids and animals, great body, fun sense of humor, fantastic at his job . . . Were the women around here crazy? He'd be an amazing husband and dad too.

"Maybe you should have a couple kids of your own," I suggested. "Since you love being an uncle so much."

He groaned and picked up his beer. "You sound like my mother. The best part about being an uncle is that you get to give them back when you're done with them."

"Ah." I picked up another rib and licked some sauce off my fingers. "So kids are fine, as long as they're only on loan."

"Exactly." He stared at my hand for a moment and took

another gulp from his glass. "What about you? Do you want kids?"

I sighed. "Yeah. But it doesn't look like it's going to happen any time soon."

"Are you still upset about Brooks?"

I thought for a moment while I took a bite. "Not really. I mean, I'm upset that the relationship didn't work out. I don't like being alone. But in the end, I don't think he was the one."

"Why don't you like being alone?" he asked.

The question surprised me. "Does anyone like being alone?"

"Sure. I do. I'd much rather be alone than in a relationship that's going nowhere."

I thought about it some more as I sipped my beer. "I guess I just like the feeling of knowing someone is there for me. Knowing someone has my back." I paused. "And sex. I like the feeling of sex."

He gave me a sideways smirk. "You don't have to be in a relationship for that."

"I know. And even if you are, there's no guarantee the sex will be good."

"It wasn't good with Brooks?" He picked up his beer and finished it.

"Well, I can't say it was *bad*. It just wasn't . . . a must-have."

Noah snorted as he set down his empty glass. "That sounds pretty bad."

I laughed as I finished my rib and licked my fingers again. "It was just . . . not boring, but . . . kind of like how I feel about—" I looked around, trying to think up a good metaphor, and saw our server passing by with a tray full of food. "Potato salad."

Noah nearly choked on his fries. He reached for his beer,

but it was empty, so he signaled the waitress, then wiped his eyes. "Oh my fucking god, you did not just say sex with him was like potato salad."

Now I was laughing too. "What I meant was, I could take it or leave it. I like potato salad, it's perfectly tasty if it's well done, but I never crave it. Like, even if I was hungry and I knew it was in the fridge, I'm probably not going to get out of bed and go get some potato salad. Or if I was already on my couch in my sweats watching Law & Order, I wouldn't go to the store for it. Know what I mean?"

"Sort of." He shook his head, still chuckling. "Jesus, that poor bastard. Did he not know what he was doing?"

"It wasn't that. I guess I'm just looking for a different feeling. I want to *need* it. I want to crave it like . . . like . . ."

"Like a Twinkie?"

I giggled and finished my beer. "No, a Twinkie is a comforting feeling. A Twinkie says, 'This too shall pass, and you will be okay.' I want sex that's unpredictable, that maybe even scares me a little. Sex that makes me feel like I might not be okay."

Noah went still, his eyes on mine.

Had I gone too far?

"I mean, I like it sweet and comforting sometimes too," I said quickly, "but there's something about being a little nervous that really gets the adrenaline pumping, you know? I like being riled up."

Still he said nothing. Just looked at me, his expression serious, possibly even a little shocked.

"That probably sounds bad, huh?"

He cleared his throat. "No. I get it."

The server came over and Noah quickly ordered another beer. "Want another?" he asked me.

I hesitated. The beer here was strong, and I didn't want to get tipsy, since I would eventually have to drive home, but I was enjoying myself so much, I didn't want to break the spell.

"I'll drive you home," he said, "if that's what you're worried about."

"Okay. Thanks." I smiled at the server. "I'll have another too."

When we were alone again, I snapped my fingers. "Shishito peppers!"

"What?"

"Shishito peppers. It's this Japanese pepper that's sort of like a guessing game as to its heat. It can be, and usually is, relatively sweet. But every once in a while, one of them packs an extra fiery punch. It's like Russian roulette for the tongue."

"Interesting."

"There's a restaurant in DC that serves them with steak. They're called 'blistered peppers' on the menu, and I swear they're different every time—sometimes so hot I can hardly stand it, and sometimes more sweet. So there's like this moment before you take the first bite when you're kinda scared that it might actually be too hot to handle and make you scream, or it'll be deliciously sweet and make you moan."

Noah nodded slowly. "Sounds good."

"It is."

Our beers arrived, and Noah grabbed his right away, taking a long drink.

"I suppose," I said as I picked up my glass, "I should be glad Brooks left, right? I mean, he saved me from a life of potato salad sex."

Noah set down his beer. "That does sound pretty fucking terrible."

I took a sip. "So what about you? Are you seeing anyone?"

"Not since Holly."

Nodding, I ran my thumb up the condensation on the side of my glass. Pictured his ex—a beautiful, blond preschool teacher with dimples and a big chest. To be fair, the couple times I'd met her, she'd seemed perfectly nice, and I had no good reason to dislike her . . . and yet, I kind of did. "What happened there? You've never really told me about the breakup."

He shrugged. "It wasn't any one thing."

When he didn't go on, I groaned. "You're *such* a guy. Can you elaborate, please? If it wasn't any one thing, there were probably several things. Can you talk about any of them?"

His expression told me talking about this breakup was his least favorite thing in the world. But to my surprise, he opened up a little. "She wasn't very supportive when my dad died."

My jaw dropped. "What? How can that be? You guys had been together for years, and she had to know how important your dad was to you, to everybody! How could she be so completely heartless?"

He grimaced and drank again, and I felt terrible.

"I'm sorry, Noah." Reaching across the table, I put a hand on his arm. "That was shitty of me. I never really knew her, and I'm sure she wasn't completely heartless."

He stared at my fingers on his wrist for a moment. "It felt that way to me. We *had* been together for a couple years by then. And she *did* know how close my family was—that was part of the problem. I think she was jealous."

I sat back. "Of your family? Are you serious?"

"Yeah. She kind of always resented how much time I spent with them. Not at first, maybe, but after a while, especially after my dad's cancer diagnosis. There were times when I'd have to break plans she and I had made in order to take Asher somewhere so my mom could be with him, or watch my sister's kids, or take a shift with my dad at the hospital."

I couldn't believe what I was hearing. I was stunned silent.

"Then when my dad died, I think she was expecting things to get easier, like she'd get more of me. She used to say things like that, and I knew it was supposed to make me feel good, like she just wanted to be with me, but it only made me feel worse." He drank again. "So I was either letting her down or letting my family down—which felt like letting my dad down. There wasn't enough of me to go around."

"Jesus, Noah. That sucks." My throat tightened up as I recalled how devastated he'd been after his dad's death. He needed support, not judgment. How could she have treated him that way? My eyes filled. "I'm so sorry."

"Yeah, well . . ." He focused on the wooden table's scarred surface. "The final straw came right after that."

"What was it?"

He took a sip of his beer before answering. "I made an offhand comment about Asher coming to live with me one day. I mean, my mom isn't getting any younger. And I want her to be able to travel, like she and my dad always planned. She's spent her entire life taking care of everyone."

"Sure."

"And I'm his brother. His twin. It *should* be me taking care of him. I *want* it to be me."

I smiled, even though that lump was still stuck in my throat. "Of course you do."

"Well, she didn't see it that way. She said we weren't doing him any favors by babying him, and that if I was serious about having him live at my house one day, she wasn't sure she could stay with me."

"She gave you an ultimatum?"

"Yeah." He frowned. "She didn't phrase it like that, but it was clear I had to choose. And I did."

"You broke up with her?"

"Yep. And I've never once been sorry."

I nodded slowly. "That's . . . that's good. But I feel bad you went through that."

"Don't. It taught me some valuable lessons."

"Like what?"

"Like what I'm capable of and not capable of."

I tilted my head to one side. "What aren't you capable of?"

"Never mind. Forget I said anything." His expression said *REGRET*.

"No." I kicked him gently beneath the table. "Tell me."

He grunted in frustration. "Okay, but then we're moving on to something else."

"Deal. Now what aren't you capable of?"

"Maybe capable isn't the right word." He paused to finish his beer. "Maybe it's more like I learned what I'm not interested in."

"Which is . . ."

"A relationship. At least, a long-term relationship."

"So like, a girlfriend or wife?"

"Right."

"Because . . ."

"Because it's too hard. There are too many expectations. I'd always be letting her down because of . . ." He struggled for words. "Because of promises I've made to other people. Because of the circumstances of my life and family. Because of the kind of man I want to be."

"You don't think you could be a good man to a wife *and* your family?"

He wiped his hands on his napkin. "It wouldn't be fair. There's Asher, for one. Where I end up, he does too, and I get it. No woman wants that kind of package deal. She wants a husband who doesn't already have that kind of built-in responsibility to someone else. And being married to a cop isn't easy, either. There are times when I'd have to put others' needs ahead of hers. That's just the nature of my job. I can remember my parents fighting all the time about that stuff—don't get me wrong, they loved each other and made the marriage work—but it was fucking hard."

"Was it?"

"Hell yes. My dad wasn't always there when he said he would be. Dinners got cold. My mom had to discipline us on her own. He missed games and concerts and my sister's ballet recitals—although he lucked out there, if you ask me."

I laughed and sipped my beer, hoping he'd keep talking. It was like old times, only in person instead of on the phone. I felt sixteen again.

"Anyway, I just made the decision that I do better on my own. And it's not like I'm lonely." There was a touch of defensiveness in his tone.

"No?"

"No. I've got family around all the time. I've got friends. I've got my dog. I work twelve hour shifts—sometimes more—and I love what I do."

"That's awesome. So no regrets about leaving the Army?"

"Fuck no." He shook his head. "I'm glad I did it, I think every able-bodied man should serve his country, but eight years and three combat tours was enough."

"What about every able-bodied woman?" I prodded.

He sighed loudly. "I'm old-fashioned, okay? But if a woman wants to serve, she should."

Satisfied with his answer, I nodded. "I agree. And I'm happy to hear you love being a cop. But I don't think you should completely rule out marriage and kids down the road. What if you meet your soul mate?"

He rolled his eyes and mumbled some words I couldn't decipher, although I caught his drift loud and clear.

"What? It could happen. You might answer a 911 call someday and have to rescue some beautiful woman's kitten from a tree. Then she'll be so grateful to you, she'll hand over her heart forever and ever. The end. Happily ever after."

He cocked his brow. "I'd settle for a blowjob."

I laughed, kicking him under the table again. "Fine, I give up. Come on, let's pay the bill and go get some ice cream at First Mate down by the harbor. I'm dying for a waffle cone."

I tried to give Noah some cash for dinner, but he wouldn't take it. He also insisted on paying for my single scoop of Superman ice cream, even though he didn't get anything for himself.

"You don't eat sweets?" I said, licking around the top of a giant mound of red, blue, and yellow ice cream.

"Sometimes, but ice cream isn't really my thing. Want to walk out on the pier?"

"Sure." It was a nice early fall night and the sun was just about to set, although the breeze was picking up a bit. "I should have brought a sweater."

"Are you cold? Wait here." Noah jogged over to his SUV and grabbed something from the back seat. When he came back, he handed me a gray zip-up hoodie that said ARMY on the front. "It's mostly clean. I had it on this morning before my run, but left it in the car because today was so warm."

"Good enough for me. Thanks. Can you hold this?" I handed him my cone and pulled on the sweatshirt. It was huge on me, but definitely cozy. It smelled nice too.

"Looks good on you," he said, giving me back my ice cream.

"Thanks. This reminds me of the time you came to see me in DC when you were in the Army."

He frowned. "Was I wearing it?"

"No, you were in uniform. But we walked around the city and I got cold, so you bought me an I-heart-DC sweatshirt and a hot chocolate." It was also the day I'd thought he might finally kiss me, but he hadn't.

"Oh yeah. I remember." He grinned. "You spilled the hot chocolate on the sweatshirt."

"I did. And I had to walk around wearing a stain for the rest of the day."

As we walked, we caught each other up a little more on our families, reminisced about teenage memories, laughed at inside jokes. At the end of the pier was a bench, and we sat down. The wind was stronger out here, and I was glad for his sweatshirt. Finished with my ice cream by then, I pulled the elastic from my wrist and tugged my hair into a ponytail. When I was done, I brought my heels up to the bench and wrapped my arms around my legs.

"God, this reminds me so much of summers when I was young," I said. "My sisters and I used to ride our bikes into town and just hang out and eat ice cream. Then we'd have to race home like crazy to avoid missing curfew. Except Chloe. She missed it all the time."

"But you never did?"

I shook my head. "Never. I was a rule follower. Scared to do anything wrong. Although," I went on, laughing a little. "I did have my first kiss on this very bench. He copped a pretty good feel too. I thought I was going to die."

"Who was it?" Noah asked. He sounded kind of mad about it, like he might go kick the guy's ass.

"His name was Austin Brown. He moved away shortly after that." I sighed. "Our romance was cut tragically short." I looked over at him. "What about you? Who was your first kiss?"

"I have no idea."

"What? Yes, you do. Come on."

"No, I really don't." He squinted out at the bay. "If I had to guess, I'd say it was eighth grade and her name might have been Sarah. Or Samantha."

"Sarah or Samantha," I mused, surprised at the flare of jealousy in my gut. "Did you cop a feel?"

"I doubt it. It took me a while to get brave enough to do that. Former altar boy and all."

"You were an altar boy?" I squealed. "How did I not know that?"

"You don't know everything about me."

Our eyes met, and a hot little current buzzed between us.

"I guess I don't," I said slowly. "An altar boy, huh?"

"Yep." A smile tipped his lips. They were full and looked soft. I wondered what his kiss tasted like. What his scruff would feel like on my cheek, or moving down my throat. When he caught me staring at his mouth, I quickly looked out at the water and kept talking, mostly out of nerves.

"I remember going home the night Austin first kissed me, rushing up the stairs to my bedroom, locking my door, and staring at myself in the mirror above my dresser, desperately hoping I looked different."

"Different how?"

"I don't even know exactly. More mature. More experienced. Like I was in on the secret."

"God, that's such a girl thing. How the hell was one kiss from some skinny-ass, barely pubescent teenage boy, who probably came in his pants the second he touched your boob, going to make you look more mature?"

"I don't know." I lifted my shoulders. "You really think he came in his pants?"

He laughed. "Chances are good. And if he didn't, he probably went home and finished himself off thinking about you."

"Seriously?" I wasn't sure whether to be flattered or creeped out.

"Sorry. That's probably too much information about teenage boy brain."

I thought for a second before braving the question. "Is that what you did with Sarah/Samantha?"

"Uh, it's likely. I did it all the time back then. And afterward I always felt guilty about it—my inner altar boy thought it was a sin. For the longest time I worried I'd cause something bad to happen. Or that I'd go to hell."

"But you did it anyway."

He nodded. "Oh yeah. Every night."

We laughed, and then sat there for a minute or two in silence, the sky growing darker. It was funny, we'd talked about girls he'd liked and boys I'd had crushes on during our teenage phone conversations, but we'd never gotten into details about sexual exploits. At the time, either I was too shy to ask or possibly didn't really want to know. Sex stuff used to scare me. But now I was curious. And kinda turned on. "What about your first time?"

"You mean sex?"

"Yeah." I looked over at him. He had a great profile, with a strong, masculine jawline.

"I was a senior. She was a junior. My parents' basement."

His parents' basement. Where we used to sit and watch TV. Envy tightened my gut. "Was it good?"

He winced. "It was fast."

"Mine was too. Freshman year of college. His dorm room. It smelled like socks and Abercrombie and Fitch cologne." I wrinkled my nose at the memory.

Noah smirked. "Sounds about right."

I paused, wanting to ask a question, but nervous it was going too far. In the end, curiosity won out. "What about Holly?"

"What about her?"

"Was it good? The sex?"

He shrugged. "You know. Potato salad."

I tipped my head onto the back of the bench and laughed. "Yeah. I know exactly."

Seven

Noah

WHEN MEG STARTED TO SHIVER, WE WALKED BACK TO my car. I was tempted to put my arm around her but refrained. In the past, I probably would have just done it, but there was something different about tonight that made me hesitate to touch her.

You want her too much. That's what.

I tried to silence the voice in my head by clearing my throat, and I stuck my restless hands into my front pockets. *I shouldn't have made the joke about the blowjob at the table. Or told her I jerked off every night as a teenager.* Now I had sex on the brain, and Meg was a little too tempting tonight. Too cute. Too familiar. Too easy to talk to.

And too unaware . . . she had no idea what she did to me. What she'd always done to me. Watching her lick that ice cream cone was fucking murder on my self-control.

On the short drive back to my house, I was silent, which was fine, because Meg talked a mile a minute about everything she had to do this week and all the wedding shit going on. I listened with half my brain while the other half continued listing all the reasons it would be a terrible idea to invite her in.

You'll end up touching her. You'll end up kissing her. You'll end up fucking her. You'll ruin this friendship, this amazing, nearly two-decade-long friendship just because you like the way she sucks barbecue sauce off the bone and you haven't gotten laid in so long. Leave her be. Drop her off. Go home alone and jerk off to some other woman.

"Want me to take you home?" I asked her.

"No, that's okay. Thanks, but I can drive."

"Are you sure? I really don't mind."

"I'm sure."

At my house, I pulled into the garage, hoping she'd get on her way fast. "I better go let Renzo out."

"Speaking of that, can I just use your bathroom real quick?" she asked as we got out of the car.

"Sure." I vowed to stay in the yard with Renzo while she was in the house, and I did.

"Thanks," she said when she came out, smiling at me in the dark. "Guess I'll take off now."

"Okay." I shoved my hands into my pockets again. "Thanks for hanging out."

"I had a good time. Thanks for dinner. And dessert."

"You're welcome." *Now stop looking so adorable in my sweatshirt and get the fuck out of here before I lose my mind.* I wasn't about to ask for it back because watching her strip off an article of clothing was liable to put me over the edge.

"So you don't have to work tomorrow?" she asked.

"Nope."

She glanced at her phone. "It's not even ten yet. Want to watch TV or something? You know you've missed watching Law & Order with me." She poked me in the stomach, and I took a step back.

I smiled, barely trusting my tongue to say the right thing.

"Sounds like fun, but I'm kind of tired. I'm used to going to bed early and getting up before sex."

"Before what?" She looked confused.

Fuck you, brain. "Before six."

"Oh. Okay, no problem. Are we still on for a run?"

"Sure." Running was fine. Running would be in public. In the sunlight. With clothes on. And it did not involve sitting close to her on the couch. "Do you want me to pick you up or should we meet at the park?"

"I should be able to get a car. If I can't, I'll text you. What time?"

"Is seven too early?"

"Seven's good. See you then."

"See you then."

For a second, she just stood there, and my heart hammered with fear. My entire body was tense. Was she ever going to leave?

"I'll walk you to your car," I said, trying to move her along.

"Okay. Thanks."

Renzo followed us down the driveway to the street, where a dark Cadillac was parked along the curb. She unlocked the door and gave me a sheepish grin. "Got my dad's Caddy."

"Nice."

"Well, goodnight." She came toward me and raised her arms for a hug.

Suppressing a groan at the feel of her body pressed close to mine, I took one hand from my pocket and returned the hug *very* loosely, leaning forward so our hips didn't touch. "Night."

Before she let me go, she pressed her lips to my cheek. "This feels really good," she whispered close to my ear.

Fuck yes, it did. Too good. And if she didn't let go of me, I was going to do something we would both regret.

It actually reminded me of that day we'd spent together, the one she'd brought up earlier when I'd gone to DC on leave. She hadn't been dating anyone at the time, and we'd spent the entire day walking around the city. One of the places she'd taken me was the World War II Memorial. Both of us had grandfathers that had fought in that war, and even though both of them had returned, the memorial was a reminder of heroes and sacrifice. Since I was still in the military at the time, back from one combat tour and due to deploy again soon, I was conscious of it all in a way I never had been before. And so was she.

For the first time, she'd taken my hand as we walked near the fountain. "I don't want you to go," she said.

I liked the feel of her fingers interlocked with mine. "I'll be back."

"You don't know for sure."

"That's true."

"Noah!" She stopped walking and turned to face me. "You're supposed to say something more reassuring than that."

"Sorry. I didn't know there was a script. I was just agreeing with you that I don't know anything for sure." But as I looked into her eyes just then, I *did* know something for sure—that I wanted to kiss her. That I'd miss her. That I cared for her more deeply than I'd ever admitted. That if she'd wait for me, I'd always come back for her.

She grinned. "I guess I wanted you to argue with me."

"I don't want to argue with you right now," I said quietly.

Her smile faded. "What—what do you want?"

I looked at her lips, and my heart skipped like a stone on the water.

But I didn't kiss her, and the moment passed us by.

A moment later we were walking again, and she'd let go of my hand.

Now, here in the street, I stood as still as if I were frozen, praying she couldn't feel my dick starting to get hard, and eventually, she backed away. I thought her face looked a little disappointed, but I couldn't be sure—might have been wishful thinking on my part.

She got in the car, and I shut the door after her. Two minutes later, I watched her tail lights disappear into the dark and breathed a sigh of relief. "Come on, boy. Let's go in."

Upstairs in my room, I stripped off my clothes, brushed my teeth, and got in bed, promising myself I'd ignore my hard-on and go straight to sleep.

But my erection refused to cooperate. Hating myself, I reached into my boxer briefs and starting giving myself a very angry hand job.

Don't think about her. Don't think about her. Don't think about her.

But she was like gravity—no matter what I did, I couldn't fight the physical pull of her. I was never going to win.

Thoughts of her dragged me down deep and wouldn't let go. Her mouth, her eyes, her hair, her legs, her scent, her laugh, her tears, her touch.

One night, my traitorous mind thought as I yanked furiously on my aching cock. *That's all I need. One night, and I'll give her everything she ever wanted.*

All my desire for her converged inside me demanding

release, and as I reached the breaking point, my eyes shut tight, my breath ragged and rasping, my jaw clenched, I imagined her body arched above me. I came hard and fast onto my own stomach, groaning as I thought about how good it would feel to come inside her, to make her come with me, to feel her body ripple and pulse, hear her softly sighing my name.

God, I wanted her. I fucking wanted her. I'd never wanted anyone so badly in my entire life.

But did I want her badly enough to risk losing her?

Eight

Meg

I DROVE HOME FEELING EXHILARATED, HAPPY, and . . . confused.

The entire night had been so much fun, but something had felt off at the end. I couldn't pinpoint exactly what it was or when it had happened, but Noah was definitely different when we said goodnight. Tense. Quiet. Almost like he was nervous.

But why? What had changed?

I racked my brain the whole way home. Was it something I'd said? Had I asked too many personal questions? Had I poked too deeply into his breakup with Holly? I knew guys didn't enjoy talking about their feelings like some women did, but Noah and I had always been able to talk openly about things.

And I still couldn't believe the selfish way his ex had behaved. Generally I didn't like to judge people I didn't know, but honestly, I didn't feel that guilty for judging Holly. Noah had always been protective of his brother—protective of everyone. From the day they met, I was certain she would have known that. It was one of the sexiest things about him.

He was definitely better off without her.

After parking my dad's car in the garage, I let myself

into the house, locked the door behind me, and trudged up the stairs to my room. That's when I realized that I'd forgotten to give Noah his hoodie back. Sighing, I took it off and tossed it onto the back of a chair. I'd return it tomorrow morning.

After plugging in my phone and setting the alarm, I laid out my running clothes for the morning and got ready for bed. But when I slipped between the sheets, I was too restless and uneasy for sleep.

I wished Noah had invited me in. Maybe he'd have admitted what was bothering him at the end of the night. Maybe we could have talked more about it. Maybe we'd have sat close together on his couch and laughed some more about first kisses. First times. Fantasies.

Maybe, I thought, my skin beginning to hum, I would have put my hand on his thigh. And maybe he would have leaned a little closer. Maybe we would have kissed, and it would have been *our* first time.

I couldn't deny that I'd been thinking about it tonight. Because even though being with him had that familiar cozy feeling, that whole big-brother-little-sister vibe we used to have was gone. Instead, there was something else between us tonight. Some kind of chemistry that had only simmered beneath the surface before. And I liked it.

Before I knew what I was doing, I got out of bed and grabbed his sweatshirt, bringing it back to bed with me. I slid beneath the covers again and brought it to my face, hoping it still smelled like him.

It did. I closed my eyes and breathed him in.

My right hand moved down my stomach, inching inside my underwear. I felt a little ashamed at first, like getting myself off to the idea of Noah was something I shouldn't be doing in my parents' house, but as soon as I began to touch myself, I got over it.

Fuck it, this was my room, my bed, my body. If I wanted to get off with Noah in my head, it was my business. Maybe it would never happen in real life, but my mind was my personal playground.

I'd never fantasized about Noah before. Not that I did this very often, but when I did, my go-to dudes were nameless, faceless people I wouldn't have to worry about facing the next day at Starbucks or the gym or the office. Cowboys. Firemen. Knights in shining armor.

Tonight, however, no anonymous hero would do. Tonight, the body above me, the hands on my skin, the tongue between my legs, the cock sliding inside me, belonged to Noah.

And he was fucking *fantastic*. He knew exactly what to do, how to touch me, what to whisper in the dark. He moved like he owned me. *I've always wanted you*, he said. *And tonight, I can't hold back.*

My orgasm tore through me, its strength taking me by surprise. It was powerful enough that I gasped into his sweatshirt, which I still had pressed to my face. Usually it took a lot longer than just a few minutes for me to come, especially without the help of a vibrator—which I'd gotten rid of after moving in with Brooks, because he said it made him "uncomfortable."

I decided that would be my first purchase when I got back to DC.

If only I could take this hoodie with me too.

My alarm went off at 6:15 the following morning, and I bolted upright in bed. I hit snooze, but I didn't need any more sleep. I felt wide awake. Excited. Happy.

I dressed quickly in leggings, a sports bra, a loose tank, and pulled on Noah's sweatshirt as well. I knew I'd have to give it back, but damn I wished I could keep it. Heat rushed into my cheeks as I made my way downstairs. I still couldn't believe what I'd done last night—or how good it had been. Would it be terrible if I did it again tonight?

My parents were already in the kitchen, sipping coffee and reading the news—my mom on her laptop and my dad holding up a newspaper. "Morning," I chirped as I went over to the Keurig and made myself a to-go cup.

"Morning," my dad said, turning a page.

"Morning, dear. You're up early," my mother observed.

"I'm going for a run with Noah. We're meeting at seven. Dad, okay if I borrow your car again? I should be back by nine."

"Sure, honey."

"Thanks."

My mother smiled at me. "Did you two have a nice time last night?"

"Yes. We had dinner at Hop Lot. It was fun."

"Feel free to invite him to the wedding," she said. "There's an extra chair at your table since . . ."

Since your boyfriend dumped you. My good mood threatened to deflate at the reminder, but I refused to dwell on it. "He probably has to work."

"But you could *ask*," my mother said.

"I'll think about it." I took my cup from the machine and snapped a lid on it. Then I kissed both my parents on the cheek and headed out. "See you later."

On the drive to the park, I thought about asking Noah to the wedding as my sort-of date. I wasn't standing up for Frannie (Chloe was her maid of honor, and Mack's daughters were her junior bridesmaids and flower girl), so it's not like he'd be left alone constantly while I did wedding party things.

But would it be weird? Would it make him uncomfortable? The last thing I wanted to do was to introduce awkwardness into our friendship. The whole reason our bond had never been tested, even across time and distance, was because we'd never crossed the line. Would going on a "date" wreck what we had? Would it even be considered a "date" if he just sat with me at my table? It's not like I'd make him dance with me or anything. It would be more like dinner with a group of friends. We could handle that, right?

In fact, it would be fun. He'd keep me from feeling sorry for myself. He'd make me laugh—we made each other laugh. I bet he didn't get out much socially, either, since apparently he didn't date and his closest friend was married to his sister and had a houseful of kids.

By the time I pulled into the parking lot and spotted Noah's car, I'd made up my mind. I'd ask him.

"How's the pace? You doing okay?" Noah asked as we jogged along the dirt trail, Renzo joyfully leading the way.

"I'm fine," I said, although I was huffing and puffing a bit. His legs were longer than mine, and it was clear his stamina was better. In fact, I had to use all my energy and lung power to keep up, so conversing wasn't really an option during the run. Every now and then, he'd check in with me and make sure I was okay, or issue a command to Renzo (usually "slow down, buddy") but mostly we ran beside each other in peaceful silence, the sun warm on our faces.

In fact, it had been warm enough that I'd already given Noah his sweatshirt back—after sneaking one more big sniff of it. He'd offered to let me keep it, but I couldn't really think of a good reason. It was too warm to wear it while we ran (plus that would make it smell like me), and I couldn't very well tell him I wanted to keep it because inhaling his scent while getting myself off last night had given me a fantastic orgasm, so I sadly handed it over, sighing inwardly as he tossed it onto the passenger seat of his SUV.

After we finished the run, I asked him if he'd like to have breakfast with me in town. Everything between us felt perfectly normal this morning—I hadn't sensed any of the weird tension that had existed between us when we'd said goodbye last night. In fact, I almost wondered if I'd imagined it.

"My treat," I said, grabbing my right foot to stretch my quad. "You got dinner last night."

"I could do that." He thought while he stretched his calves. "But I need to drop Renzo off. And I should probably grab a shower first."

"No problem," I said, switching legs. "I guess I could go home and do that too. Why don't I meet you back at your house?"

"I can pick you up."

"Are you sure? It's out of your way."

Noah rolled his eyes. "Sawyer, it's like fifteen minutes from here. Not a big deal."

I laughed. "Okay. Text me when you're on your way."

At home, I quickly showered, aimed the blow dryer at my

hair for ten minutes before putting it in a ponytail, and threw on jeans and a fitted red short-sleeved shirt. The top was *slightly* cropped, but it had a mock neck and my jeans were high-rise, and I looked at myself from all angles in the mirror to make sure I didn't look like a belly-baring teenager. Satisfied it didn't look too come-hither, I sat down and pulled on my sneakers.

When I got his text, I was trying to decide about putting makeup on . . . I didn't want to look like I was trying to impress him, but I did want him to think I was cute. At least, cute enough to say yes to being my wedding date. I decided that a little makeup would be okay, but I stayed away from any bold colors. I *did* spritz on a little perfume, but I did that every day. So it wasn't really just for him.

But I hoped he liked it.

When he texted again that he was in the drive, I hurried down the stairs and out the door.

"Hi," I said breathlessly as I jumped into the passenger seat. "Thanks for picking me up."

"No problem. You smell good." He snuck a glance at my midriff before putting his eyes back on the road—fast. I nearly teased him about it but thought twice. And I suppose I could have been wrong. He was wearing a cap, which shaded his eyes a little.

But I hoped I was right.

"Thanks. Do you have a place in mind for breakfast?" I asked him.

"Yes, but if you have an idea, I'm open." He circled around and headed back down the long road leading from the farm to the highway.

"If you've got the time, let's drive into Traverse and hit Coffee Darling, where Frannie works. I don't know if they have eggs and bacon, but they have amazing pastries."

"We could do that," he said.

On the twenty-minute drive into town, I told him all about how Frannie had gone from simply supplying pastries for weddings at Cloverleigh to running a shop out of Coffee Darling and taking over the management duties there as well while her partner took some maternity leave. "I always thought of her as such a baby, but she's really come into her own. When I look at her now, I hardly recognize her."

"I hear you. I can't believe my little sister has a successful business and all those kids. She's amazing, even if she drives me fucking nuts."

I liked the note of pride in his voice. And the way he filled out his shirt. I couldn't stop looking at his upper arms. He had nice thick wrists too. And he wore a baseball cap, which made him look even more boyish and cute. "That's right, I forgot Nina took over the salon. I actually have an appointment there this week—Wednesday, I think. I hope I see her."

"You will, she's there every day. Unless she goes into labor before then." He shook his head. "I'm telling you, she is massive. Big as a house."

"I hope you don't say that to her."

"She's my sister. Of course I say that to her."

"Noah!"

"Trust me, she gives it right back. It's how we are." He chuckled a little. "Don't worry about Nina. She might be a house, but she's made of bricks."

We arrived at Coffee Darling a little before ten, and Frannie came out from behind the counter to give me a hug. "Hey! Thanks for coming in, you guys."

"Frannie, I don't know if you've ever met my friend Noah McCormick before." I turned to Noah. "Noah, this is my youngest sister, Frannie."

He held out his hand. "Nice to meet you."

She took his hand and gave him a friendly smile. "I know all about you. I live in Hadley Harbor, and you and Renzo are pretty famous there. Plus Mack has talked about you."

Noah nodded. "Mack's a great guy."

"Thanks. Did you guys come to eat?" Frannie looked hopeful. "We've got the best cinnamon buns around, and the coffee is hot and fresh."

"Perfect," I said. "We'll just grab a seat."

The shop was crowded, but we snagged two stools at the counter, and Frannie hurried over with the coffee pot and two menus. Turns out, they did have eggs and bacon, which Noah ordered along with a potatoes and toast, while I ordered a cinnamon roll.

"That's all you want?" Noah asked.

"They're huge," I said. "Trust me, I saw them last time I was here. And I have to fit into my dress Saturday night."

"Oh right, the wedding." He picked up his mug and sipped. "Mack really is a good guy."

"He is. Do you know him very well?"

"Not too well. But I sometimes see him at the gym I go to. And recently he's gotten interested in a cause I'm involved with."

My ears perked up. "I love a good cause. Tell me."

"It provides service dogs to post-9/11 veterans with PTSD or traumatic brain injuries."

"That's amazing," I said, my heart melting. "Where do you find the dogs?"

"They're rescue dogs."

"So it's like you're rescuing two souls in one swoop. I love that."

"It's a good cause. Preventing suicide is a major goal

of the program, and I guess Mack had a Marine buddy that killed himself after he came home and struggled to adjust."

Setting my coffee down, I put one palm over my heart. "Oh my God. I had no idea."

"It's common, unfortunately. I was lucky to have the support of family and friends, but even with that, a lot of guys need some help returning to civilian life." He took a drink of his coffee and set down the mug, but kept his eyes on it. "It was actually after I lost my dad that I struggled the most. But right after that, I got Renzo, and my life turned around."

I heard the catch in his voice. "Really?"

He nodded. "So I know firsthand how much bonding with an animal can help."

Reaching over, I placed a hand on his arm. His skin was warm, but gooseflesh rippled up my arm, making me shiver. "What can I do to help? Do you need a connection in Washington? Increased awareness? Fundraising?"

"Hell. All of the above, probably." He lifted his cap off his head and replaced it. "I can ask the leadership on that. Mostly I've just done community events with Renzo, helped find foster homes to raise puppies, donated money. We've actually got an event coming up this month, a 5K race."

"Ooh, when? Can I run in it?" I bounced on my seat.

"Sure, but when do you go back to Washington? The race is Saturday the 19th."

"Oh." My excitement died down. "I'm already back in DC by then. I leave Sunday, the day after the wedding."

"Quick visit."

"Yeah. I have to get back for work. Fall is always a busy season." And usually one I looked forward to for its action and excitement. But then I remembered what I'd face when I got back there—I had to move, find a roommate, or ask for a raise in order to afford the townhouse Brooks and I'd shared. I wasn't ready to deal with that yet.

"Maybe another time, then." Noah took another sip of coffee. "And I'll let you know about making a connection in Washington."

"Yes, please do that." I rubbed his arm. "I want to help."

He smiled at me. "Of course you do." He was teasing me, but it was a sincere compliment too, and it made my entire body tingle.

I smiled back, feeling my cheeks grow warm. "So I want to ask you something. And you can say no."

"Uh oh. Should I be worried?"

Laughing, I took my hand from his arm and clasped my fingers together in my lap. "No. It's nothing crazy. I just wondered if you would maybe want to hang out with me on Saturday night . . . at the wedding."

Just then, Frannie appeared. "Here you are." She set two plates down in front of us—eggs, bacon, and potatoes for Noah, cinnamon roll for me. "And I'll be right back with your toast, Noah."

"Thanks," he said, a little distracted. "So would that be . . . like a date?"

"It wouldn't have to be," I replied quickly. "More of a favor to me. We could just go and hang out like we usually do."

Frannie reappeared and set the toast down with a smile. "Can I get you two anything else?"

"No, thanks," I said, my stomach too knotted up to eat anyway. Had asking him been a horrible idea?

Noah picked up his fork. Took a bite of his eggs.

"Listen, forget I asked. It was just an idea. There's an empty seat at my table, and my mother thought—"

"Wait. It was your mother's idea to ask me?"

"No. I mean, yes, but no." I sighed, closing my eyes. "This is stupid. I don't know why I'm getting flustered." I looked at him again, reminding myself it was just Noah. "Yes, my mother mentioned it this morning, but *I* want you there. I think you'd make the whole night more fun."

"Well, that's a given."

The joke made me relax. I poked his shoulder. "Does that mean you'll come? It's okay if you have to work. You could come by later, even if it was just for a little while."

He set his fork down and reached for his coffee again. "I don't have to work Saturday. I have to work Sunday though."

"I'll be sure you make your curfew." I grinned. "You can arrest me if I don't."

He laughed. "That might be fun."

My belly flipped over. *Holy shit.* "Does that mean you'll come?"

"I guess I could come."

"Yay! Thank you." I clapped my hands. "It will be fun, I swear. Good food, good booze, good music."

Giving me the side eye, he declared, "I'm not dancing, Sawyer."

"No dancing, I promise."

"Then you've got yourself a date—or whatever you want to call it."

I couldn't help smiling as I dug into my cinnamon roll, which was the best thing I'd ever tasted. Fluffy and sticky sweet, with just the right amount of icing dripping off the top. I devoured it, moaning with delight.

"Good?" Noah asked.

"Hell yes," I said, licking icing off my thumb. "Even better than a Twinkie."

He laughed and shook his head. "Some things never change."

But some things do, I thought, as my heart raced. *Some things do.*

Nine

Noah

JESUS CHRIST.

Did she have to lick her fingers like that? Was there no food she could eat with utensils? Next time, I'd take her to a Japanese steakhouse or something. Some place I could put a goddamn fork and knife in her hands. Maybe some chopsticks.

And that icing was even worse than the barbecue sauce. It looked more sexual. I tried not to let my mind go there, but fucking hell, now she was sucking it off her thumb!

I shifted in my seat, the crotch of my shorts suddenly tight. This morning, I'd promised myself I'd control my mind and my body and *be-fucking-have*. I would treat her with the respect that she deserved and expected of me. I would hold myself to the highest standards, like I always did at my job, and quit allowing my thoughts to run away from me. She was my friend, she mattered to me, she trusted me. It was up to me to protect her. From me, if necessary.

It was not going well.

First, I'd had a hell of a time keeping my eyes on the path in front of us while we ran. Her ass looked fucking spectacular in those skin-tight leggings she had on. I kept glancing back at it over my shoulder without even realizing it. And now she had some kind of little top on that showed a sexy strip of her bare belly above her jeans. It made me want to lick it.

Second, when she made that comment about arresting her, I'd said, *That might be fun.* What the hell? I had a dirty mind and cracked those kind of jokes on the phone with her all the time, but in person, it was different. I needed to lay off that shit. She was going to think I was some kind of pervert—which, let's face it, I was. Not to mention the fact that now I was trying not to imagine her handcuffed to my bed.

And I'd agreed to take her to the wedding. At least there would be lots of people around—that was the main reason I agreed to go with her. That, and the fact that I knew she was right about having a good time. I was pretty sure she and I could have a good time anywhere, fully clothed or buck naked, vertical or horizontal or any angle in between . . . but if I stuck to public places, we'd be safe. *She'd* be safe.

I glanced at her one more time and amended my statement: public places where she would *not* eat with her hands. No ribs, no ice cream cones, and especially no dripping hot icing.

"So what do I have to wear to the wedding?" I asked, trying to distract myself.

"A suit, if you've got one." She wiped her hands on her napkin.

"Yes, I've got one. I've actually got two. Despite what my mother and sister think, I'm not a total Neanderthal."

She laughed. "Sorry. I'm sure you'll look great. If it helps, my dress is a cinnamon color."

I squinted at my plate. "You mean brown?"

"No, I mean cinnamon," she said like I was a first grader.

"Cinnamon is brown, Sawyer."

She rolled her eyes and gave me an exasperated sigh. "Okay, it's a shade somewhere between brown and red. Does that compute?"

"Better." I reached for my coffee. "How about a dark gray suit?"

"Perfect," she said, picking up her phone from the counter. "Sorry, my mom is texting me."

"Go ahead." While she replied to her mom, I finished eating, hoping her dress was long enough to cover her legs and showed no cleavage. With any luck, it would have a turtleneck.

"Confirming appointments for the salon on Wednesday." Meg set her phone down. "What do you think, up or down?"

"Huh?"

"My hair. Up or down?" She yanked out her ponytail and let her hair swing loose around her shoulders. "This is down, although it's not very pretty right now, so just picture it smooth and curled. Or up." She lifted it off her neck and piled it on the top of her head, then looked at me expectantly.

I laughed. "I've got no opinion on this. You always look good."

"Come on! Up or down, I need help. And you have to look at me all night."

I stuck the last bite of potatoes in my mouth. "Is your dress long or short?"

"Why does that matter?"

"Just asking."

"It's long."

"And how about the top? Does it have sleeves? Or is it strapless?"

"It has sleeves," she answered.

"Good."

"Good?" She looked confused, her hands still nested in her hair. "Why are sleeves good?" She let her hair fall and examined her elbows. "Is there something wrong with my arms?"

"No." I set my fork on my empty plate and pushed it away. "I was just curious." *And I want to make sure I'll be able to control my unsavory urges around you.* "Wear it down, I guess."

"Why?"

"For fuck's sake, Sawyer." I gave her a menacing look. "I don't know. Because it's natural. And it smells nice."

"Okay, okay." She put her ponytail back in. "So what should we do now?"

I checked the time. "I should go back and let Renzo out."

"Oh. Right."

"And then I have to head over to my mom's to pick up Asher. I'm taking him to work today."

She smiled. "I'd love to see him while I'm home."

"He'd like that," I said, happy that she'd asked. "He remembers you. Asked me if you still like to watch true crime shows."

"Really?" That irresistible smile got bigger. "That's so sweet. And the answer is *yes*, of course."

"How was everything, guys?" Frannie came over and cleared our plates.

"Excellent," said Noah, pulling out his wallet. "We're all set, and I will definitely be back."

"Good." Frannie smiled. "Put your money away, breakfast was on me."

"Frannie, you don't have to do that." Meg tugged on my arm. "And Noah, I invited you to breakfast, so I'll buy."

"Neither of you are buying, because it was on the house." Frannie shooed us toward the door. "Now go on. Get out of here and enjoy the day."

I pulled a twenty from my wallet and placed it on the counter. "Tip. Thanks for everything."

"That's too much!" Frannie cried indignantly.

"The service was exceptional." I flashed a grin at her and took Meg by the shoulders, steering her toward the door before she could get out her wallet or her sister could get around the counter and give me my money back.

"You're too nice to me," Meg said as we walked to the car. "I'm getting spoiled."

I wished I could spoil her in all kinds of ways. She had no idea. I unlocked the car and opened the passenger door for her.

She slid onto the seat and looked at me. "Why don't I come with you to let Renzo out and then over to your mom's? Like I said, I have no plans today, and tomorrow Sylvia gets in, so I think it's all wedding wedding wedding after that."

Instead of answering right away, I shut the door and took my time going around to the driver's side. It wasn't that I didn't want to hang out with her, but the more time we spent alone together, the harder it was getting to treat it like my job. Could I manage to keep my hands to myself all day? I wasn't too sure. I was still thinking when I started the engine.

She noticed my silence—of course she did.

"Hey, forget I asked," she said. "You've got things to do on your day off. You don't have to entertain me all day."

"It's not that. I just . . . You're only home for the week. I don't want to monopolize all your time," I lied.

"Hey." She reached over and put a hand on my arm. "I'm exactly where I want to be."

Our eyes met. My whole body warmed. And I knew at that moment that today would test me in ways I'd never even imagined.

And in ways I had—but then, that was the problem.

My mother, as I'd expected, was overjoyed to see Meg.

"Meg Sawyer, I don't believe it!" she squealed, coming right over to give her a hug as Renzo bounded past us into the house. "Just look at you. You haven't changed a bit since you were a teenager."

Meg laughed as she returned the hug. "It's good to see you, Mrs. McCormick."

"It's Carol, please. You might look sixteen, but you're a grownup now."

"I try." Meg looked at me. "I'm making Noah drag me around today. Everything is all wedding craziness at Cloverleigh."

"Good. He could use the company." My mother nodded in satisfaction. "And I bet it is. A wedding is so exciting—and is it right there on the farm? You mother must be going nuts with all the preparations."

"It's pretty nuts," Meg agreed. "But my sister April is planning everything, and she's a pro." She elbowed me. "I convinced Noah to come along with me."

My mother's eyes lit up. Possibly even teared up. "You did?"

"Yes, although I had to promise not to make him dance," Meg said with a laugh. "So I don't think my shoes will see much action."

"Oh, for goodness sake." My mother gave me a dirty look and stuck her hands on her hips. "Noah McCormick, you ask this young lady to dance, do you hear me?"

"I hear you, Ma. But I'm not dancing." Clapping her on the shoulder of her nurse's scrubs, I moved past her into the kitchen, where Asher was finishing lunch, dressed for work. Renzo was sniffing around the floor beneath the table, probably hoping for scraps. "Hey, Ash."

He reached for his SGD. "Hi. Who's here?" he asked.

I sat down next to him. "I brought Meg over to say hi."

He smiled. "Does she remember me?"

"Of course she does. Hey, Meg!" I called. "Come on in here."

Meg came into the kitchen room and gave Asher a big grin. "Hey, you. Long time no see." She bent down to give him a hug, and he hugged her back. Once she was seated next to me, he reached for his device again.

"Hello. How are you?" he asked.

"I'm great," she said. "In town for the week to see my younger sister get married."

"Do you still watch true crime?" he asked.

"You know it! Hey, do you like podcasts? You need to listen to My Favorite Murder."

Asher's face lit up even brighter. "I love that podcast. My friend Alicia loves it too."

I blinked. Asher had a friend? A *girl friend* named Alicia? That was news to me.

Meg clapped her hands. "So good, right? I can't believe Noah's never even heard of it."

Asher typed frantically, a gleeful look on his face. "He doesn't have good taste in shows."

Meg burst out laughing. "So you're headed to work today?"

"Yes. I work at Logan's."

"And you like it?"

"I like my job a lot."

"Cool. And what else are you up to these days? Do you still like swimming?"

"Yes. I swim on Fridays. That's where I met Alicia."

Ah. It had been a few weeks since I'd taken him to the rec center for swimming, so maybe that's why I hadn't heard about her. But it was obvious Asher really liked this girl. Why hadn't he ever mentioned her? Was it because I'd never asked him about girls? It wasn't that I didn't care or didn't think he could go on dates, I simply hadn't wanted to put that kind of pressure on him. But maybe by treating the subject as if it was nonexistent, I'd made him feel funny about it. I felt like a shitty brother.

"That's great," Meg said. "Friends are awesome." Then she punched me on the shoulder. "Even if they have bad taste in shows."

My mother appeared, tugging a sweater on over her scrubs. "Asher, dear, go brush your teeth and your hair. It's almost time for you to go."

Asher got up from the table, looking embarrassed in front of Meg—not that I blamed him. He was thirty-three. His mother should not be telling him to go brush his hair in front of other people. He grabbed his device and headed for his room with his distinctively stilted, tip-toed walk.

"Mrs. Reynolds is picking him up at five?" I asked my mother.

My mother nodded as she dug through her purse for something. "Yes, and warming up his dinner, which I left in the fridge. I won't be back until after six."

"Okay. Let me know if you need anything else this week. I'm off Thursday, Friday, Saturday."

"How about taking him to adaptive swim on Friday?"

I nodded. That would be the perfect time to ask him about this Alicia. "That works. Usual time?"

"Yes." She came over and kissed my cheek. "You're an angel. Mostly." Then she rubbed Meg's shoulder. "And it's *so* lovely to see you, dear."

Meg smiled up at her. "Thank you, you too."

"How nice the two of you are still such good friends after all this time. It makes you wonder, doesn't it?"

"Bye, Ma." I gave her a warning look.

"I mean, really, what a special, *special* relationship you two have," she gushed. "You've cared for each other all these years. It's really something. Are you single, Meg?"

Meg pressed her lips into a line. "At the moment."

"What a coincidence, so is Noah! And if you ask me, when two people—"

"We didn't ask you. Goodbye, Ma." I got up from my chair and collected Renzo. "Come on, boy. Let's go. You ready, Meg?"

She stood too. "Sure. Bye, Mrs. McCormick—I mean Carol."

My mother sighed and looked at the blank space on the mantel, and then heavenward. "Goodbye, dear."

After dropping Asher off at work, we drove back into town and walked around with Renzo on his leash, ducking in and out of shops (I waited for her outside if the shop didn't allow dogs) and stopping practically every few feet to chat with people who recognized Renzo and me.

"You should totally run for sheriff," Meg said as we strolled in the afternoon sun. "Everyone in this town adores you."

I shrugged, although I'd thought about it a million times. "I don't know about that."

"Didn't your father like the job?"

"He loved it."

"So why wouldn't you?"

"I don't want a lot of people poking in my business. And I've never liked politics. The thought of having to campaign for something pretty much makes me want to vomit."

She rolled her eyes. "Oh come on. It's not that bad. You've got a squeaky clean record, right? You're a hometown boy, a combat veteran, a sheriff's deputy—not to mention the son of the most beloved sheriff this county ever had. And no skeletons in the closet! Jesus, you're a shoo-in. Who'd even run against you?"

"How do you know I don't have any skeletons in the closet?" I asked her.

"I guess I don't. Do you?" She elbowed me. "Are there bodies in your basement? A wife chained up in the attic? Are you a Russian spy?"

"No."

"Then you should do it." Excited, she grabbed my hand. "I could even help you! I've got a ton of experience as a campaign strategist. I can't believe I didn't think of this before. We could do it together! We'd make a great team!"

"You're crazy," I said. *"You don't even live here."*

"Well, I'd help you hire the right people locally. I'm sure we could find someone to manage everything. Just give it some thought, okay? I bet your dad would love the idea."

I didn't answer right away as I thought about some of those conversations with my dad in the end. "Yeah. We talked about it a little."

"And?"

"And he was all for it," I confessed.

"See?" She tugged on my hand. *"It's meant to be."*

"I'll think about it."

"Good."

We walked all the way to the edge of town, then crossed the street and headed east toward the harbor and beach.

She didn't let go of my hand, and I liked it.

It reminded me of another day, a missed opportunity. If I could do it over again, would I kiss her?

I couldn't decide.

Ten

Meg

WHEN WE REACHED THE SAND, NOAH TOOK RENZO off the leash and let him run around the empty beach. Right away he found a stick and brought it over to us, wanting to play fetch. Noah threw it for him.

But he didn't let go of my hand.

My breath was starting to come a little faster. My arms were blanketed in gooseflesh. My knees felt a little weak. I had that crazy urge to kiss him, just like I'd had last night. I just wanted to know what it would be like to feel his lips on mine. I allowed myself a brief From Here to Eternity fantasy, picturing Noah and myself as Burt Lancaster and Deborah Kerr, rolling around in the surf.

Good Lord, Meg. Get a grip.

"It looks so different in the fall, doesn't it?" I asked, glancing around at the deserted beach. "In the summertime, it's always so packed."

"Yeah."

"Want to walk a little?"

"Sure."

Still hand in hand, Renzo happily trotting ahead of us, we strolled to the north, the wind in our faces. I pointed at the water. "And right there, lady and gentleman voters, is where the future Sheriff Noah McCormick saved my life."

Noah shook his head. "God, that was fucking scary."

"It was." I squeezed his hand. "I don't mean to make light of it. I'm grateful every day."

"I'm just glad I was there and happened to be looking in the right direction."

"What?" I stopped walking and stared at him. "That's not what happened at all, Noah. It wasn't an accident you were looking in the right direction—it was fate!"

He chuckled and adjusted his cap. "Okay."

I clucked my tongue as we started walking again. "Fine, if you don't believe me. But I have always known deep down that the universe meant for you to save me."

"Yeah?"

"Of course! There's no other way to explain it. We went from being perfect strangers to being the best of friends in a matter of days, didn't we?"

"I guess."

"And we're still close, even though we live far apart and don't talk every day. I love that about our friendship. I love *everything* about our friendship. I don't tell you often enough, but I'm really glad you're in my life."

"Jesus, Sawyer. That's really fucking sappy."

I laughed. "Well, it's true! And I'm trying to get better about prioritizing my relationships. Letting people know how much they mean to me." I nudged him with my elbow. "So how am I doing? Do you feel special and appreciated?"

"Uh, yes. So you can stop now."

"In a minute." I tipped my head against his shoulder for

a few seconds. We walked until we hit a patch of the shore-line where the sand had been eroded and the waves came right up to the trees. For some reason, I didn't want to turn around and go back yet. "Want to sit?"

"Okay."

We dropped down onto the beach a little ways from the water and watched Renzo chase a bird, dig a hole, and fling sand around. No longer holding my hand, Noah sat with his forearms draped over his knees, looking out at the bay. Looked like I had to face the fact that this whole kissing in the surf thing wasn't going to happen.

In fact, I had to close my eyes and chastise myself. How ridiculous could I be? If he hadn't tried anything when he was seventeen and all jacked up on adolescent hormones, he certainly wasn't going to do it now that he was older and more mature. I had to face reality—he simply didn't look at me like that.

And maybe it was better this way. But still . . .

"Can I ask you a question?" I ventured, the wind blow-ing my hair all around my face.

"If I say no, will you ask it anyway?"

I thought for a moment as I gathered it over one shoul-der. "No. I won't. Because it's personal."

He exhaled. "Go ahead and ask. There's not much I don't tell you."

"You might not want to tell me this."

"For fuck's sake, Sawyer. Just ask already."

"Okay." I bit my lip for a second. "Why haven't you ever tried to kiss me?"

He didn't answer. He didn't even look at me.

When a five full seconds had passed—which felt like five years—I got nervous. "Never mind. I shouldn't have asked.

It's a stupid question, and the answer is none of my business. Obviously, you've just never felt that impulse or you'd have done it. And that's fine, it's totally fine. I don't know what's going on with me. I think I'm just feeling bad about myself, and I—"

He moved so fast, I didn't even see it coming. One second I was sitting there gripping my hair over one shoulder, burning with humiliation and wishing a hole would open up in the sand and swallow me, and the next I felt his lips on mine, his hands on either side of my face.

My pulse went haywire as the shock and thrill of his kiss moved through me like lightning. His mouth was warm and firm, and covered mine completely. His lips moved with slow, strong confidence, and his tongue sought mine with hungry strokes. I couldn't breathe, couldn't think, couldn't even kiss him back. My hands remained wrapped around my hair as heat pooled at my center and my mind spiraled with happy, dizzy, unimaginable excitement. A small sound issued from the back of my throat—a gasp for air, a plea for more, a cry of blossoming desire.

Suddenly Noah let go of me, breaking the kiss, and I fell back on my elbows in the sand. I hadn't even realized he'd been holding me up. I blinked at him as the wind whipped my hair around my face again.

"Fuck," he said. "I'm sorry."

I shook my head. "No, don't be—"

"I don't know what I was thinking." He jumped to his feet and moved a few feet toward the water, readjusting his cap. Renzo came running over with the stick again, but Noah didn't throw it.

For a few seconds, I just lay there on my elbows, staring at Noah's broad back and trying to figure out what the fuck had just happened. Last I could remember, I'd said something stupid and embarrassing, and he'd gone silent. Then all of a sudden, his lips were—

I closed my eyes as my core muscles clenched. God, he was a good kisser. Even better than in my fantasy. And I loved the way his hands had grabbed me that way. Possessively. Hungrily.

Why had he apologized?

When I opened my eyes again, Noah was walking slowly toward me, his face grim, his jaw set. His dark eyes were shadowed by the bill of his cap, but I didn't need to see them to know they were full of regret. His body language was clear.

I started to get up, and he offered me a hand. Placing my palm in his, I rose to my feet, but I still didn't feel all that steady.

"I'm sorry," he said again.

I took my hand back. "It's okay."

"No, it's not. Let me say this." He exhaled. "Your question threw me off balance. Because it's not true that I haven't thought about kissing you. I've thought about it a thousand times."

I stared at him. "You have?"

"Yeah." He looked down the beach in the direction we'd come from. "But I talked myself out of it every time."

"Why?"

"Because I don't want to ruin what we have."

I nodded slowly. "I get that."

"You might think you're not good at letting people know what they mean to you, but you are. I don't *need* very many people in my life, and I don't need them often, but you've been there for me."

"Just like you've been there for me."

"Which is exactly why giving in to whatever physical attraction we feel is a bad idea, Meg. It would change things. Probably ruin them."

Meg. He never called me Meg. Things were different already.

"But—"

"It wouldn't be worth it," he said. "Believe me, I've gone over and over this in my mind. Because as much fun as it would be to say fuck it all and take you to bed, I'd be too afraid of losing what we have."

I don't care, I thought stubbornly. *Say fuck it all and take me to bed.*

But he was right to be scared.

"I'd be afraid too," I admitted. "Although I agree—it probably would be fun."

"Oh, there is no probably," he said with the touch of that cockiness I was used to in his voice. "It would be epic."

I had to laugh a little. "Right. But we can't."

Part of me was hoping he'd argue, but he never did that when he was supposed to.

"No," he said firmly. "We can't."

I sighed. Why'd he have to be such a good man?

Renzo came sniffing around us again, and Noah finally gave in and threw the stick. Then he looked at me again. "So are we okay?"

I nodded and smiled, although I sort of felt like crying. "We're okay."

We walked back down the beach and through town to his car, and then he took me home. The conversation stayed light, and although there was an awkwardness between us, I didn't feel like we'd wrecked anything. We'd get back to normal. In fact, maybe we'd even be glad we'd gotten that kiss out of our systems. At least we could stop wondering.

Except . . . I didn't stop wondering.

I spent the entire rest of the afternoon moping around the house, mooning over him, and replaying the kiss in my head. Finally, I got so fed up with obsessing over it that I threw on a sweater and walked across the orchard to the tasting room to see if Chloe needed help. I needed a distraction.

Since it was a Monday, she wasn't very busy, and the last tasting was just finishing up. But when she looked closer at me, she could sense something was wrong.

"What's with the face?" she asked. "You look like you swallowed a goose egg."

"I had a weird day," I confessed. "I think I need to talk about it."

"What happened?"

"I kissed Noah."

Her mouth fell open. "Say no more. Dinner tonight?"

I nodded, relieved. "Yes. Thanks."

While Chloe finished the tour and closed up the tasting room for the night, I wandered around the farm a little. I stopped in the barn to pet the horses, walked along the hilly path that skirted the vineyards, peeked into the building that would serve as Frannie's reception spot. It was silent, barren and dark today—no linens, no lights, no flowers, no music. But on Saturday, it would be full of life and love as everyone gathered to celebrate Mack and Frannie's marriage. Would Noah still want to be my date?

I hoped so. I still wanted him to be there with me.

I still wanted him, period.

What the hell was I going to do about it?

"Tell me everything." Across the table from me, Chloe lifted her glass of pinot noir, her eyes wild with delight and curiosity.

"Don't you want to order food first?"

"Oh, right. Food." She glanced down at the menu of the bistro we'd chosen and gave it precisely five seconds. "Okay, I know what I want, do you?"

I gave it a one-minute scan and decided on salmon with a honey-maple glaze, roasted potatoes, and a house salad. Once the server had taken our order, I picked up my wine glass too. "I don't know where to start. I guess with yesterday."

"What happened yesterday?" Chloe asked eagerly, taking a sip.

"Nothing. Nothing physical, anyway. We just had a really good time."

"You guys always did have great chemistry." Chloe nodded knowingly. "I always wondered why you two never banged."

"Because it wasn't ever like that with us. And I never really questioned it, because we had more of that brother-sister vibe. Which was fine with me."

"He never tried *anything*? Not once in all those times you guys sat around watching TV late at night?"

"Never. I always assumed I wasn't his type."

Chloe took another sip. "Okay, so go on. You were having fun together yesterday . . ."

"Right. And I couldn't stop looking at him and thinking how hot he was. I started to imagine what it would be like to kiss him. And then by the end of the night, I sort of tried to get him to do it."

She looked surprised. "But he didn't?"

"No."

"Like, you puckered up and closed your eyes and did a dreamy thing with your face, like this . . ." She imitated a kiss-me-you-fool expression and swayed side to side. "And he did nothing?"

I burst out laughing. "Okay, no. I definitely did not do that. It was more like I asked him if he wanted to keep hanging out, and he said he was tired."

She shrugged. "Maybe he was. Or maybe he didn't know that by *hanging out*, you meant you wanted to put your hand in his pants. I bet he'd have said yes to that."

"I'm just not like that—I can't be that forward." I frowned. "I did give him a really good hug at the end of the night."

Chloe blinked at me. "A good hug? Meg, a good hug says *friend zone*. It says *bye, thanks for coming*. It does not say *my body is ready, let's get it on.*"

"It doesn't?"

"No! Men do not read minds. They don't pick up on subtlety. They see red light—stop. Green light—go. They do not see fifty shades of gray. At least not the good guys like Noah. If he's not one thousand percent positive you're into him like that, he probably wouldn't try anything." She put her glass down. "You have to make the first move."

"I can't make the first move." I gulped wine at the thought.

"Give me one good reason why not."

"Because . . . because I've never made the first move. I don't know how. What if I do it wrong? What if he doesn't understand?"

"Grab his balls. He can't misunderstand that," Chloe said, laughing.

"It's not funny, Chloe. You don't know what happened today." Our salads arrived, and as we ate I told her about how I'd flat-out asked Noah at the beach why he'd never kissed me before.

"Damn." She looked impressed. "That took some guts. So what happened?"

"At first, he just went silent, and I was dying a thousand deaths in the sand. Then I started babbling about being sorry, and how I shouldn't have asked, and then all of a sudden—he did it."

Chloe gasped, her fork halfway to her mouth. "He did? With no warning?"

"No warning. Out of the blue."

"And? How was it?"

I set my fork down and sighed. "Amazing. Breathtaking. Hot. It made my head spin. But then he jumped up and apologized."

My sister groaned. "That's the worst."

I nodded. "He said he'd always wanted to kiss me, but never had because we were such good friends."

Chloe sighed. "That's noble. But not much fun, huh?"

"No. But I mean, I get it. He explained to me all the reasons why it would be a bad idea to mess around with each other, and I agree with all of them. Neither of us wants to throw away seventeen years of friendship just to scratch an itch, no matter how long that itch has been there."

"No matter how good it would feel to give it a good, hard clawing?"

A tingle started between my legs and raced up my spine. I shifted around in my seat. "No matter what."

Our entrées arrived and we began to eat, although I hadn't even finished my salad and didn't feel that hungry. "I wish I had better advice, Meg. I can see that you're really into him, and I've always thought you two would be good together, but if you don't want to risk what you have now, it's probably best to remain friends."

I thought about that as I pushed a potato around on my plate. "Can't we remain friends *and* scratch the itch?"

"You mean like friends with benefits?"

"I guess."

Chloe shrugged. "You could. I mean, as long as both of you understood exactly what the nature of the relationship was and didn't have any additional expectations."

"What other expectations could there be?" I sat up a little taller, the possibility sparking something in me. "I mean, I'm only here for the week. After the wedding, I go back to DC. And he told me last night he's not interested in dating anyone long term. Since his last relationship fell apart, he doesn't date at all."

"So this would be just a fling? Something for fun?"

"Right." I took another drink, feeling more courageous by the minute. "I feel like we both could use a little fun with someone we trust."

"Then I say go for it. As long as neither of you is in danger of being hurt, I don't see why you shouldn't." Chloe lifted her glass to mine. "Go get him, tiger."

I tapped my glass to hers. "But how? Tell me what to do. How did you seduce Oliver?"

"Which time?"

I laughed. "Come on. Help me."

"Okay, okay. Let me think. Our first *kiss* was kind of mutual. But our first *time*, I definitely took the lead—at least at first."

"What did you do?"

"I showed up at his dorm room and told him to take my virginity."

I nearly choked on my wine. "What?"

"Yeah, it was amazing." Chloe looked happy at the memory. "At first he was mad and said he wouldn't do it."

"Seriously?"

"Yes, but he changed his mind pretty fast."

"I bet." I took a bit of my dinner and tried to think how I could apply her advice to be more proactive. "I'm not sure how I would go about it. My virginity is gone, alas. And I'm not used to being the aggressor."

"You don't need your virginity, silly. And you don't even have to be that aggressive. Just show up and make it clear you've changed your mind. That despite the risk, you *do* want him. You can't resist him. You have to have him or you'll go crazy." She nodded knowingly. "He'll lose his mind thinking he's all that."

"Really?" I bit my lip.

"Trust me. All you have to be is yourself, but be brave. Be confident. Be shameless in wanting him. He will *eat it up.*"

I set my fork down and picked up my ice water. Suddenly I felt hot and a little sweaty. "When should I do it?"

"If it were me, I'd surprise him at home tonight."

Setting the glass down with a thump, I stared at her. "Tonight?"

"Yeah, why not? You've made up your mind haven't you? And it's not like you've got endless time here. The clock is ticking." Her eyes danced. "Let the shenanigans begin."

An hour later, around nine o'clock, Chloe pulled up in front of Noah's house. I still wasn't exactly sure what I was going to say. I was hoping the right things would come to me spontaneously.

"If it goes wrong, will you come back and get me?" I asked her. My insides were already tied in knots. And I should have used the bathroom at the restaurant before we left—it wasn't an emergency, but I'd drunk that glass of wine fast, and then downed my ice water.

"It's not going to go wrong. Don't even put that out there. Think about what you want, and go get it." Chloe patted my leg. "Call me tomorrow."

"Okay. Wish me luck."

"You don't need it, champ."

I wasn't so sure, but I opened the door and got out.

There was a light on in an upstairs room, which I assumed was Noah's. At least he wasn't asleep yet. As I walked up the driveway, I rehearsed a few opening lines.

I changed my mind.

I can't stop thinking about you.

Fuck our friendship.

Then fuck me.

Nothing seemed quite right, and I reached the back door without a firm plan. I was surprised to find it slightly ajar, knowing how vigilant Noah was about safety. I knocked lightly and expected Renzo to come bounding over. He didn't, but I could hear him barking somewhere in the house. Was he shut inside a room?

On high alert, visions of serial killers in my head, I pushed open the door. "Noah?"

He didn't answer, but I heard water running and then pipes squeak, as if the shower was being turned off. I relaxed—he was fine. He was just upstairs taking a shower. And Renzo was in the spare bedroom, where Noah always put him when he showered, or else the dog would follow him into the bathroom. Hadn't he just told me that last night?

Laughing at my overactive imagination—I really needed to lay off the true crime—I shut the back door behind me and hurried toward the downstairs bathroom. With any luck I could use it quickly enough to arrange myself in some kind of seductive pose on the couch before he came downstairs to let Renzo out one last time.

It didn't register that the bathroom door was shut. Or that the light was on. Or that steam billowed out to meet me the moment I opened the door.

Which happened to be the precise moment Noah slid the shower curtain aside.

And there he stood. Buck naked. Dripping wet. Hot as fuck.

My jaw fell open.

He looked slightly alarmed for a second—after all, I *was* an intruder in his house—but then he saw it was me.

"Sawyer," he said, like he wasn't at all surprised to see me standing there in his bathroom with my lower lip on the floor. "Are you going to hand me a towel?"

A nice girl would have.

She probably would have apologized too.

At the very least, she would have covered her eyes. Maybe turned around and walked out.

I did none of those things.

"No," I said, my body catching fire. "I'm not."

Eleven

Noah

I ALMOST LAUGHED. "You're not?"

She shook her head, looking like a kid who had inadvertently found the hidden stash of Christmas presents. Kind of guilty, but also gleeful as fuck. Her eyes traveled over every inch of my wet skin, lingering on my cock.

I could easily have reached for a towel myself, but I didn't. I was enjoying the look on her face too much. And I'd been kicking myself all afternoon for being such a fuckup on the beach. After dropping her off, I'd come home and spent three hours raking leaves and cleaning out the gutters, then I went over and did my mother's gutters too—I felt like I needed the punishment.

Back at home, I ate a shitty frozen dinner, watched the World Series without really paying attention to the game—and it was the final—and gave myself hell for messing up the one chance I'd ever really had with Meg. I told myself that if I were somehow offered another one, I'd do things a lot differently.

And here she was, still in that hot little red top.

And here I was, stark fucking naked and starting to get hard as I thought about ripping it off her.

"Are you in the habit of breaking and entering?" I asked her.

Again, she shook her head. "I didn't break in. Your back door was open."

It wasn't like me, but it was possible, since I'd been so damn distracted all night.

"And I was just going to use the bathroom real quick," she went on, obviously flustered. "I didn't know you'd be in this one."

"There's a problem with the drain upstairs, so I came down here."

"Oh."

Jesus. The girl could *not* keep her eyes off my dick. It was both hot and hilarious.

"So you're not here to steal anything?" I asked.

"No."

"Were you planning to vandalize the property?"

"No." She lowered her chin, but finally met my eyes. "I'm more interested in bodily harm."

Done fooling around, I went at her, threw her over my shoulder, and carried her up the stairs.

Inside my bedroom, I laid her down on top of my comforter, pausing only to remove her shoes.

"You make your bed?" she asked, clearly surprised.

"With hospital corners in thirty fucking seconds or else."

"I'm impressed."

"Good." I stretched out above her, settling my hips over hers.

She giggled. "You're getting me all wet."

"That's my plan." Brushing her hair aside, I buried my face in her neck and kissed her throat.

She moaned softly, writhing beneath me. "Oh God, that feels good. You're not mad?"

I picked my head up. "Why would I be mad?"

"Because of what you said today. How giving in to what we feel would be a bad idea, because you're afraid it would ruin things."

"Fuck what I said. I'm not afraid." I looked down at her. "Are you?"

"No." Her denim-clad legs twined around me and she lifted her lips to mine. "I want you. I want this. Please don't stop."

She didn't have to tell me twice.

I kissed her like I'd always wanted to, like I'd dreamed of, like I'd fantasized about. She tasted faintly of honey, or maybe maple syrup, something sweet and sexy at the same time.

I couldn't get enough.

And neither could she. I loved the way she moved beneath me—her arms might have been pinned above her shoulders, but she had those runner's legs, and she used them, rubbing her heels up the back of my legs, crossing her ankles behind my thighs, opening her knees wide and bringing them up toward our chests.

Eventually, I kissed my way down the front of her shirt and ran my tongue along that narrow little ribbon of bare skin that had been driving me nuts all day. "Did you wear this on purpose?" I asked. "Knowing it would turn me on?"

"Truth?" she breathed. "Yes. At least, I hoped it would."

"It did. From the second you got into my car." I pushed the shirt farther up her stomach and kissed her ribcage. "You evil temptress."

She laughed, the sound resonating through her chest to my lips. "I wanted you to look at me differently. To want me like this."

I grabbed the shirt by the hem and lifted it over her head. When I looked down at her lace-edged nude bra, her breasts spilling over the top, my desire surged, and I said a little prayer of thanks I'd left the light on in my room. "It worked." I lowered my head to her chest and moved my mouth over flesh and satin and lace. "I've never wanted anyone so badly in my entire life."

Her whole body shivered. "Me neither."

God help me, I tried to go slow.

I took off her bra and lavished each of her perfect breasts with all the attention they deserved, with my hands and lips and tongue. I slid her jeans and underwear down her legs and licked my way back up one inner thigh and then the other, reveling in the way she caught her breath, and gasped for air, and whispered my name like a plea. I pushed her legs apart and buried my face between her thighs, devouring her with long, leisurely strokes before sucking gently—and then not so gently—on her clit while she moaned and rocked her hips and fisted her hands in my hair.

And when she said, *Oh God, Noah, it feels so good, and it's been so long*, I got even harder and even more determined to make her come again and again tonight.

Fuck that asshole who left her. Fuck *anyone* who'd ever had this chance and messed it up. Fuck *everyone* who'd ever been lucky enough to taste this woman I'd been dreaming about since I was goddamn sixteen years old.

Tonight she was mine.

I slid my fingers inside her. I listened. I paid attention

to the way she moved, the way she cried out, the way she grew even wetter and firmer beneath my tongue. And when she came, her cries at a fever pitch, her clit pulsing against my tongue, her grip tightening in my hair, I nearly lost control and made a mess all over my bed.

She was still breathing hard when I moved back up her body. Her skin was warm and damp, her mouth open and waiting. I kissed her deeply, driving my tongue between her lips, grinding my erection against her hot, wet skin. I wasn't going to last much longer.

She reached down between us and sheathed my cock with her hand. I groaned as she let my flesh slip through her fingers, tightening her grip as I thrust inside her palm. "You're so big," she whispered against my mouth. "So hard. And I want you inside me so badly."

My dick threatened to come right there in her hand and sent a serious 911 emergency call to my brain. *NOW or else, asshole.*

Prying myself from her, I leaned over and grabbed a condom from the box in my nightstand drawer. It had been so long since I'd needed one, I was surprised the box didn't creak when I opened it. The thing was probably covered with dust.

I tore the packet open with my teeth and rolled it on, loving the way she watched me. The way she caught her bottom lip between her teeth. The way her chest rose and fell with every anticipatory breath.

Ten seconds later, I was easing into her, every muscle in my body tensed with the effort of maintaining control. I went slow, giving her time to adjust to me, listening as her sharp gasps became soft sighs of pleasure.

"Yes," she whispered as I began to move in an easy,

rhythmic, rocking motion above her. She slid her palms down my back and over my ass. "Yes, just like that."

Sustaining *just like that* took some effort on my part, since my body was desperate to abandon this slow, decadent pace and gallop for the fucking hills. But I took deep, measured breaths, inhaling the scent of her skin and hair. I forced myself to think of all the times I'd longed to feel this very thing—my body inside hers, at her invitation. I stayed intensely aware of her every breath, her every word, her every move, wanting this to be perfect for her.

"Oh God, Noah. You're gonna make me come again," she panted in my ear, her hips meeting mine thrust for thrust. "Fuck me, fuck me, fuck me . . ."

Annnnd that was the end of *just like that*.

Her words snapped the last frayed rope tethering me to self-control, and the beast in me was unleashed. I grabbed her wrists and pinned them in an X above her head. I drove into her hard and fast and ferociously. I took perverse pleasure in the way she struggled and failed to free her arms, in the way her piercing cries could be those of pain or ecstasy, in the slick, hot layer of sweat that covered our skin.

And then I went deeper, using the weight of my pelvis over hers to sink even farther into her body and fucking her with tight, quick thrusts of my hips. "Come again for me," I demanded. "Let me feel you."

I knew when it happened, because her head dropped to the side and her mouth fell open. Then she screamed my name, and I was lost.

My orgasm was a detonation felt in every bone, every muscle, every cell of my body. I gave myself over to it, my vision going black, my groans long and loud, my cock throbbing inside her again and again and again. I never wanted it to end.

When my senses returned, I propped myself up and looked down at her. "You okay?"

Her eyes were closed, but they popped wide open. "No. I really don't think I am. But it's a good thing."

She was fucking adorable—flushed cheeks, messy hair, swollen lips. Her expression a mix of self-satisfaction and awe. "You're beautiful, you know."

The pink in her complexion deepened. "Stop."

"I'm serious. You're fucking beautiful."

"You're just saying that because your dick is still inside me."

"I will admit, that is something I'm very happy about, but it's not why I'm telling you what I see. It's the truth."

A smile made her lips curve slowly, like she was really letting my words sink in. "Thank you. I feel beautiful right now."

"Good." I pressed my lips to her forehead. "Can you stay? Or will you be in trouble if you miss curfew?"

She laughed. "Thankfully, I no longer have a curfew. Do you want me to stay? I know you have to get up early for work. I don't want to be a bother."

"Fuck off, Sawyer. I wouldn't have asked you if I didn't want you to stay. But I can drive you home right now if you'd rather."

She took my face in her hands. "I'll stay."

"Good." I kissed her lips. "Let me take Renzo out one last time, and I'll be right back."

"Okay."

Carefully pulling out of her, I grabbed a pair of sweatpants, stopped in the bathroom to clean up a little, then let my poor dog out of his room. He was all agitated, probably because he'd heard all the noise, and wanted, of course, to race up to my bedroom and see what all the fuss had been about. But I'd spare Meg from a second animal jumping all over her tonight, shepherding Renzo right outside. After we came back in, I made sure to shut and lock the back door.

When I got back upstairs, the bathroom door opened and Meg stood there, looking very naked and a little sheepish. "Do you happen to have an extra toothbrush?"

"Sure. Bottom drawer on the right."

"Thanks."

While she brushed her teeth, I made sure my room was clean, although I kept things pretty neat and tidy in there— old Army habits die hard. Then I ran downstairs again for two bottles of water, ignoring Renzo's dramatic whines, and hurrying back up to set one on each nightstand. Would she need anything else? It had been so long since I'd had a woman in my bed—for any length of time, let alone all night—that I couldn't think. I was turning down the blankets when she came in. My heart pounded double time.

"Hi," she said, crossing her arms over her chest.

"Now you're shy?" I teased her. "After breaking into my house to spy on me in the shower?"

"I didn't break in! And I'm not shy, I'm just . . ." Her arms fell to her side. "Not used to someone looking at me naked with the lights on."

"Can't say I'm sorry about that. But here, will this help?" I ditched my sweats and tossed them onto a chair. "Now I'm naked with the lights on too."

She smiled and nodded. "Yeah. It does."

Instinctively, we moved for each other, as if pulled by magnetic force. She looped her arms around my waist and pressed her cheek to my chest, and I wrapped her up in my arms, resting my lips on her head. We stayed like that, skin to skin, for a solid minute without saying anything.

Then she looked up at me. "I love your body. It's perfect."

"Then we're even."

"You're much more muscular than you were in high school."

"I fucking hope so. I was a bean pole back then."

"And you have hair on your chest."

"As every man fucking should."

She smiled before planting a kiss over my heart. "I also really like your ass."

"What a coincidence." I moved my hands down to her butt and squeezed. My dick was showing signs of recovery already, swelling against her hip.

"Should we go to bed?" she asked, her voice a little huskier.

"Definitely. I'll be right in." I ran into the bathroom and brushed my teeth, and by the time I came back into my bedroom, she'd turned off the lights and slipped between the sheets.

I shut the door, set my alarm, and crawled into bed. At the same time I reached for her, she nestled in closer, tucking herself along the side of my body with one palm on my stomach. I lay on my back, one arm draped around her shoulders and the other hand stroking her hair. "So are you going to tell me?" I asked.

"Tell you what?"

"What made you come over here tonight."

"Same thing that made me ask you why you'd never tried to kiss me before—I was curious. I wanted to know what it would be like."

"And now that you know?"

She kissed my chest. "I'm glad I was brave enough to do it."

"Me too. I'd been beating myself up ever since I dropped you off."

"Really?" She picked up her head and looked up at me.

"Fuck yeah. You'd just basically *told* me to make a move, and I'd been too chicken shit to do it, despite the fact that I'd always wanted to."

"So that part wasn't bullshit."

"None of it was bullshit. Every single thing I said to you this afternoon was true. I *am* worried about losing what we have. Because . . ." I told myself I had to be able to look her in the eye and say this. "I can't make you any promises, Meg. I care about you, but what I said at dinner yesterday was true. I can't be your boyfriend."

"You know what? I just had one of those, and I can't say it was much fun in the end. I'm looking for something else right now."

Relief rushed through me. "Oh yeah? What's that?"

"A good time. I'm only here for a week, and I don't want to spend it wallowing in misery over my failed relationships or worrying about what's down the road. I just want to be with someone I like and trust, and have some fun."

"In that case, I'd like to apply for the position of that someone."

"The position is yours, Deputy McCormick. But I warn you." She sat up and swung her leg over me, straddling my hips. "I've got high expectations."

"Is that right?" My hands moved up her thighs and rib-cage, my thumbs flirting with her hard pink nipples.

"Yes." Her eyes closed, her back arched, and she moaned

as I sat up and brought my mouth to her breasts, teasing one stiff peak with my tongue.

"How am I doing so far?" I asked.

"Oh God," she breathed as I moved a hand between her legs and drew little circles over her clit with my thumb. "It's perfection."

"As long as it's not potato salad."

Dropping her head back, she laughed breathlessly as she started to grind against me. "Not. Even. Close."

Twelve

Meg

I HADN'T DONE IT TWICE IN ONE NIGHT SINCE I TURNED thirty—and that was nearly four years ago.

And multiple orgasms? Forget it. I always considered myself lucky if I got one, and gifted by God if I got two. But Noah was a whole different level of sexual euphoria.

He was attentive. Talented. Patient.

He put my needs first, every single time.

But when it came to his own pleasure, he took it how he wanted it, and he wasn't always gentle.

I fucking loved it.

By the time we fell back onto the sheets after round three, it was nearly two o'clock in the morning, and I knew Noah had to get up at six. "You're going to hate me tomorrow," I said, still trying to catch my breath.

"Nope." He grabbed my hand and squeezed it. "I'll be tired, but I won't hate you. In fact, I'll be wondering when we can do it again."

I giggled. "Fiend."

"Sticks and stones, Sawyer."

Smiling, I let my eyes drift shut and fell asleep next to him, my hand in his, my entire body humming.

I felt happy and beautiful and alive.

"Why don't I call Chloe and see if she can pick me up on her way to Cloverleigh?" I asked Noah as he raced around his bedroom getting ready for work. I was dressed already, sitting at the foot of his bed, admiring him in his uniform.

"I'll drive you," he said, fastening his watch to his wrist.

"But you're already running late, and it's my fault!"

He stopped what he was doing, came over to the bed and kissed me. "I'll drive you. End of discussion."

I sighed and stood up. "Okay, fine. Can I do anything for you?"

He smirked. "Many, many things. But I'm just about ready to go."

Downstairs, he collected Renzo and we piled into his SUV. On the ride to Cloverleigh, he held my hand and asked what I was up to for the day.

"I'm not sure, exactly. Sylvia gets in at some point this afternoon with her whole family, so probably some sort of family dinner tonight. It's been years since we've all been together under one roof."

"Sounds like fun."

"It will be. But I'd still rather be with you." I whispered behind my hand. "Don't tell anybody."

He grinned. "Your secret is safe with me."

At Cloverleigh, he pulled around back by my parents' house and gave me a quick kiss. "Enjoy the time with your family."

"Thanks. I'll text you later."

As he drove away, I said a quick prayer of hope that my parents would not be at the breakfast table as early as they had been yesterday.

No such luck.

When I let myself in the back door, wearing the outfit I'd been in yesterday, my dad was in his usual spot reading the paper and my mother was slicing a grapefruit at the counter—and she happened to have a perfect view of the driveway where Noah had just dropped me off. Had she seen us kiss?

"Morning," I said, wishing I'd at least had a hairbrush in my purse. I knew I looked completely rumpled and totally *last night*.

"Morning, dear. Late night, hmm?"

I smiled sheepishly. "Yeah. I had dinner with Chloe and then hung out at Noah's for a while. It got late and he had to work early, so I just stayed the night at his house." I considered adding something about staying in his spare room or on his couch, but caught myself. For heaven's sake, I was thirty-three! Why did I did think I needed my mom's permission to spend the night with a man?

But somehow I did, so I avoided their eyes as I bee-lined through the kitchen and headed for the stairs. "I'm going to grab a quick shower."

"Okay, honey."

Upstairs in my room, I couldn't resist my bed and ended up crashing facedown in it for two hours. When I woke up, I was groggy and disoriented, but the moment I remembered why I'd needed the nap, I smiled. What a crazy turn of events.

I cleaned up and went down to the kitchen, which was empty. Ravenous, I made myself some lunch and scarfed it down standing at the counter while checking my messages. I had several work-related texts; a few from Chloe, who was dying to know what had happened after she dropped me off; one from Brooks, who wanted me to know he'd be back in DC this weekend to clear out the rest of his stuff; and one from Noah containing a single word.

You.

My heart fluttered wildly.

I knew today was a family day, but I also knew I'd go mad if I couldn't spend another night in his arms.

Somehow, I'd make it happen.

I spent the afternoon with Chloe in the tasting room, and in between tastings when the room was empty and we were preparing for the next guests on the tour, I managed to tell her about last night.

She laughed her ass off. "Oh my God, that's priceless. You must have died when you opened that bathroom door!"

"I about did. And any other time, I would have slammed it shut and run away—but I made myself stay."

"Good for you." Chloe held up a glass to the light to double check it was perfectly clean. "So now what? Will you see him again tonight?"

"I hope so. Do you know what the plan is?"

"Dinner res at eight. I guess Sylvia's plane gets in around six-thirty."

"And the reservation is at eight? That's cutting it close. What if the flight is delayed?"

Chloe gave me a look. "It's *Sylvia*. That shit doesn't happen to her. Hashtag blessed."

I laughed, although I knew our oldest sister hated it when we made fun of her that way. But we couldn't help it—Sylvia's life was charmed. A beauty queen from childhood, she was still stunning at thirty-seven, married to a handsome, successful investment banker, and had the house of her dreams in Santa Barbara. Did I mention the slope-side condo in Aspen, annual European vacations, and two smart, well-behaved children, my niece Whitney, and my nephew Keaton, aged twelve and ten?

"True," I said. "So I guess I'll plan on dinner at eight. Maybe I can see Noah after that."

"Why not invite him to dinner?" Chloe suggested as the next tour group made its way into the tasting room. "What time is he off work?"

"I think seven, but I don't know that I'd subject him to dinner with our entire family," I said. "He'll be dealing with all our crazy at the wedding."

"Then late night it is." She wiggled her eyebrows. "I'm happy to drop you off again on my way home from here."

"Thanks," I told her, smiling as an elderly couple approached the counter holding hands. "I'll let you know."

Later, when I had a moment to myself, I texted Noah back.

Me: How's your day, gorgeous?

Noah: The usual. Except I keep getting hard every time I think about you. It's very inconvenient.

Me: Not sorry.

Noah: Of course you're not. You look like a nice girl, but I'm onto you. I know what you want.

My stomach whooshed.

Me: Can I see you tonight?

Noah: Now who's the fiend?

Me: Haha. Chloe said she could drop me off after dinner, but it would be late. Maybe around ten.

Noah: Call me. I'll come get you.

Me: But that's out of your way.

Noah: For fuck's sake, Sawyer. When are you going to realize that I will always go out of my way for you?

I smiled at my phone like an idiot. I felt like dancing.

Me: Okay. I'll call you.

As predicted, Sylvia's flight arrived on time, and my parents returned from the airport with her family right around seven. April, Chloe, and I were sitting out on our parents' patio with a bottle of wine when we heard them pull up, and we set down our glasses to head around front and greet them.

"Sylvie!" April cried, throwing her arms around our big sister, who looked tired and harried after a long day of traveling, but gorgeous nonetheless. "It's so good to see you."

While they embraced and my parents took luggage from the back of the car, I hugged my niece and nephew, who'd sprouted up like weeds since I'd seen them last. "God, you guys. Stop growing already. You're going to be taller than I am by the time you leave."

My niece, a carbon copy of my sister except with braces and her dad's dimpled chin, smiled shyly. "My foot is already as big as my mom's."

"I believe it," I told her. "And that's awesome, because your mom has an amazing shoe collection."

Whitney's eyes went wide. "She so does."

When it was my turn to hug Sylvia hello, I couldn't help

noticing how thin she'd gotten. Embracing her was like hugging a scarecrow. But when she smiled, her face lit up and her eyes misted over. "I'm so happy to see you guys, and to be home," she said, grabbing my hand. "And you have to catch me up on everything. I feel like we haven't talked in forever."

"Where's Brett?" Chloe asked. I hadn't even realized my sister's husband wasn't with them.

"He couldn't come this early," Sylvia explained as we headed into the house. "Work commitments. But he'll be here this weekend. He's taking the red-eye Thursday night."

My parents led the way inside, with Sylvia's kids racing ahead like puppies, Sylvia and April arm and arm behind them, and Chloe and I bringing up the rear. Sylvia's sundress hung on her tiny frame like wash on the line, and Chloe and I exchanged a worried glance.

While my parent helped Sylvia and her kids get settled into their bedrooms for the week—my sister and brother-in-law would have her old room, Keaton would be in April's old room, and Whitney got Chloe's—April, Chloe and I returned to our patio chairs and glasses of wine.

"She's so thin," Chloe whispered right away. "She must have lost twenty pounds since I last saw her—and she was slender then!"

"I thought the same thing," I said, glancing toward the house to make sure the bedroom windows weren't open. "It's kind of alarming."

"I think she looks great," said April, "but I agree she's definitely skinnier."

"I didn't say she doesn't look great," Chloe defended. "She's Sylvia—she always looks great. On my best day, I couldn't look as great. But I feel like something is off with her."

"Brett?" I guessed. "Is it weird that he didn't come with them? Maybe she's mad about it."

"I think it's more than that." Chloe glanced up at the windows too. "Frannie and I were talking the other day about all those photos from their summer vacation in Italy that Sylvia posted on Instagram. She's not smiling in *any* of them. It was one sad face after another! Sad in front of the Coliseum. Sad in front of the Leaning Tower of Pisa. Sad in a boat heading for the Blue Grotto on Capri. How the fuck is anyone sad in a boat off the coast of Capri?"

"Shhhhhh," April admonished her. "She'll hear you."

The patio door slid open, and Frannie stepped out of the house. "Hi, guys. What's going on?"

"We're just having a chat about Sylvia," I said softly. "Have you seen her yet?"

Frannie nodded, biting her lip. "Just now. She looks kind of . . ."

"Emaciated?" I supplied.

Frannie shifted her weight from one foot to the other. "I don't want to say that, because she still looks beautiful. But she *has* lost a lot of weight."

"Where are Mack and the girls?" April asked.

"He's in his office, and the kids are moping in the lobby because he told them no when they asked to run down to the barn before dinner and pet the horses."

I laughed. "That used to be Chloe."

"Yeah, except I'd go anyway." Chloe grinned mischievously. "Want a glass of wine, Frannie? We've got a few minutes before dinner, and I have another bottle here."

"Sure," she said. "Let me go get Sylvia."

"Good idea."

Frannie returned with Sylvia and our mom a minute

later, and we opened the second bottle of wine. Our dad, the old softie, had convinced Mack to give in to the kids and together they'd taken them all down to the barn to say hello to the horses—with strict instructions from my mother and Sylvia to watch where they stepped and wash up *very well* before coming to dinner.

For the next thirty minutes or so, the Sawyer women sat on the patio, sipping Cloverleigh wine, laughing about childhood memories, and chatting about all the wedding details. At one point, Chloe turned to April and said, "Oh, by the way, remind me to tell you about a conversation I had with Mia Fournier over at Abelard Vineyards last week. I might have a lead on someone who can fill in for you here so you can take that vacation."

"Who is it?"

"It's a close friend of hers who runs an event planning business down in Detroit but is looking at moving up here with her family."

April smiled. "Okay. I'll get in touch with Mia after Frannie's wedding. Thanks."

Eventually, we moseyed over to the inn, where we'd reserved the small private dining room normally used for small receptions or rehearsal dinners. There were thirteen of us around the table, and when my father stood at the head and raised a glass to his five daughters and all the love and joy they'd brought to his and my mother's lives, I immediately choked up. Thank God I'd come home early—not only would I have missed this dinner and all the extra time with my sisters, I wouldn't have had more than a couple hours over a beer with Noah.

In that moment, I felt with one hundred percent certainty, I was exactly where I was supposed to be.

Thirteen

Noah

Chris: Dude. I gotta get out of my house. Can you meet me for a beer after work?

The text came in around six, just when I was starting to look forward to a post-shift nap. Usually, on a nice day like today I'd have taken Renzo for a run and done some training in the park, but I was wiped the fuck out after staying up so late with Meg. And since I had big plans for us tonight, I really could have used the rest.

But I hadn't seen Chris in a while, and a friend was a friend.

Me: Sure. I can meet you at 7:30 or 8.

Chris: Thanks. Let's do 8 so I can still do kids bedtime routine. And let's meet at Jolly Pumpkin so I can stay close to home just in case.

Me: Jesus. Is she STILL pregnant?

Chris: Dude.

After my shift was done, I took Renzo home, changed out of my uniform, and let him play around in the yard for a few minutes. Then I fed him, said goodbye, and promised I'd be back soon.

When I walked into the Jolly Pumpkin, Chris wasn't there yet. I took a seat at the bar, ordered a pint, and checked my phone to see if Meg had called or texted.

For the fiftieth time that day.

Christ, get a grip, I told myself. I'd never been this way over a woman. But I couldn't get last night out of my head. I just wanted to be with her again.

I felt a hand on my shoulder, and Chris slid onto the seat next to me. "Hey. Sorry I'm late."

"That's okay. Kids asleep?"

He grimaced. "Well, they're in bed. I didn't exactly wait to make sure they were asleep. I had to get out."

"What's up?"

"Fuck." He rubbed his face with both hands. "I love your sister, dude. I fucking love her to death, but she's killing me with this nesting shit. She cannot get the house clean enough. I have scrubbed every toilet twelve times this week. The tub. The shower. The kitchen floor. The sinks. The counters. There is not one surface in that house that could possibly have a single germ on it."

I laughed and waved the bartender over, and Chris ordered an amber ale.

"It's unbearable," he went on. "Tonight she wanted me to steam clean the carpets and couch—*again*."

"How'd you get out of it?"

He looked guilty. "I told her I had to help you move an appliance."

"She's gonna know you were drinking. She'll smell it."

"I know. She can smell what the neighbors five doors down cook for dinner. Her nose is fucking bionic when she's pregnant." He grabbed the glass the bartender set down in front of him and gulped it. "But you were nice enough to offer me a beer after I helped you. That's my story, and I'm sticking to it."

I shrugged. "I'm that kind of guy."

We ordered burgers and fries and caught up a little, since it had been a few weeks since we'd seen each other. "Asher is doing really great at work," he told me. "My mother loves him. If he wants more hours, let us know."

"I will, thanks." I felt proud of my brother, and thankful to have Chris as a friend. "He does get tired easily, but he loves the job. I'll ask him."

"Good. So I hear Meg Sawyer's in town."

I rolled my eyes. "My sister has a big mouth."

He laughed. "Have you seen her?"

"Uh, yeah. I saw her last night." I took a long drink, debating how much I should tell him.

"And?"

"And what?

"Don't be a dick. Did you guys finally bang?"

"Jesus, Chris. I've told you a million times. It's not about that with her." I took another drink. "But yeah, we did."

Chris swallowed too fast and nearly choked. He set his glass down. "Fucking hell, I was kidding. Are you serious? You did?"

"Yeah." I gave him a warning look from the side of my eyes. "But that is not public knowledge. And by public, I mean my sister. She'll go right to my mother. And my mother will probably go right to the priest."

He held up both hands. "I won't tell. Scout's honor. But holy shit, I can't believe it."

"Me neither." I stared into my beer, the caramel color of

which was the exact shade of the streaks in Meg's hair. "But it's been a long time coming."

"No shit." Chris picked up his glass again. "So how was it?"

I shook my head and drank again. There weren't words.

"That good, huh?"

"Better."

Our food arrived, and we dumped ketchup on our plates and dug in. "So is it casual?" he wondered after a few minutes.

"Completely."

"She still lives in DC, right?"

"Yep. She's only here for the week. I'm taking her to her sister's wedding on Saturday."

Chris laughed. "Uh oh. The wedding date. Better be careful."

"What do you mean? We're just going as friends. It's not even really a date." I picked up my beer and finished it. "Why would I have to be careful?"

"Maybe you don't. I'm just saying that single women get all weird at weddings. They start thinking about their own futures, and how they're not getting any younger, and feeling like it's time to settle down. It's like a subliminal message transmitted by the sight of a white dress or something. They get all . . . rabid to be a bride and start hinting around."

"Meg will not get rabid," I scoffed. "We're just having some fun together. She knows how I feel about relationships, and she's not interested in one either. She lives halfway across the country, for fuck's sake."

"Okay, okay. Don't get mad, dude. Have your fun. It's about time you got laid."

I shook my head, laughing a little. "Asshole."

Around nine, Chris got a text from Nina asking when he'd be home, and I told him to go ahead and take off, I'd settle up with the bartender.

"Thanks," he said, pulling his keys from his pocket. "I'll get you next time."

"Sounds good." I was just signing the check when I got the call from Meg.

"Hey," I said. "You ready?"

She groaned. "This dinner is taking forever. We haven't even had our main course yet. I snuck out to the lobby to call you."

"Oh." Disappointed that I might not see her, I headed out the door into the dark. "That's okay. We can do it another time."

"But I really want to see you tonight. I'm just worried it will be too late when I get out of here. You have to work tomorrow, and you must be tired today."

"I don't care how fucking late it is, Sawyer. If you want to see me, I'll come get you."

"I do."

"So call me when you're done, and I'll be there in fifteen minutes." I lowered my voice as I walked to my car. "I've got plans for you."

She gasped. "What kind of plans?"

"I'm not going to *tell* you. That would take all the fun out of it." Actually there wasn't really anything that would take the fun out of what I was going to do to her. But the element of surprise would add a little extra something.

"Oh, you're so mean." She lowered her voice to a whisper. "But I can't wait. I'll call you as soon as I can."

We hung up, and I drove home humming a song that had been playing in the bar. When I got there, I let Renzo out, gave him some attention, and then put him into the spare bedroom. He let me know in no uncertain terms that he was *not* pleased.

"Sorry, buddy. But I need a little more room to myself tonight. And since things might get kinda rough and I don't want you to get spooked, you've gotta stay in there." I scratched behind his ears. "I'll make it up to you tomorrow, okay? Extra play time at the park after work."

Once Renzo was taken care of, I took a quick shower, threw on some jeans and a T-shirt, and went downstairs to make sure everything was in place. Surprisingly, I wasn't even that tired anymore. Thinking about the night ahead had adrenaline running through my veins, and my imagination was working overtime thinking up things I wanted to do to her, say to her.

The other night she'd told me she wanted sex that was a little unpredictable, sex that made her feel like she might not be okay. I had *years'* worth of fantasies saved up—all kinds of things I never in a million years thought I'd get the chance to act out, with Meg or anyone else. Her words were like an invitation. And we had the necessary kind of trust between us.

When she texted me just after ten-thirty, I was ready. I turned off all the lights, pulled all the blackout shades, and left the handcuffs on the counter.

I was going to push her boundaries tonight.

Fourteen

Meg

"**W**HAT'S WITH YOU? GOT A HOT DATE LATER?" Chloe poked me in the side and gave me a knowing look.

"Huh?"

"You keep checking your phone."

"Oh." Heat rushed my face, and I glanced around the table, where everyone was still finishing up dessert. "Yeah, kind of. Noah is coming to pick me up and I can't figure out how to get out of here. He'll be here in like fifteen minutes."

"Say you're tired and want to turn in."

"You think?"

She shrugged. "Why not? Is your bedroom door closed?"

I thought for a second. "Yes."

"Perfect. When they get home, they'll just assume you're already asleep." She glanced around the table. "You start. I'll back you up."

I flashed her a grateful smile. "Thanks."

"Don't mention it."

I put my phone away, waited about sixty seconds, and yawned dramatically, stretching my arms for good measure.

"Wow, I am *beat*. All that food and wine did me in. I think I'll head back and hit the hay."

"Me too," said Chloe, pretending to stifle a yawn of her own.

"Really?" my mother asked, eyeing us both a little suspiciously. "It's not even eleven. I thought we'd go back to the house for coffee."

"Sounds nice, but I'm really tired," I said, jumping to my feet.

"Same, and I've got a bit of a drive home." Chloe stood too.

"It's the same drive I have," April pointed out, one brow arched. She had to know something was up.

"I know, but I'm a baby about my sleep. I'll walk out with you, Meg." Chloe grabbed my elbow and tugged me toward the door. "Thanks for dinner, Mom and Dad. See you guys tomorrow. Night, all."

We hurried through the restaurant, which was fairly empty at that hour. Hitting the lobby, we burst out laughing. "God, that was so bad," I said, cringing.

"It was," Chloe agreed. "We are not very good actresses. You've got zero chill whatsoever."

"You're no better! And I can't help it. I'm excited to see him."

"I can tell."

We said goodnight to the evening desk receptionist, walked down the back hallway past the executive offices, and used the employee exit. "I mean, I knew it was going to be good," I said once we were outside. "But it was more than that. It was the best I ever had."

"Wow." She looked around, but Noah's car wasn't there yet. "Want me to wait with you?"

"No, you can go. I'm fine." I glanced at April's car in the employee lot. "I just hope I'm out of here by the time April leaves. She totally suspects something."

"You're not going to tell her?" Chloe pulled her keys from her purse.

"There's not really anything to tell. We're just . . . messing around for the fun of it. And because we kind of always wanted to."

She smiled like she knew something I didn't. "Right."

"What? What's that face?"

"It's nothing." She headed toward the parking lot, calling over her shoulder, "Enjoy, sis. Don't do anything I wouldn't do . . . which really isn't much."

I laughed. "Night. Drive carefully."

Noah pulled up just a few minutes later. My heart raced as he reached over and opened the passenger door. I jumped in and pulled it shut. "Hi."

"Hi." The smile he gave me could have melted butter, he was so fucking hot. "You ready?"

I nodded. "Let's go, before my parents catch me."

He laughed as he drove away from the inn. "You snuck out?"

"Kind of. I told them I was really tired and wanted to go to bed."

"How was dinner?"

"Good. But I wasn't that hungry. I was too excited to eat."

"Excited about what?"

I poked his shoulder. "Being with you."

"Ah." He gave me a crooked little smile and ran a hand up my bare thigh. "I like your outfit."

"Thanks." I'd hoped he would. I was wearing a light

brown suede skirt with tall brown boots and an off-the-shoulder sweater in ivory.

"So what color is your skirt? Is that cinnamon?" he asked, his hand inching higher.

I laughed. "No, I'd say this is more like . . . gingerbread."

"Mmmm. And the boots?"

"The boots are definitely chocolate."

"You're making me fucking hungry." He slid his hand between my thighs, his fingertips rubbing me through my panties. "I want to taste you."

I opened my knees a little more. "Good."

He growled and hit the accelerator as his fingers edged inside my underwear. "Fuck. You're already wet."

"Told you I was excited." I grabbed the edge of the seat, my mouth falling open. His touch had me breathing hard and wanting more. "You're going so fast. Won't you get busted for speeding?"

"The only one of us getting busted tonight is you—for bad behavior."

"Bad behavior?"

He slipped a finger inside me. "Don't play innocent with me."

"But I—"

"No excuses. Just sit there and think about what you did."

"What are *you* going to think about?" I asked, struggling for words as he slid his finger inside me.

"How I'm going to punish you for it."

He teased me with his hand all the way home. I was so hot and bothered by the time he pulled into his garage, I hoped he'd fuck me right there in the front seat.

But he had other ideas.

"Don't move," he told me.

I stayed where I was, and he came around to open the passenger door. Then he grabbed me by the arm and yanked me out of the car. "You're coming with me."

His grip was tight, and he moved with long, quick strides toward the house, almost like he was angry. I could barely keep up. He unlocked the back door without letting go of me, pushed me inside, and slammed it behind us.

Then he let me go.

It was pitch black inside the kitchen. I couldn't see a fucking *thing*. From the spare bedroom, Renzo began to growl. "Noah?" I whispered, moving deeper into the room, my skin prickling with a mix of uncertainty and anticipation. "Where are you?"

Suddenly I found myself being spun around to face the wall, my arms being twisted behind me, and something being snapped around my wrists.

Oh my God. Handcuffs.

He pressed close behind me and spoke low in my ear. His voice was deep and commanding. "You have the right to remain silent. Anything on my body can and will be used against you."

"Oh, fuck," I whispered.

"But feel free to scream if you want. No one will hear you." He flattened his body against mine, pressing his erection against my hip. "Bad girls who break the rules need to be taught a lesson."

"What lesson?" My voice trembled.

"Actions have consequences." He grabbed a fistful of my hair and tightened his fingers at the base of my skull. "And sometimes consequences are painful."

I winced at the sting on my scalp.

"But they can feel good too." With his other hand he reached beneath my sweater and unhooked my strapless bra with an easy flick of his fingers. It fell to the floor as he filled his palm with one breast, kneading it gently. My nipples were tingling and tight, and I cried out when he pinched one. "See?"

I wanted to nod, but he was pulling my hair so hard I couldn't even move my head. The pain was enough to bring tears to my eyes, but then his other hand was under my skirt again, his fingers pushing aside the damp silk of my panties.

With some kind of cop move that made me gasp, he kicked my heels apart so my feet were planted wide. "That's it. Spread your legs for me like a bad girl should."

Then his fingers were sliding in and out of me again, and I whimpered as he rubbed slick, hot circles over my clit. My brain was torn between focusing on the pleasure between my legs, the pain on my scalp, and the frustration of being completely at his mercy. I'd never experienced anything like this before, never been treated like a bad girl, a prisoner, a plaything.

Panic hovered at the edges of my mind, but my body responded to his touch, and I moved against his fingers. "Yes. Do it," he told me. "Come. Right here. Right now. All over my hand."

My legs began to tingle. My core muscles tightened. Harder and faster, his fingers working me into a tight, hot frenzy until the tension coiled inside me sprung and unspooled in wave after wave of pleasure.

"God, I fucking love your body," he growled in my ear, finally loosening his grasp on my hair. "I love the way you move. I love the way you taste. I love the way you do exactly what I tell you to."

I could barely breathe. My legs were ready to give out. My cheek was pushed so hard against the wall I thought I might have a bruise tomorrow.

But I didn't care.

"Was that my punishment?" I panted.

He laughed, a low, gravelly sound from the back of his throat. "That was just the beginning."

Immediately I was pulled off the wall, spun around, and bent forward over the kitchen counter. I still couldn't see a goddamn thing. Why the hell was it so *dark* in here? I felt like my eyes were closed when they were open.

Noah pressed my head down so my cheek rested on the stone counter. Then he placed a hand on my back. "Are you okay?"

"Yes."

"If you want me to stop, what will you say?"

"Can't I just ask you to stop?"

"No, because that turns me on."

My stomach jumped. "Even if I say please?"

"*Especially* if you say please."

A shiver moved up my spine.

"Are you nervous?"

I hesitated. "A little."

"Good." He hiked my skirt up to my hips, grabbed my panties, and fucking *tore them off*. "If you want me to stop, say cinnamon."

"Okay," I whispered, imagining the scrap of shredded lace now lying on his kitchen floor.

"Now," he said. "Are you sorry for what you did last night?"

"No. Ouch!" I cried as his hand spanked my ass so hard I saw stars.

"Try again, Sawyer. Are you sorry?"

I gritted my teeth. "No."

He delivered a second smack, then held his hand over my hot, stinging flesh. "And now?"

"*No.*"

That earned me a third spanking. And then a fourth, on the opposite cheek. My eyes filled with tears, but whatever hormones or endorphins were coursing through my body made the pain indistinguishable from the pleasure. I felt like someone else, someone who did bad things and liked it. And *he* felt like someone else too—a sinister, sexy stranger. A man I didn't know if I could trust, whose mind went places I'd never imagined, whose voice sounded like one I'd never heard, and whose body could deliver torment or gratification at his whim.

I fucking loved it.

"What were you hoping to see last night, huh?" he whispered. "When you snuck in here, quiet as a mouse."

"You," I managed. "I wanted to see you."

He leaned over me, pressing his body close to mine. He still wore his clothes—as far as I knew—but I could feel his cock pushing against my ass. "Liar."

It was a lie. I smiled in the dark, my breath hot and heavy and fast.

"I saw you staring at my cock," he said. "You wanted me to fuck you. Admit it."

"I wanted you to fuck me."

His weight lifted from my back, and I could breathe

slightly easier. A second later I heard a belt being unbuckled. A zipper descending. "You are such a bad girl." The tip of his cock swept across my skin. Slid down the crack of my ass. Stroked between my thighs, as if he were guiding it with his hand. "Wicked. Shameless. *Filthy* dirty."

He leaned over again and whispered in my ear. "But I can't resist you, and you know it."

"Noah." Desperate to get my hands on him, my arms around him, I tried to straighten up.

He pushed me down again. "No. I'm in charge here. And you're going to stay right where I want you while I give you exactly what you came for."

I heard the crackle of a condom wrapper, and five seconds later his cock was sliding into me from behind, both of us moaning at the tight, hot friction.

"Is this what you wanted?" he growled. "To make me so hard it hurts? To feel my cock deep inside you? To get fucked like the wicked little thing you really are?"

"Yes," I whispered as my legs trembled. *"Yes, yes, yes . . ."*

He went deliciously, agonizingly slow at first, making me feel him inch by inch. He buried himself deep. He used his fingers on me again, rubbing my swollen, sensitive clit while his cock hit some heavenly spot inside me that had my entire body clenching up with unbelievable intensity, until I was on the edge and panicking I might never feel relief— and then gloriously, miraculously, it began to unravel. It was unlike any orgasm I'd ever experienced before—rather than hitting me all at once, it came on slowly, from some place so hidden within me I couldn't even pinpoint its origin. My entire world went still and sirens went off as my body contracted around his cock over and over again.

When the sirens subsided, which I realized were my

own cries of ecstasy, Noah moved fast. He grabbed my hips with both hands and began yanking me backward as he drove in hard and deep. He was rough and relentless, his rasping breaths and rugged growls making him sound more animal than human. I was wet and swollen and sensitive, and every single thrust threatened to tear me apart. Part of me was afraid I'd have to use my safe word and beg for mercy.

But another part of me loved every second, despite the pain. Or maybe because of it. It was beyond belief that *I* was driving him to this furious, uncontrollable fever pitch. Noah, who'd always been so honorable, so trustworthy, so *good*. I'd turned him into a slave to his own desire, who *had* to have me or go mad.

It made me feel beautiful. Sexy. Strong.

And when he couldn't hold on anymore, his body going stiff behind me, his fingers digging into my hips, I felt every single throb of his orgasm as deeply as I'd felt my own.

I never wanted this to end.

After taking the cuffs off me, he set me on the counter and kissed circles around my wrists in the dark. Sweet, soft kisses that made me wish the lights were on so I could have watched him do it.

"You okay?" he asked.

"Yes."

"I wasn't too rough with you?"

"No. I mean, you were rough, and I might have a couple aches and pains tomorrow, but I loved every second of it."

"You did?"

"I didn't say cinnamon, did I?"

"Actually, you might have. I don't even think I could hear by the end."

I laughed. "I didn't. I promise."

"Good." He pulled me closer, hugging me to his warm, solid chest and gently stroking my hair. "Can you stay?" he asked.

I could feel his heart beating through his shirt. I wanted to feel it all night long. "If you want me to."

Sweeping me off the counter, he carried me up the stairs to his bedroom, cradling me like a baby. After laying me in his bed, he undressed me the rest of the way and looked at me in the lamplight. "Shit," he said, brushing his thumb softly across my sore cheek. "You have a bruise."

"Granite counters are hard."

"And here too." My hips bore deep red marks from where he'd gripped them.

"It's okay. I kinda like them."

He looked angry with himself. "I didn't mean to get so carried away."

"Noah, I *loved* it. I'd have stopped you if I didn't. Honestly, I've never had that much fun during sex on both a mental and physical level. The fact that you tested my limits turned me on."

"Are you sure?"

"Yes. I trusted you the entire time, I promise." I smiled. "I was maybe a little scared of you for a minute or two, because you almost seemed like someone else, but it was hot. You were strange and familiar all at once."

He was quiet for a few seconds, then he leaned down and kissed me. "I'll be right back."

He left the room and a moment later I heard him taking Renzo outside. Taking advantage of the time alone, I dashed into the bathroom, cleaned up a little, washed my makeup off, and used my same toothbrush from last night. Examining my face in the mirror, I noted the faint blue-purple mark on my cheek, the crimson fingerprints on my hips, and when I turned around, I could see the bright pink skin on my ass.

Damn. I was branded. All over.

It made me smile—Noah had *pounced*. And I hadn't felt this sexy in my skin since . . . well, ever.

How wrong was it that I wanted to do it again already?

How bad would it be to hope he left more marks on my body?

How was I ever going to get enough of him and us and this feeling in only five more days?

Fifteen

Noah

WHILE I STOOD OUTSIDE IN THE COOL DARK WAITING for Renzo, I couldn't stop thinking about what Meg had just said.

You were strange and familiar all at once.

I knew exactly what she meant. Although for me, it wasn't Meg herself that was strange and familiar. It was more like the way I felt about her. But I wasn't sure how to put it into words.

Renzo finished up and we went back into the house. Much to his dismay, I closed the door to his room again and renewed my promise to give him extra time and attention tomorrow. Upstairs, I used the bathroom and noticed that it smelled faintly of her perfume. I inhaled deeply before turning out the light, although the scent turned me on and my dick started to get hard. But I told myself not to be an asshole and start poking at her with it so soon. My God, she had bruises on her body. What kind of monster was I?

The bedroom was dark when I entered it, and Meg's breathing was slow and deep. I thought she might have fallen asleep already, and part of me was a little disappointed. After making sure my alarm was set, I peeled off my clothes and crawled into bed next to her.

She immediately snuggled up to me. "Hi."

"I thought you were asleep."

"Nope. I was waiting for you. Can we cuddle?"

"Sure." I pulled her alongside my body. "Although being right next to your skin tends to rile me up."

"I don't mind."

I kissed the top of her head. "I feel bad about those bruises."

"Well, don't."

"You say that, but—"

"Hey." She picked her head up suddenly. "Don't do that. Don't tell me I don't mean what I say. I get to decide what's too much for me. I get to decide how I like it. Yes, you made these marks, but it's still my body. I own it. I just wasn't . . . *in charge* of it for a few minutes down there. But I liked it. I'd have stopped you if I didn't."

"Okay." I pushed her hair off her face. "You know, I kinda like it when you get mad."

She stuck her tongue out at me and put her head down again.

We were silent for a full minute before I spoke. "I was thinking about what you said."

"About what?"

"About me being strange and familiar all at once. That's what it's like for me too, only . . . kinda different."

"Different how?"

I exhaled, trying to find words. "It's not *you* so much that's strange and familiar, but it's like . . . my feelings about you. I've always been really protective of you, which was why I never allowed myself to touch you back then. I didn't want to be just another asshole trying to get in your pants. I wanted to be better than that, even at sixteen."

"You were, Noah," she said softly. "You *are*."

I frowned. "Yes and no. Because I still have that feeling about you—like I want to protect you. But at the same time, now I want to do all these bad things to you . . . and it's fucking with me."

She laughed and kissed my chest. "You're being too hard on yourself." Her hand drifted south. "This is all for fun. Just do the bad things."

I groaned as she teased my thickening flesh with her fingers, then I flipped over, pinning her beneath me. "You don't know what you're asking for, Sawyer."

"I'm not asking." She squeezed my cock hard. "I'm begging for it."

Despite what she'd said, I couldn't bring myself to be as rough with her the second time, and I made sure she came twice before I even thought about my own orgasm. Still, it was wild and passionate and intense, and my sheets were a twisted fucking mess by the time we toppled right off the foot of the bed onto the floor.

So was my brain—I didn't stop for a condom.

Stop, my conscience said. *It's risky and reckless and you can't afford a mistake. Don't be an irresponsible asshole.*

But my body wouldn't listen. She was velvety soft and snug around my cock, so warm and wet, and she took me so deep, her hands on my ass pulling me into her, and her pleading cries—*don't stop, don't stop, don't stop*—were so sweet and sexy and all-consuming, I came inside her under a minute later with nothing between us.

Right away, I realized what I'd done and pulled out fast, as if it mattered at this point. "Oh, fuck."

She paused. "It's okay."

"No, it's not. I'm sorry. I got too carried away."

"Noah, it's *okay*. We're fine. I'm on the pill."

It was a relief, but I was still mad at myself. "Next time, I'll be more careful."

While Meg used the bathroom, I straightened up the bedding as well as I could in the dark, and got back into bed. My sheets smelled like her too now. I fucking loved it.

A minute later, she came back to bed, but instead of snuggling up with me, she lay on her back on her side of the bed. I thought maybe I'd hurt her somehow, and I was about to ask if she was okay when she spoke up.

"I have to tell you something."

"What?"

"I didn't forget about the condom."

"You didn't?"

"No. I thought of it, and I could have said something, but I didn't want to."

Turning onto my side, I propped my head in my hand. "Why not?"

"Because I wanted to be that close to you." She looked over at me. "But now I feel like I did something wrong."

My chest grew tight, and I reached for her. "Come here."

She rolled toward me and we lay face to face, chest to chest. I slung my arm around her lower back, and pulled her body tight to mine.

"Listen to me," I said firmly. "You didn't do anything wrong. I love that you wanted to be that close to me. I feel exactly the same way. I only apologized because I worry about you. I want you to feel safe."

"I always feel safe with you."

"Good." Hearing her say those words felt like a gift. I kissed her forehead, and a moment later she was asleep in my arms.

For a half a second, my mind started to drift in the direction of Sunday, when she'd leave to go back to DC and I wouldn't be the one holding her at night. Or anytime at all. Sunday was only five days away.

But I quickly flipped that switch off, and told myself to go to sleep. Meg didn't seem worried about it. *This is all for fun*, she'd said. It was exactly the kind of arrangement I'd been craving. Phenomenal sex with a not-crazy woman I actually happened to adore that didn't live in this town and had no expectation of me other than orgasms.

What more could I ask for?

Sixteen

Meg

ON THE RIDE TO CLOVERLEIGH THE NEXT MORNING, I looked at my text messages. "Oh, no."

Noah glanced over at me from behind the wheel. "What?"

"I'm busted. My mother called me a bunch of times last night, and then I got this text from Chloe: 'Hey, sorry about this but just wanted you to know that I had to tell Mom where you were. She was worried about you because you seemed out of it at dinner LOL so she checked on you when she got home and your room was empty. Then she freaked out and called me when you didn't answer your phone. I told her the truth because she wanted to call the police, which cracked me the fuck up.'"

Noah laughed at that too.

I groaned, looking down at last night's dinner outfit. I tried to pull down on my skirt and make it cover more of my legs. "It's not funny, Noah! They're going to take one look at me and know exactly what I was doing last night."

"Not unless they have *really* dirty minds," he joked.

I hit his leg. "Stop it. This is going to be seriously

awkward. I already did the walk of shame into the kitchen *yesterday* morning. It was not fun."

"Oh, Jesus." Noah shook his head. "You're a grown woman. Grown women have sex." He glanced at me and winced. "But if you have any makeup, you might want to put some on that cheek."

"Oh, God." I pulled down the visor and checked my face in the mirror. In the sunlight, the mark was even more obvious, but it wasn't horrible. "I don't have any makeup, but I do have sunglasses. I'll just wear those."

Noah pulled up at the house. "You gonna be okay?"

I took a breath. "Yeah."

"Hey. Look at me." He took my chin in his hand and turned my head toward him. "If you don't want to go in there, you don't have to. I'll take you back to my house and you can stay there as long as you want."

My belly flip-flopped at the sight of him in uniform, like it always did. What would it be like to kiss him goodbye every morning? Be there when he got home? Talk about our days over dinner and share the same bed every night?

I couldn't let myself think about it.

It was impossible, and it wasn't what we were doing. "I'm okay. I promise. Today is supposed to be sister day. Salon and spa and all that stuff, so I better stay here."

"Sounds like fun. Say hi to Nina for me."

"I will." I leaned over and kissed him. "I'm not sure if I'll be able to get away tonight."

"I suppose I'll survive. I owe Renzo some time anyway, don't I, buddy?"

I glanced at Renzo in the back seat, who looked excited at the prospect. "Have fun. And thanks for the ride home."

"Anytime, Sawyer."

I got out of the car and shut the door, and as he drove away, I fought off a wave of loneliness that swept over me. I'd miss him today. That was a feeling I hadn't counted on.

Sighing, I dug around in my purse until I found my sunglasses. Shoving them onto my face, I tried to arrange my messy hair to best cover my right cheek while I worked up the nerve to walk in.

Maybe they'll still be asleep, I thought hopefully as I unlocked the back door, slipped inside, and pulled it silently shut. *Maybe I can tiptoe right upstairs and not have to endure a conversation about this at all.*

Nope.

Not only were my parents at the breakfast table when I attempted to sneak in, but my sister Sylvia and both her kids were there too. All five of them blinked at me. My father's brow furrowed. My niece's mouth hung open. My sister looked slightly appalled for a second, and then hid a smile behind her coffee cup.

"Well, good morning, sunshine," my mother said, taking in my bedraggled, be-sun-spectacled appearance. "Did you have a nice time?"

"Uh. Yes."

"I wish you'd have told me you were going out. Or at least left a note or something," my mother said with a bit of a huff.

"Oh come on, Mom." Sylvia stuck up for me. "She's thirty-three. She can come and go as she pleases."

Thank you, I mouthed at her.

"I know how old she is, Sylvia, but she's still my daughter, and when she stays under my roof, I worry about her." My mother sent a withering glance toward Sylvia's end of the table and looked back at me, but I was already through the doorway leading to the front hall. "Hey, where are you going? Don't you want breakfast?"

"I'll get something later!" I called, racing up the stairs.

"We're leaving for the salon at ten, so be ready."

"Okay!"

Once I was safely in my room, I whipped off the glasses and flopped facedown onto my bed. Again, I fell asleep immediately and didn't wake up until I heard a soft knocking at my door. "Meg?"

Shit! Was it my mother? Frantically I looked around for my sunglasses. "Yeah?"

"It's Sylvia. Can I come in?"

I relaxed. "Oh. Sure."

She opened the door, slipped into the room and shut it behind her, leaning back against it. "Hi."

"Hi."

This time she didn't even try to hide her grin. "Have fun last night?"

I nodded, leaning back against my headboard. "Yes."

"I can tell. Either that or you got mugged, but since you came in with your purse, I'll hazard a guess you had some really good sex."

I laughed and touched my hair. "Pretty obvious, huh?"

"Yes. And good for you."

"Come on in." I gestured at the bed. "Sit."

She ditched her flats by the door and sat cross-legged near the foot of the bed. She looked a little better this morning—more color in her face. Less tension in her brow. "So tell me about this guy. Mom said he's the lifeguard who pulled you out of the bay that time?"

I nodded. "Yeah, that's him. Noah McCormick. We

were close in high school. He joined the Army after graduation, and he's a sheriff's deputy now."

A flicker of recognition crossed her face. "Was Sheriff McCormick his dad?"

"Yes."

"He was so nice."

"He was. They were close. His dad passed away about three years ago, and Noah took it hard."

"I bet."

"We don't see each other much, although we keep in touch by text pretty regularly." But now the thought of just text messaging him made me feel a little sick.

Sylvia took a pillow onto her lap. "So you've always just been friends before?"

"We're still just friends." I sighed. "I think. Things have shifted somewhat this week. I'm actually a little . . . confused about what we are right now."

She gave me a look. "I'd say so. That bedhead hair and mark on your cheek definitely do not say 'just friends.'"

I couldn't resist. "You should see the marks on my wrists from the handcuffs."

Her eyes went wide. "Shut up!"

Laughing, I pulled up the sleeves of my sweater and showed her. "I'm serious."

"Oh my God!" She shook her head. "Did it hurt?"

"Not as much as the spanking."

She buried her face in the pillow she held and screamed. Then she looked at me again, slack-jawed with shock. "I can't believe this."

"Why not?" Enjoying this, I leaned back against my pillows and put my hands behind my head. "You should try it sometime."

"Have you done that before? Sex with handcuffs and . . ." Her cheeks flushed pink. "Spanking?"

"No," I said. "But I told him the other night I like sex that isn't always predictable and safe. He must have been paying attention."

She looked down. "I guess so."

"You guys should totally try it. Spice things up after all those years of sweet married sex. I bet you'd like it." Actually, I wasn't sure she would. Sylvia was pretty vanilla in all aspects of life, and I didn't know anything about Brett's sexual appetite.

"I'd settle for sweet married sex. We don't even have that anymore."

"No?"

She shook her head, her eyes still on the pillow in her lap. "He gets his kicks elsewhere."

Now it was my turn to be shocked. "You can't be serious."

She shrugged, and when she looked at me, her eyes were shining. "Just because I look the other way doesn't mean I don't know."

"Why would he go somewhere else when he has you? You're gorgeous!"

Her eyes dropped again, and she shook her head. "Thanks, but I don't feel it. I feel tired and anxious and old."

"You're only thirty-seven!"

"I know, but I've had two kids, and—"

"Syl, you can't think you're overweight. I've never seen you so thin."

She tucked her hair behind her ears, looking miserable. "Yeah, turns out stressing about your husband having an affair is a great appetite killer. When I try to eat more, I'm just nauseated. And if I stop exercising, I get antsy. But I know I don't look good."

"Listen." I scooted toward her and put my hand on her knee. "You do look good. You look better today than you did last night, and I bet that's because you enjoyed a nice family meal and got a good night's sleep."

"I did," she admitted. "I haven't been sleeping well at home. I just lie there and think all these terrible thoughts. I don't want him to leave me. I don't want to be a single mother. I don't want to be single, period." Her panicked eyes met mine. "I don't like being alone."

My heart broke for her. "Listen, I know how you feel, at least partly. I don't have kids to think about, but I don't like being alone either, and Brooks just up and left me last week."

She nodded. "I heard about that. I'm sorry."

"Don't be. I'm over it." I pointed at my cheek. "Clearly."

Sylvia laughed a little. "I don't mean to unload all my baggage on you. I just wanted to hear about your fun night."

"Unload all you want. That's what sisters are for, right?"

Her smile was sad but genuine. "Right."

"And when's the last time we all got together like this? Your wedding? That was what, twelve years ago?"

"Fifteen."

"See? This is long overdue. Family is always there for you, and coming home feels good. Believe me, I needed this reminder too. When I was a kid, I couldn't wait to get out of here, but now I'm like, when's the next time I can come back?"

She smiled. "Sure that's not because someone hand-cuffed you to the bed last night?"

I laughed. "That *might* have something to do with it. But

it was in the kitchen, not the bedroom. *Later*, we did it in his bed—and also on the floor."

That got a laugh out of her. "Oh my God, you're a maniac."

"Possibly. But it feels so damn good with him, Sylvia. I've never felt so free with anyone before."

She tilted her head. "Better be careful. Sounds like there are some feelings beyond friendship there."

I hopped off the bed and busied myself going through my suitcase for clean clothes. "That can't happen. We agreed at the start, this is just friendly fun and ends when I go back to DC."

"And when is that?"

"After the wedding. Sunday." Dropping to my knees, I rummaged through piles of underwear and jeans and tops, not seeing anything. Sunday was way too close. So close it made my throat hurt.

My sister sighed. "I don't even know if Brett will come for the wedding."

I looked at her over one shoulder. "Seriously? He'd blow off Frannie's wedding?"

She shrugged. "He just keeps saying how busy he is, and what an inconvenient time this is for him to travel. But I think it's just an excuse to avoid time with me. And I'll be *so* embarrassed if he doesn't show. What will I even do?"

I wanted to punch Brett in his smug handsome face for making her feel bad about herself. It was inconceivable to me. This was *Sylvia*, the leader of the pack, the beautiful one, the pageant queen. The one who did everything right. The one we all aspired to be. How had life beaten her down this way?

"Hey." Getting to my feet, I went over and sat on the

bed again. Took her hands in mine. "You know what we're going to do today?"

"What?" She sniffed.

"We're going to go to the spa and get facials and massages to relax us. We're going to drink champagne and tell dirty jokes and fun stories. We're going to hit up the salon and get gorgeous. And then we're going to go out on the town, just us—the Sawyer Sisters on tour."

She laughed. "Sounds like fun, but I have kids, remember?"

"Mom and Dad can watch them."

"Mom will probably want to come," she pointed out.

"So the kids can stay here with Dad and veg out on the couch and eat junk food and watch movies with him."

"They'd love that." She sighed. "I don't allow them to eat junk food at home."

"Of course you don't. I need to remember to ship them each a case of Twinkies every Christmas."

She looked horrified. "Oh God, are you still eating those things? Meg, they have a shelf life of like two hundred years!"

"I know." I smiled. "But they are *delicious*, and during the zombie apocalypse, I'll be all set. I'll be able to wait it out in my pantry."

"You're insane." But her smile matched mine. "But you're having great sex and you seem really happy, so maybe I should stop with all the non-GMO, gluten-free, organic bullshit and start eating Twinkies."

I patted her knee. "Now you're talking."

On our way to the spa, I convinced my mother to pull into the grocery store parking lot. "I'll be right back," I told her, jumping out of the back seat.

In the passenger seat, Sylvia laughed. "Why do I have a feeling I know what you're running in there to buy?"

"Hush," I told her before shutting the door and hurrying into the store. Ten minutes later I came out carrying bags full of champagne bottles and boxes of Twinkies.

"Oh, Meg, for heaven's sake." My mother looked at the bags and shook her head. "You're not ten years old anymore."

"I know, Mom. That's why I got the champagne."

She clucked her tongue and frowned at me. "Good grief. And what's that mark on your face? Is it dirt?" For a second, I thought she might lick her finger and try to wipe it off like she used to do when we were kids.

"It's nothing, Mom."

"I hit her this morning," Sylvia said, cracking up. "We got into a fight."

My mother backed out of her parking spot, muttering, "This place is going to think we're crazy."

"They're going to think we're having fun," I corrected her.

And we did have fun.

April, Chloe, and Frannie met us at the spa, which was connected to the salon that Noah's sister Nina owned and ran. We spent the morning getting facials and massages and waxes, had a light spa lunch that was entirely Sylvia-approved, and then sipped champagne and ate Twinkies while we got pedicures. I gave up trying to hide the bruise on my face and told them all I walked into a door in the dark at Noah's house.

My mother might have believed me if my two sisters in the know hadn't started in.

"Was it a big door?" Chloe asked.

"A big, *thick* door?" echoed Sylvia.

"A big, thick, *hard* door that goes bang bang bang?" Chloe's eyes were alight with mischief, and Sylvia was laughing so hard she nearly choked on her Twinkie.

"What is going on that I don't know about?" April looked from me to Chloe to Sylvia and back at me. "Why don't I get the joke?"

"I don't get it either," Frannie said.

"Well, we know *I* don't get it." My mother rolled her eyes and took another sip of her champagne. "Can someone please clue your old mother in?"

"Okay, fine." The champagne had me tipsy enough to tell the truth. "I was with Noah last night, and things got a little rough."

"Rough?" My mother looked confused, which sent Sylvia and Chloe into hysterics.

"Yes, Mom. We were messing around, and things got rough." I tried to give her a meaningful look. "And that's all I want to say about it."

Suddenly it clicked. "Oh. *Ohhhhhh*. Oh, goodness." Then she laughed, her cheeks coloring. "Forget I asked. I don't want to know!"

"*I* do. You and Noah? After all this time?" April grabbed the bottle of champagne from the ice bucket next to her chair, leaned over and poured me some more. "Let's get her drunk so she keeps talking."

"Yes!" Frannie shouted.

"No!" I shook my head. "Not while Mom is here."

"Thank you, Meg." My mother sighed. "I know you

girls are all grown up and have sex lives by now, and I hope they're wonderful, but I can't bring myself to think about it. You can talk about it after I go home."

"Aren't you going to come out with us tonight?" Frannie asked. "You're invited, Mom."

"I know, and I appreciate the invitation, but you girls go ahead. You need some time together, and I need some time with my grandchildren. I don't see them enough." She looked concerned. "But how will you get around? None of you should drive."

"We'll get rides, Mom. Don't worry," April assured her. "So what are we all going to do with our hair today?"

I sent her a thankful smile for changing the subject, and we all discussed what we might do with color or cut. When our manis and pedis were done, we moved over to the salon side, bringing our champagne and Twinkies with us.

"Hey, you!" Nina came over to me right away and gave me a hug. "I heard you were in town."

"And I heard you were having a baby any day now." Laughing, I gestured toward her round belly. "Guess it was the truth."

"Oh God, I hope so. This baby needs to come out." She knocked on her stomach like it was a door. "Do you hear that? Get out already! I want my body back."

I laughed. "You look great, Nina. You're glowing."

"That's probably because I'm so damn hot all the time," she said grumpily. "I'm like one giant halogen lamp. I could heat this entire building. Maybe give you guys all tans." She waved a hand in the air. "But enough about me. I hear you were at the house the other day."

"I was," I said. "Noah and I have been hanging out quite a bit. It's been really fun."

"That's awesome. He needs some fun." Then she laughed. "And Lord knows that boy has always been hung up on you."

Flustered, I flapped a hand in front of my face. "It's not like that. We're just friends."

"Friends. Right. God, you're as bad as he is." Shaking her head, she sighed. "So what are we doing today? You're with me."

"Really? Wow, I'm honored."

She held up one hand and whispered behind it. "Yeah, I rearranged some other clients. I can do that. I own the place."

Laughing, I followed her to her chair. "Awesome. I'm all yours. I was thinking about some highlights. Can I be a hot, sexy blonde when I leave here?"

"Absolutely," she said. "Have a seat, and we'll get to it."

While she worked, putting foil after foil after foil on my head, I imagined surprising Noah later with my siren hair, my bright red toes, and my smooth-as-silk skin. Then I remembered I probably wouldn't see him tonight.

Disappointment balled up in my stomach, and I found myself thinking up excuses to potentially cut out early. But I didn't want to do that to my sisters. I wanted time with them—and I wanted time with Noah too.

Unfortunately, time was the one thing in short supply.

Seventeen

Noah

WEDNESDAY AFTERNOON, I GOT A TEXT FROM MEG.

Meg: Your sister is awesome.

Me: Don't tell her that. Her ego will be as big as her belly.

Meg: I already told her.

Me: Are you at the salon?

Meg: Yes. She is transforming me into a hot sexy bombshell.

Me: You do not need her help in that department.

Meg replied with a kissy-face emoji, and I checked the time. It was just after one, and I was starving, but instead of thinking about lunch, I was considering dropping by the salon.

I wouldn't stay long or anything—I just wanted to say hi. We probably wouldn't see each other at all today if I didn't. Maybe not tomorrow either. She was probably going to be all tied up with lots of wedding stuff now that everyone was here.

Plus, there was a deli on that block I loved. I could pretend that I'd been heading there for lunch. I'd go in, say a quick hello, and get out. Then I'd grab a sandwich and get back to work.

I'd been thinking about her nonstop since I'd dropped her off, replaying all the little details that had made the last two nights so fucking amazing. Everything she said, everything she did, everything she let me do to her . . . it was better than a dream.

And the coolest thing was that nothing had changed. Nothing was awkward or weird or uncomfortable between us. I could still be myself around her. If anything, we were even closer friends than we'd been before. We were still *us*, but new and improved us, with one hundred percent more sex included.

I found a parking spot on the street near the deli, told Renzo I'd be right back, and walked up the block to the salon. As soon as I opened the door, I spotted her reading a magazine in my sister's chair, her head under a dryer and *full* of tin foil. There had to be a hundred pieces of it sticking out in every direction.

Waving to the receptionist, who was on the phone but gave me a smile, I snuck up behind Meg and studied her in the mirror. Even with a head full of foil, she made my heart beat faster.

"If that's my sister's idea of sexy bombshell, you might want to ask for a refund."

She looked in the mirror and gasped, hiding her face with the magazine. "Noah! You're not supposed to see me like this! Get out!"

Laughing, I moved in front of her and leaned back on Nina's station, crossing my arms over my chest. "Having fun?"

"I *was*." She lowered the magazine to her lap. "What are you doing here?"

"I'm about to grab a sandwich for lunch at the deli up the street. Since I was in the neighborhood, I figured I'd stop in and say hi."

Her cheeks went pink. "Well, I wish I looked better. Can you come back in three hours?"

"Three *hours*? It takes that long to get your hair done?"

"It's a process. But it will be worth it."

"Jeez. Where's my sister?"

"In the back, I think. She had to get off her feet for a bit."

I nodded. "What are your plans tonight?"

"Painting the town with my sisters, who are probably all looking over here right now, wondering what is going on."

I glanced around the salon. Sure enough, every eye in the entire place was on us. "Should I arrest you? Give them a little excitement?"

She swatted me with her magazine and lowered her voice. "Don't you dare put those cuffs on me in public."

Our eyes shared the memory of last night, making the crotch of my uniform pants threaten to get tight. Not a good look. "I better go," I told her. "Have fun tonight."

"Thanks. What will you do?"

"Nothing much. Hang out with Renzo. Watch baseball." *Miss you*, I thought, but didn't say it.

"Okay. I'll call you tomorrow."

"Sounds good." I wanted to kiss her, even if it was just on the cheek, but I couldn't. Tongues were already going to wag about us. So instead, I took her hand and gave it a squeeze. "I better get out of here before people start asking why I'm wasting their tax dollars talking to pretty girls in salons."

Her mouth fell open. "Do people really say that kind of thing?"

"Sometimes."

"Jerks." Her face was angry, and it looked so funny with all that foil on her head I had to laugh.

"Oh my God, get out of here," she said, giving my ass a shove and hiding behind her magazine again. "And forget you saw me like this."

"I'm going. I'm just going to say a quick hello to Nina." I headed for the salon's break room, conscious of the way Meg's family was staring at me—not rudely or anything. In fact, her mother and a couple of her sisters smiled and said a casual hello.

But it was clear they *definitely* knew what was up.

I'd told Meg it didn't matter if they knew we'd spent the night together, but damn if I didn't feel naked as a jaybird as I passed them. I nodded cordially at anyone who made eye contact and returned their hellos, but didn't stop to chat.

When I reached the break room, I poked my head in. Nina was sitting in one chair with her bare feet up on another, her phone in her hands. "Hey," I said.

She looked up in surprise. "Hey. What are you doing here?"

"I was in the neighborhood. Thought I'd come by and say hi."

"To who?"

"To you, my ever-loving sister. Who else?"

"Ha." Her smug expression told me she knew better. "You're *so* obvious."

"About what?"

She rolled her eyes. "You didn't know Meg Sawyer was going to be here?"

"No. I mean, she might have *mentioned* something about it . . ."

"Please." Nina held up one hand. "Don't embarrass yourself. You're a terrible liar. We both know why you're here and it's not to see me. So what's with you two?"

"Nothing."

"Really? Then why has every other word out of her mouth for the last two hours been Noah? Why does she turn a lovely shade of pink when she talks about you? Why do her eyes light up every time she tells me about something you said to her or something you've done or about how you're taking her to Frannie's wedding?" She shook her head. "Face it, Noah. That girl adores you. And you've always adored her. The only question is whether you're going to be too stubborn to admit it."

"Bye, Nina."

She groaned. "Men are the worst. Why do you all refuse to admit you have feelings?"

"Say hi to Chris for me," I called, heading back toward the front of the salon.

Catching Meg's eye in the mirror one last time, I winked at her, waved again at the receptionist and went out the door. Up the street, I grabbed a sandwich and cup of coffee at the deli, and while I ate, I couldn't get the thought of Meg hiding behind that stupid magazine out of my head. Or the thought of her cuffed and bent over my kitchen counter while I spanked her. Or the thought of her bursting into my bathroom and seeing me naked. Or the thought of how nice it had been the past two nights to have her close to me as I fell asleep.

So nice that I was already missing her tonight.

It started to bother me a little. What the hell was wrong with me? I'd slept alone every night for the past three years and now two nights with Meg had me so messed up I couldn't even get through a day without seeing her? It was fucking ridiculous. I didn't need someone in my bed every night.

Determined to put her from my head, I finished up lunch, threw out my trash, and headed back to the car. I was nearly there when I heard the dispatcher call my number on the radio.

Thank God. Work would distract me.

Eighteen

Meg

MY SISTERS WENT NUTS THE MOMENT NOAH WALKED out, jumping out of their chairs and surrounding me, all talking at once.

"Oh my God!"

"I can't believe he came in here!"

"He's so cute in that uniform!"

"Seriously, those arms!"

"How about that heat he was packing, if you know what I mean?"

"Did you see the way he looked at her?"

"I know! And with all that foil on her head! She looks ridiculous, and he still couldn't take his eyes off her!"

"For real, he is *totally* in love."

"Okay, enough," I said, moving the dryer off my head. "It's not that big a deal. He was in the neighborhood and came to say hi."

Nina broke through the Sawyer sister offensive line. "Which he has never done before," she said with a grin. "Just so you know."

My face flushed with heat. "Okay, fine, he might have

come here to see me. But he's not *in love* with me. We're just friends." I had to keep saying it if I was going to keep believing it.

The gaggle of women around me honked and snorted like barnyard animals. There was plenty of eye rolling too . . . Clearly, *they* did not believe it, which only made me more determined to dig my heels in.

"I have male friends," April said wryly. "That is not what it looks like."

"I think it's so sweet," gushed Frannie. "You've been friends for so long, and now you're falling in love." She bounced around so the foils on her head flopped. "It's so Beauty and the Beast!" She broke into song, giddily and off key. "There may be something there that wasn't there before!"

"Oh, Lord. You guys, we are *not* a fairy tale," I insisted, squirming a little in my chair. "We are not a song, and we are not falling in love. We're just two people who feel really comfortable around each other having a good time. It's more like a vacation fling than anything else. The only thing it has in common with a fairy tale is that it's not real."

"I don't know, Meg." Sylvia gave me a rueful smile. "It looked pretty real to me."

"Why wouldn't it be real?" Chloe asked. "You just said you feel comfortable together. That's real."

"Okay, yes, our *feelings* are real." I was starting to get hot under my clothes. Why did I feel so confused all of a sudden? "We do genuinely care about each other. But neither of us wants to mess with our friendship, so we have agreed that this is temporary fun while I'm in town and nothing more. The end."

"I don't like that ending." Frannie pouted.

"Well, sorry, but that's what it is. And we're supposed to be celebrating you today anyway. Can't we talk about the wedding or something?"

Her face lit up again. "Yes. So I was going to wear my hair down, but now I'm thinking I might like it like this . . ." Frannie rhapsodized dreamily about her wedding day hairstyle, after which everyone drifted back to their chairs or the sinks to be rinsed, leaving me alone with Nina.

She checked under one foil. "Almost done. A couple more minutes."

"Okay."

She set the dryer back in place and moved over to the chair next to her station, which was currently empty. "You look a little stressed out."

"Yeah, well. Sisters love to torment each other, and mine are good at it."

"We love to torment our brothers too." Nina grinned mischievously. "I gave Noah plenty of shit back there too, don't worry."

I groaned. "You're all merciless."

"I know, but it's fun. Listen, he's been calling me Shamu for months."

"I told him to stop doing that. You do not look like a whale."

She shrugged. "Eh, it's fine. He's my brother, and that's what he does. We still love each other. He's a good guy."

"He is."

"You know, this is the happiest I've seen him in a long time."

"Really?" I sat up a little taller. I liked thinking that I made him happy.

"Yes. I don't know how much he told you about his ex . . ."

"Holly?" I tried—and failed—to say her name without disdain.

Nina nodded. "I think it really messed him up the way it ended with her. She really got to him. Made him feel bad for wanting to take care of his family."

"That's what he said." I shook my head. "I don't get how anyone could treat him that way. It's so selfish."

"It was. And it all fell apart at the worst possible time for him—we'd just buried my dad, and Noah took that loss *so hard*. So I think he associates being in a relationship with pain and failure. He thinks being alone is easier."

"Yeah, he mentioned he's not interested in marriage or kids or anything." I fussed with one corner of the magazine cover. "Says he's got enough people to take care of already."

Nina sighed heavily. "We've had that conversation before too. And it stinks, because he's so good with kids. He'd be *such* a great dad."

"Yeah." I could see it—Noah lifting a little girl onto his shoulders, pushing a little boy on a swing. It was a sweet and happy image . . . so why did it put a big empty pit in my stomach?

"He'd be a great husband too," Nina went on. "I mean Holly was clearly not the one, but we're all holding out hope that the right person is out there. It would have to be someone special. Someone compassionate and understanding for sure. My mother always said being married to a cop was its own kind of job."

"Noah mentioned that as another reason he's determined to stay single."

"Did he?" Nina's forehead wrinkled. "You know, it was tough for my mom sometimes, but she'd tell you herself it was worth it. I mean, yes, they used to fight—they both had those stubborn Irish temperaments, but there were more good times than bad. And everybody needs a little love at the end of a hard day."

"Yeah." But I refused to let myself imagine Noah and I coming home to each other after a hard day—after *any* kind of day. My feelings for him were already veering into baffling and dangerous territory. If I let my hopes start to rise, I was bound to be disappointed, wasn't I? He'd told me flat out what he wanted and didn't want. We'd agreed on no expectations, no promises, no commitments. When he said, *I can't be your boyfriend*, I'd replied I that wasn't looking for one.

It had been the truth at the time. Was it still?

Nina must have sensed my unease. "Listen, forget I said anything. Noah's personal life is none of my business, and I respect his devotion and loyalty to his family. I wish he didn't think it had to come at the expense of his own happiness, but he's stubborn as hell and that's never gonna change. I'm just glad to see him having a good time with you, that's all. He deserves it. Now let's get you rinsed and gorgeous."

After leaving the salon, we all went home to change, agreeing to meet for cocktails at Low Bar in Traverse City at five. Grateful for the alone time, I locked myself in my room, undressed, and lay down on my bed for a few minutes. I'd had a great day with my sisters and I was looking forward to our evening out, but I couldn't exactly say I felt relaxed, even after all the luxury spa treatments. Something was gnawing at me, and I didn't know how to handle it.

Had I changed my mind about what I wanted from

Noah? Was I going to be able to leave here on Sunday and forget about the way he made me feel? Was I crazy to even entertain the idea that maybe—*maybe*—we could be something more than friends?

Or was all the fantastic sex clouding my brain? Could too many orgasms in a matter of days make you nuts? Weren't there some sort of mind-altering chemicals that your body released when you came that made you feel good? Maybe that's what this was. And maybe when I left and this week-long sexcapade was concluded, my brain would go back to normal, and I wouldn't have these weird feelings anymore. I wouldn't be questioning things that had already been decided.

Bolting straight up, I decided that's exactly what the situation was, and I didn't need to worry about it. Everything was fine. I hopped out of bed, changed into my bachelorette party outfit, did my makeup, and studied my reflection in the mirror.

Sexy black blouse? Check.

Skinny jeans that showed off my butt? Check.

Beautiful lingerie worn just for me? Check.

High heels that hurt to walk in but looked fabulous? Check.

Bombshell salon hair with big, tousled curls that I'd never be able to reproduce on my own? Check.

Eyebrows waxed, eyeliner even, bruise concealed, and lips pink and shiny? Check.

I felt beautiful. Confident. Sexy. I wished Noah could see me.

Stop it, I told myself as I threw a few things in a small black evening bag. *You can go one night without him. You're not a junkie, for heaven's sake. You don't need a dick to have a good time. Not even if it's Noah's dick. His big, hard, perfect dick that feels so good and makes me come so fast and—*

"Meg?"

I opened my eyes and realized I'd stopped halfway down the stairs, my feet on different steps, my hand gripping the banister. And had I just moaned out loud?

At the foot of the staircase, Sylvia stood looking up at me, her expression bemused. "Um, are you okay?"

"Yes," I said, clearing my throat as I descended the rest of the way. "I just . . . had a cramp."

"Aha." She gave me a knowing look. "A cramp. Well, if you're ready to go, Mom offered to drive us into town."

"I'm ready." I followed her to the garage and got into the backseat again, vowing not to think any more about Noah's dick.

But it was *really* hard.

(See what I mean?)

Turns out, the Sawyer sisters aren't very wild partiers. After cocktails at Low Bar, several bottles of wine during dinner at Trattoria Stella, and after-dinner drinks with dessert at Poppycock's, we were *done*—and it wasn't even ten.

"Are we lame?" April said as we all stood outside the restaurant waiting for Mack, who had generously offered to drive all our tipsy asses home. She stifled a yawn. "I'm pretty sure we are."

"I can't help it." Sylvia yawned too. "I go to bed every night at nine o'clock. I'm old."

"So what's my excuse?" Frannie looked like she might fall asleep on her feet. "I'm not even thirty. But you know what I *am*?" She hiccuped. "Drunk."

"I think it's Mom's fault," said Chloe. "She always made us go to bed so early as kids. We never developed a tolerance for late nights."

While they lamented our party-pooper genes, I snuck a look at my phone. Noah hadn't texted or called, and it worried me. Granted, I hadn't contacted him either (although I'd failed miserably at trying not to think about him), but I couldn't shake the feeling that something wasn't right.

Moving slightly away from the group, I broke down and called him.

"Hello?" His voice sounded different to me. Quieter. More raw. Maybe he'd been asleep?

"Did I wake you?"

"No."

"How was your night?"

"Okay."

I expected him to ask about mine, but he didn't. "Everything okay?"

"Yeah."

I bit my lip. "Doesn't sound like it."

"It was a rough day. I'm tired."

"Oh." I wasn't sure what to say. "Want to talk about it?"

"Not really."

"Okay," I said, although it didn't feel okay at all. "Well, I'll let you get some sleep."

"Where are you?" he asked, and I was relieved he finally showed some interest.

"Downtown Traverse. In front of Poppycock's waiting for Mack to pick us up."

"He's driving you home?"

"Yeah. We've all been drinking since like, ten A.M. or

something." I laughed through a yawn. "We're pretty much toast. Kind of pathetic for a big night out, huh?"

He didn't laugh. Or agree. Or say anything at all. I almost thought we'd lost our connection.

"Hello?"

"I'm here," he said. "Sorry. I'm just . . . I don't know what the fuck I am right now."

"You sound really down. Do you want company? I could have Mack drop me at your place."

"Nah."

I tried not to be too hurt. "Okay. Just wanted to offer in case you needed a friend or something."

"I'm fine."

More tense silence.

"Okay, well, Mack is here, so I better go," I lied. "You get some sleep and let me know how you're doing tomorrow, okay?"

"Okay."

"And I'm here if you need me." I waited for him to offer something more, but he didn't. All I could do was let him go. "Goodnight."

"Night."

I ended the call and stood there for a moment in the dark, listening to my sisters laugh and wondering what the hell could have happened today to make him act so distant and sad. Was it something at work? With his family? His ex?

Whatever it was, he hadn't wanted to confide in me about it. And he hadn't wanted to see me. I felt stupidly selfish for being hurt, but I was.

Was this the end? Had we ruined things? But how? This afternoon at the salon, everything had been fine. What could have happened in between then and now to make him shut down that way?

"Everything okay, Meg?" Sylvia called.

Attempting to swallow the lump in my throat, I nodded. "Yeah, I—" My phone vibrated in my hand, and I looked at the screen. *Noah McCormick calling.*

"Hello?"

"Fuck, Sawyer. I'm sorry." He sounded a little more like himself.

"It's okay."

"Are you in Mack's car?"

"Not yet."

"Stay there. I'm coming to get you."

My heartbeat quickened. "Okay."

"But wait inside, do you hear me?"

"Yes."

"Give me twenty."

"I'll be here."

I went over to my sisters and told them Noah was going to pick me up and suffered another round of good-natured teasing peppered with lots of obscene gestures and dirty jokes. After about ten minutes, Mack pulled up, and my sisters piled into his Chevy Tahoe, giggling like children.

He came around to open the passenger door for Frannie, kissed her cheek, and helped her in. After shutting the door, he turned to me, an amused look on his face. "You need help getting in too?"

"No, my friend Noah is picking me up."

"Noah McCormick?"

"Yes."

He nodded. "I know him a little bit. Nice guy."

Frannie rolled down her window. "Is she telling you

about her *friend*, Noah? Don't believe her. They have sex. He handcuffed her."

"Frannie!" I gave her a murderous look over Mack's shoulder. "That was a secret!"

"You can trust Mack," she said, giving me her innocent eyes, except she was so drunk it came out more like *trush*.

Mack shook his head. "How much did you guys drink tonight?"

I had to laugh. "Probably too much. But we had fun."

"Good." He looked up and down the street, which was pretty empty this late on a Wednesday night. "Are you sure I can't drop you at his house?"

"I'm sure. He's on his way, and I'm going to wait inside until he texts me he's here."

He looked relieved. "Okay. Go on in now, and stay there until you see him."

I saluted him. "Yes, sir."

Rolling his eyes, he grumbled something about Sawyer women I couldn't quite make out and hustled back around to the driver's side. I gave my sisters a wave and went back into Poppycock's to wait.

After a couple minutes, I saw Noah pull up at the curb. I rushed out as he leaned over and opened the passenger door for me.

"Hey," I said, sliding in and buckling up. "Thanks for coming to get me."

"No problem." He pulled away without looking at me or touching me. Clearly whatever was causing the bad mood hadn't lifted.

Renzo was in the back, and I leaned around to greet him. "Hi, handsome. Did you have a good day?"

The dog seemed happier to see me than Noah did.

We drove in silence for about ten minutes, until I couldn't stand it anymore. "Do you want to talk about it?"

"About what?"

"Whatever has you so pissed off."

"No."

"Did something happen at work?"

"Drop it."

I sat back and looked out the passenger window, but again, the silence grew unbearable. "Did you go to the park after work?"

"Yeah."

"Did you run?"

"Yeah."

"How was it?"

"Fine."

I sighed dramatically, crossing my arms over my chest and studying the hard set of his jaw. "Do you want to just take me home, Noah? Because it doesn't seem like you want to be with me."

"I'm just not in the mood to talk, okay?" he snapped. "Not everything needs to be talked about all the time."

"But if you don't talk about it, whatever's eating at you is just going to get worse," I said, wanting to help.

"Words aren't going to make anything better, Sawyer, they're just fucking words. Even when *you* say them." His tone was angry and bitter. He'd never spoken to me that way before.

"Why are you mad at *me*?"

"I'm not mad at you!" he roared. "I'm just mad, okay? Not everything is about *you*!"

"Fine." I looked out the window for a few more minutes, feeling confused and helpless and frustrated. Why had he even come to get me?

Ten minutes later when we pulled into his garage, he still hadn't said anything. The crickets in his yard seemed extra loud as we made our way to the back door.

"I'm going to give Renzo a few minutes out here. You can go in," Noah said.

"I'll wait with you."

"Suit yourself."

We stood side by side without speaking. When Renzo was ready, we followed him inside.

Right away, Noah took Renzo into the spare bedroom. I got myself a glass of water and waited in the kitchen for him to come back. When he didn't, I wandered toward the front room, where I found him sitting on the couch, staring at the TV, which wasn't even on. One lamp was lit, illuminating his strong, handsome profile. My insides tightened, and I knew instinctively something was *way* off.

"Can I get you anything?" I asked.

"No, thanks." His tone was a little softer.

Moving into the room, I set my water aside and sat on the ottoman in front of the couch, so I was facing him. "Hey."

His eyes closed.

"Hey." I put my hand on his knee. "It's okay. You don't have to talk to me. You don't have to tell me anything. I can just be here with you."

He reached for me. "Come here. Let me hold you."

Nineteen

Noah

I DIDN'T DESERVE HER AFFECTION AFTER THE WAY I'D TREATED her, but I pulled her onto my lap anyway. She kicked off her heels and wrapped her arms around my shoulders, cradling my head against her chest.

I took a deep breath, inhaling the scent of her perfume. "Sorry I was an asshole in the car."

"It's okay."

"No, it's not. This has nothing to do with you, I just needed to get angry at someone, I guess."

"I understand. We've all done it."

"I should have let Mack take you home. I'm not much fun tonight."

"I don't care." She stroked my hair, kissed my temple. "I'm not just here for fun, Noah. I care about you. And if you need to vent some anger at me, it's okay. I can take it."

"You don't deserve it." Still, I wasn't about to let her go. It felt too good to hold her this way, to let her hold me, to let some of the tension from this shitty day drain out of my body and take solace in her warmth and familiarity. I was a lucky fucking bastard.

I looked at her, really seeing her for the first time to-night. The hair, the tight jeans, the red lips, her bare feet with red-painted toes. "Holy shit. You're gorgeous."

She smiled. "Thanks. Told you your sister was magic."

"It's not just your hair, Sawyer. But I do like it." I took a fistful of newly golden-streaked strands and tugged gently. "A lot."

A laugh escaped her, loosening the knots in my gut even more. "I'm glad. And I'm so glad you called me back."

"I almost didn't. I was afraid I'd end up being a dick to you. But I wanted to be with you."

"I wanted to be with you too. And you're entitled to a bad day."

She continued stroking my hair, my neck, my shoulders, and pressing soft kisses on my forehead. It was soothing and sweet, and it made me want to tell her things.

"I had to go to the hospital today to interview a suspect."

"Was he injured or something?"

"No. He'd brought his six-year-old daughter in."

Meg's hands stopped. "Why?"

"She was screaming in pain and wouldn't stop. I think it was the noise that bothered him more than her suffering. Turns out she had a kidney infection."

"Poor baby."

"We were called because of all the bruises on her body. New and old. And burn marks."

Meg's arms tightened around me. "No."

"This fucker hurts her," I seethed, the fury making my blood boil all over again. "I know he does. But I have to in-terview him with respect, and be polite, and try to get him to think he can trust me so he'll admit to all the fucked up shit he does to his own kids. The girl isn't the only child in the house."

"Oh, Noah. That's heartbreaking. No wonder you were so upset."

"And the entire time, all I want to do is beat the living fuck out of this guy so he knows what it feels like."

"I wish you could have."

"Me too. That fucker deserves worse than jail time for hurting a child."

"Do you think he—" she stopped, unable to even voice the thought.

"I don't know for sure. But I suspect it." My stomach turned over. "I kept thinking about my niece, Violet. She's exactly that age. If anybody ever—"

"Oh honey, no. Don't even think it."

"I swear to God, Meg, I've seen a lot of things you wouldn't believe. Violence. Tragic accidents. War. I've watched men die right in front of my eyes." I forced the tremble out of my voice. "But nothing fucks me up like someone hurting a child."

"I know." Meg rubbed my shoulder. "I'm sorry."

"It just reminds me how fucked up the world is. I don't even know how people can bring kids into it. My sister is crazy."

"Come on, it's not all bad. And we've got heroes like you to protect us. Did you arrest the guy?"

"No. A detective was brought in. She'll get more detailed photos, a sexual assault exam, and bring the suspect to the PD for a more thorough interview. But I don't need any of that. I knew in my gut that guy was guilty, and there was nothing I could do about it."

"That has to be so frustrating. You must have wanted to put your fist through a wall."

"I nearly did, I was so wound up. And I was a total asshole to everyone the rest of the day. After my run, I went out for a beer, and I kept hoping someone would throw a punch so I could get in a fight."

"Well, I'm glad they didn't. I like your face. And you like your job. Both of those things probably would have been in jeopardy if you'd hit someone."

"Yeah," I agreed.

She took my face in her hands and forced me to look at her. "But I don't blame you for being that worked up. And I'm sorry." She kissed my lips, then my forehead before cradling my head against her chest again. "You just want to protect everybody. You've always been that way. And it messes you up inside when you feel like you can't."

I sat still, trying to stay right here in the moment. Taking comfort in her touch, the smell of her perfume, the sound of her heartbeat. The way she understood me. Listened to me. "I remember sometimes when my dad would have a bad day, he'd come home and pick a fight with my mom. Or blow up at something she said."

"Why?"

"Because unlike those ridiculous TV shows you watch, the good guys don't always win. He'd be angry and frustrated and want to beat the shit out of somebody, just like I did tonight, but he was the sheriff so he couldn't, and it would all bottle up inside him until he got home. I guess it was where he felt safe to let off the steam."

"What about your mom?"

"Oh, she knew what he was doing. Sometimes she gave it right back to him, if he was being a real dick, and sometimes she just let him rant. She's got thick skin. And most of the time, my dad was pretty calm, even when people around him were pissed off and belligerent—it's part of what made him such a good cop. He knew how to keep control. But every now and again, he just needed to blow up."

"Must have been tough for you guys as kids."

"They didn't do it in front of us. And Asher wore noise-canceling headphones a lot of the time, so I don't think he ever heard them. Nina would put on music in her room. I'd just leave the house sometimes, go for a run." I paused. "After I met you, sometimes I'd head over to your house."

"Really? You never said anything about your parents fighting."

I shrugged. "I didn't really want to talk about it. And it always passed. My dad would apologize, and my mom would accept. He'd bring home flowers the next day. Red roses, always."

"That's sweet."

"It was. They were good together. Understood each other. I wish they could have had more time." I felt my chest get tight thinking of the injustice of it. "Their big plan was a trip to Ireland for their fortieth wedding anniversary. My dad would have been retired by then."

"Oooh, Ireland. I'd love to go there someday."

I frowned. "I'm trying to get her to take the trip anyway, but she's so damn stubborn. And she uses Asher as an excuse, but I'd told her a million times Asher would be fine here. Or I'd go stay with him at her house."

"Well, it's got to be hard for her, if it was a dream she had with your dad. She has to learn to let go of that and reframe it as a new dream. That's scary, and she might even feel like she's being disloyal to your dad if she does it alone."

"But she's got to move on," I said angrily. "My dad

wanted her to be happy. He made me promise I wouldn't let her stop living, and I feel like I'm letting him down."

"You can't force someone to be happy, Noah. You have to let them decide to let go of whatever is holding them back. It's painful to see someone you love choosing fear over happiness, but it has to be her choice. All you can do is make it clear you'll be there to help when she's ready."

"I know. I'm just fucking . . . frustrated with everything, including myself." I shut my eyes. "I don't even know why you're bothering with me tonight."

"Because bothering with you is—mostly—fun. In fact . . ." She slid off my lap and onto her knees in front of me. "I have an idea."

"Oh yeah?"

"Yeah." She pushed my knees apart and ran her hands up my thighs. "Why don't you let me bother your cock with my tongue and see how you feel after that?"

My jaw dropped, and my dick jumped. "Are you serious?"

"Don't I look serious?" She gave me a stern librarian face as she unbuckled my belt, with pouty red lips and one eyebrow arched. That blond hair was tumbling all around her shoulders, and I imagined my hands in it while she had her fuck-hot mouth on me.

"You look fucking hot."

"Good." She unbuttoned and unzipped my jeans, then pulled her top over her head, revealing a black and pink bra with sexy criss-crossing straps that made me want to tie her up. "Just in case I get a little messy."

I remembered watching her sucking the sauce off the bone the other night at dinner—and she'd been wearing a *T-shirt* at the time—and thought my dick was going to burst through the crotch of my pants at the thought of her sucking me off in that bra. "Go ahead. Get messy."

She tugged at the sides of my jeans and I lifted my hips just enough for her to drag them down below my knees. My cock sprung out like it had been catapulted, and she laughed as she took it in her hands. "Are you excited?"

"Yes."

She lowered her head between my legs, keeping her eyes on mine. "Have you thought about this before?"

"Yes."

"How much?" She swirled her tongue over the tip, making my entire body hum.

"A lot."

"Even back then?"

"Especially back then."

She smiled with fire in her eyes and ran her tongue up one side of my cock, then the other. "I like that."

"But I want it even more now."

Those eyes found mine again and held them for a moment before she lowered her mouth onto me and slid her lips all the way down. I felt the tip of my cock hit the back of her throat, felt her hand begin to work along the shaft, felt her tongue against my crown, felt the muscles in her mouth suck and tease and torture me. She went slowly at first, like I was a meal she wanted to savor, and I watched as she licked and tasted and tantalized every inch of me. Unable to stop myself, I started to move, rocking my hips beneath her, holding her head where I wanted it, thrusting between her lips with deep, steady strokes.

The most amazing thing was how much she seemed to enjoy it. She moaned and sighed and gasped for air. She took me so deep, she couldn't breathe. She went at me hard and fast. She got messy, and seriously didn't give a fuck. All she wanted to do was give me pleasure. I felt like a god.

When I couldn't hold back anymore and warned her I was going to come, I wouldn't have blamed her if she didn't want it in her mouth—but if anything, she just took me in deeper. My fingers tightened in her hair, my entire body stiffened, my rhythmic exhales became one long groan that tore from my throat as my cock surged and emptied into her throat.

When I relaxed my grip, she sat back on her heels, breathing hard. "Jesus," she said, wiping her mouth with her forearm. "And I thought it was big before."

Jumping to my feet, I yanked my pants up, grabbed her beneath the arms and set her on the couch. "Lie down," I told her, except I didn't even wait for her to lie down, I just pushed her back and went right to work taking off her jeans, her panties right along with them.

But I left that bra right where it was.

"Noah, you're tired. You don't have to—"

But my mouth was already on her pussy, and the rest of her ridiculous sentence was swallowed up by a moan.

"That's better," I told her. "No more talking."

"I like talking."

"Right now, all I want to do is make you come. And words aren't going to do it."

"Yours might."

That made me smile. "Just let me fuck you with my tongue, Sawyer. We can talk later."

I didn't give her a chance to argue.

Later, we stretched out in my bed, skin to skin, our legs entwined.

"Do you feel better?" she asked, snuggling close to me the way she did at night.

"Yeah. I do."

"I don't think I've ever seen you so angry."

"Well, you're not around that much. And I don't usually get so worked up. It's only certain things that really get to me."

"I know." Her fingertips brushed back and forth across my chest. "I think the last time I saw you get that mad was when that asshole kid wouldn't stop teasing Asher about wearing those headphones at the beach. You went ballistic on that jerk."

I frowned. "Yeah, I got in a lot of trouble for that. My dad was pissed at me for losing my shit."

"I didn't blame you. I don't think anybody did. That kid deserved it."

"I'm better at controlling my emotions now. Usually."

"But you're not a robot, Noah. It's okay to feel things. Even for a man."

I was silent for a minute, then I told her something I'd never told anyone. "I feel guilty. About Asher."

He hand stilled on my chest. "What?"

"I have all this guilt I carry around. I've always had it."

"But why? You're the best brother he could have."

"Because we're twins and I got everything so easy. It's not fair. It's never been fair. Do you know what caused his cerebral palsy? A lack of oxygen to the brain during birth. We were born five minutes apart. So why him and not me?"

"Oh, Noah. Don't think that way."

"I can't help it. Every single day has been a struggle

for him. Walking. Talking. Eating. Sleeping. Just being in public. And I never struggled with anything. Not school or friends or sports or girls. My only struggle was trying to protect him. It was my only way to . . . make it up to him somehow."

She propped herself up, her hand splayed over my heart. "I get it. But you shouldn't feel guilty. Asher was born different than you, and yes, he's struggled because of it, but that isn't your fault."

"Doesn't matter."

"And look how far he's come! Doctors thought he wouldn't even walk, right? And he's got a job and friends and an awesome family. He was smiling so much the other day."

"But what did I do to deserve to be born with a normal brain while his was damaged? Since I was a kid, I've been asking myself that question. The answer is *nothing*, Meg. Fucking *nothing*. And the older I get, the more I realize it's true."

"Hey." Meg's tone grew a little sharper. "You deserve everything you are and everything you have and everything you dream about."

"I don't, Meg. Why should I get to have experiences and opportunities that he never will?"

"What kind of experiences do you mean?"

Being a husband and father.

I thought it, but I couldn't say it. It wasn't even right that I was talking about this with her. She'd never be able to understand why I had to deny myself things I wanted deep down. Nobody could.

She sat all the way up. "You listen to me. You're a good man, Noah McCormick. The best I know. Your entire life, you have put other people first, from the time you were a lifeguard to joining the Army to becoming a police officer. My God, I wouldn't even be here if it wasn't for you!"

Still I said nothing.

"And what about those experiences, huh? Asher couldn't have been a lifeguard, but that didn't stop you from becoming one. Or from enlisting. Or from being a cop."

"It didn't stop me, but that doesn't mean I didn't feel bad about it. And I'm not saying it makes sense—I'm just telling you how I feel."

"Never feel like you don't deserve to be happy, Noah. Because you do. And Asher would be the first person to say so."

It almost made me smile, the soft ferocity in her voice as she defended me against my demons, even though she couldn't possibly win. "Thanks. Sorry to dump all that on you. I've never told anyone that stuff before."

She planted a kiss on my lips and snuggled next to me again. "I'm glad you told me."

"Now it's your turn."

"For what?"

"To tell me something you've never told anyone before."

"Oh. Hmmm, let me think." Then she sighed. "You'll think this is dumb."

"Tell me anyway."

"Okay, but it's going to sound silly, especially after what you told me."

"Sawyer."

"Okay." She hesitated. "I want someone to fight for me."

"What do you mean? Like, slay a dragon?"

"See, I knew you'd make fun of me." She rolled away from me and I cuddled up behind her, wrapping my body around hers like a comma.

"Hey, I'm sorry. I'm not making fun." I kissed her shoulder. "And I would totally slay a dragon for you."

"I don't want anyone to fight a *dragon*," she said. "I just want someone that doesn't give up on me so easily. I feel like . . . I've had all these relationships that just wither and die, and there's no fight to keep it alive. No one ever cares enough." She sniffed, and I felt like the biggest asshole in the world for teasing her. I was trying to think of what to say to make her feel better when she went on.

"But it's my fault too. I've never fought to keep things alive either, and I don't know why that is. Maybe I'm too scared to put myself out there. Scared to make myself that vulnerable."

"Maybe you haven't felt anything worth fighting for," I said, certain that the DC douchebags she dated weren't worthy of her anyway. Nobody was.

"Maybe. But that could be my fault too. I think I use work as an excuse not to really lose myself in a relationship. Because it's safe. I'm good at it. I know exactly what I'm doing, and the risk of failure is low. With another person, you can never really know what they're thinking or feeling."

"You can ask him."

"But I'm *scared* to ask him." She turned onto her back and looked up at me with huge eyes. "What if he doesn't feel what I feel?"

God, this woman. I'd have torn my heart from my chest for her.

"He does," I said. "He always will."

"Noah," she whispered, and for a moment I was terrified of the words that might come out of her mouth.

If we didn't say it, there was a chance we'd still be okay.

So I kissed her, moving my body over hers. And I tried

207

to silence the voice in my head the same way, using our physical connection, our insatiable hunger for one another, as a weapon against the emotions that threatened to demolish all my defenses.

We could kiss, we could touch, we could fuck. We could make each other scratch and bite, sigh and moan. We could act out our fantasies, whisper dirty words in the dark, and make each other come all night long.

But we couldn't love each other.

Not like that.

Twenty

Meg

NOAH HAD THE NEXT DAY OFF, BUT HE SAID HE HAD BORING errands to run—dry cleaners, bank, gym, grocery store—so he took me home in the morning and we made plans to hang out that evening. I'd planned to use the day to catch up on work, but spent the entire morning staring at my laptop screen and trying to make a decision about something I'd begun thinking about last night . . . moving back.

I'd lain awake for a good portion of the night wondering if it was the worst idea I'd ever had or the best. Was I really ready to drastically change my life to be with him? What would he say if I brought it up? Did he feel what I felt? What if he didn't?

When Sylvia and April invited me to join them for shopping and lunch, I jumped at the chance to distract myself . . . Then I spent the entire time obsessing over the same questions that had kept me up last night.

"Earth to Meg."

"Sorry, what?" I was sitting across the lunch table from them, and looked up to see them glance at each other, amused. I'd been asking them to repeat themselves all day.

"Your head is really in the clouds today," April said with a rueful smile. "Mine's just cloudy with a hangover."

"Ugh, mine too." Sylvia reached for her water. "Thank goodness we have tonight to recover before the rehearsal dinner tomorrow."

"So tell us about your late night with Noah." April's eyebrows rose suggestively. "You haven't said much at all. Was it fun?"

I felt a blush creep into my cheeks. "It's always fun with Noah."

But last night had gone beyond just fun. And what had me so starry-eyed and cloudy-headed today wasn't the sex, it was the way we'd opened up to each other. Every time I thought about the way he'd confessed his guilt about Asher and how he felt he didn't deserve to be happy, I wanted to cry. But it made me happy that he'd trusted me with such a deeply personal feeling.

And I totally understood why he'd been short with me in the car—like his dad, he'd just needed to get the anger out. Did I enjoy being spoken to that way? No, but it also meant something to me that he'd trusted me with those feelings too. He hadn't felt the need to pretend everything was fine. And I didn't just want the good times with Noah. I wanted everything.

I took a breath. "You guys, I need to say something out loud, and it might sound crazy."

Sylvia's eyes went wide and she set down her water. "Go ahead."

Another breath. "I'm thinking of moving back."

April's jaw fell open. "Here?"

I nodded. "Yes."

"To be with Noah?" she asked.

"Well, yes, partly. I mean, I'd be lying if I said he didn't factor in at all, but also . . ." I twisted my hands together in my lap. "I really love it here. I've been so happy all week being around family and revisiting all my old childhood memories. When I left at eighteen, I couldn't wait to get away from all the slow-paced, small-town familiarity of it all, but now I feel differently. Now I kind of *want* to slow down. Now the familiarity of being home seems comforting and peaceful."

"I understand that," Sylvia said. "I love California, but there's something about coming back here that just feels good. It's like taking off your heels and putting your slippers on."

"Exactly," I said. "And I feel like I've lived in heels for a long time."

"What about your job?" asked April. "Would you quit?"

"That would be difficult," I admitted. "I've worked really, really hard to get where I am, and I've sacrificed a lot of things to be successful—romantic relationships, sleep, friendships, my health."

"Why do you think that is?" Sylvia asked. "Does your career really fulfill you that much?"

"I don't know anymore." My throat felt tight, and I grabbed my water, taking a quick sip before going on. "Partly I've just always been that way—I get off on overachieving because subconsciously I must think it makes me a better person. It validates me. But also . . . it's a pretty good shield."

"A shield against what?" Sylvia asked.

I took another long, slow drink of water, trying to prevent myself from breaking down. "Against putting myself out there and really trying to make a relationship work. If

I prioritize work over my relationships, then it gives me something to blame when they end—and they always do, because no one wants to feel taken for granted."

"That's true," she said.

"Then I don't have to internalize it," I went on, seeing myself much more clearly. "Then it's not, 'Oh, he just didn't want me.' It's more like, 'Oh, he didn't want me because I didn't give him enough time and attention.' It's because of something I did or didn't *do*, as opposed to who I really *am*."

"That's a really honest thing to admit about yourself," said April. "It takes a lot of courage to really look in the mirror that way."

My eyes filled. "For years, whenever my relationships fell apart, I've been feeling sorry for myself, asking, 'Why don't they fight harder for me? How can they just let me go?' But of course, I've been sabotaging it all along. It comes to the same conclusion every time, because I force it to, like a self-fulfilling prophecy."

"It's not them, it's you," said April with a gentle, teasing smile.

I nodded. "It's me, because I'm scared. I never let them get close enough to me, and I don't try to get close enough to them. Why *would* they fight to save it?"

"So what's changed?" asked Sylvia. "What's making you realize all this?"

"I really think it's Noah." I shook my head in disbelief. "It's the craziest thing, you guys. I was telling him this last night—for the first time, really opening up about it. And he totally understood me and made me feel like I didn't have to be so afraid. Plus he's gorgeous and funny and thoughtful, and the sex is *so good*."

"Wow." Sylvia looked wistful. "All that is definitely worth fighting for."

"Absolutely," April agreed. "So what will you do?"

"I'm going to stay." The words surprised me—even my decisive tone surprised me. Deep down, I must have already known what I was going to do. "I need to put myself out there and take a risk. Even if things fall apart with Noah, and right now that's hard to imagine, I don't want to live the rest of my life wondering *what if* . . . I have to take this chance."

Sylvia clasped her hands beneath her chin. "This is so romantic."

I laughed, putting my hands over my stomach. "I have all the butterflies right now. Because I have no idea what he's going to say."

"What do you mean?" April looked confused. "Noah adores you. We told you yesterday, it's totally obvious. It's been obvious for *years*."

"But there are complications. You guys don't know him like I do."

"That's the point," she said. "You know him so well."

"No, I mean, he's been really honest with me about not wanting to commit to a relationship. He doesn't want to be anyone's boyfriend. And I said I wasn't looking for one."

"Well, that was *before*," suggested Sylvia.

"That was three days ago," I told her warily. "Although it has been a very intense three days."

April reached out and put a hand on my arm. "Talk to him. It's not going to do any good to sit around worrying about what he might or might not say. You're done being scared, remember?"

"Right." I nodded defiantly, recalling what I'd just said to

Noah last night about his mom. "If I want to be happy, I can't choose fear over love."

"Do you love him?" Sylvia asked.

I didn't have to think twice. "I've always loved him," I said. "I don't know why it's taken me this long to say it."

Later, I took a jog around the farm, nothing too strenuous—my body was exhausted from the lack of sleep—to give myself a chance to think everything over. I knew how I felt about Noah, but before making any life-changing decisions, I wanted to take some time alone to really consider the consequences of what I was about to do, the risks involved, the possibilities.

If I quit my job and moved back, what would I do? Where would I live? How would this thing with Noah play out?

Before I made any permanent decisions, did I need to hear him say he was open to a future together? For me, that meant marriage and kids. I wanted a family. Would I upend my life with that issue up in the air?

I knew I couldn't force him to make promises at this point. After less than one week together, it would be ludicrous of me to expect his mind to change so quickly. And it wasn't like he'd been wishy-washy on the matter. It was a firm *no way, no how*, and he had reasons to back it up. Even if I disagreed with his reasons and thought he was just being stubborn and scared, I wasn't going to get anywhere by arguing with him.

Would more time together make him change his mind? What if it didn't? What if I moved back and fell deeper in love with him only to be brokenhearted in the end?

I reached the edge of the creek that ran through the woods at the back of my family's property and sank onto my butt for a rest. My heart rate was a little too high to turn around and run right back, and I wasn't that anxious to be around people anyway.

The creek was pretty low but still moving, and I watched the water rush over the stones and thought again about Noah's refusal to believe he was capable of being a good husband and father.

It was crazy to me. What was a good husband and father if not someone devoted to loving and protecting his family? How could Noah think he wasn't that man? Sure, his ex had done a number on him, and maybe he struggled to trust after that, but this was me. He *knew* he could trust me to accept him, family and all. I'd never be so demanding he had to feel guilty about disappointing me here and there when his family needed him.

As for his being a cop, I loved that about him. I couldn't think of a more perfect job for Noah, and I truly believed he'd make an awesome sheriff, as good as his father had been. If I moved here, I could help him with his campaign. He'd never need to worry that I wouldn't understand when his job had to come first. Maybe I couldn't promise I'd never get frustrated by it, but I could promise that I knew what it meant to him to serve and protect no matter the cost. His parents had made it work—we could too. I fell back onto the mossy ground and looked at the sky above the tops of the birch and maple and evergreen trees, imagining a life together for us.

Of course, I knew Asher would be part of that life. Someday he'd live with Noah full time, and I had to be willing to accept that. When Mrs. McCormick traveled or got older or wasn't around anymore, Asher's care would fall to Noah. He wanted it that way, and I admired him for it.

But that didn't mean he couldn't have a family of his own—if he wanted one. He said he didn't, but was it true? Or was that the guilt talking? Maybe deep down, he did want children, but fatherhood would be yet another thing that came easily to him that his brother couldn't experience. Maybe he was denying himself the opportunity because he didn't think he deserved it.

Sighing, I sat up again. All this was useless speculation—I needed to talk to Noah. I needed to be brave, even braver than I had been the night I burst in on him in the shower. I needed to tell him how I felt, what I wanted, and what I was willing to do make it happen.

I was in love with him, and I wanted him to know it.

My heart started to pound again. Our plans for tonight were nothing major, just pizza and TV. He'd promised to watch Law & Order with me like old times. But he hated that show, so I bet he'd be glad to turn off the television and just talk.

At least, that's what I hoped.

Rising to my feet, I inhaled a few lungfuls of the autumn air. I loved that woodsy fall smell—part decaying leaves, part pine sap, part smoke—and it was so particular to home. It always meant the end of a season, and as a kid, I'd been sad because it meant summer was over.

But today, it smelled like a new beginning.

Twenty-One

Noah

Thursday afternoon, I had just come out of the gym when my mother called me.

"Hello?"

"Nina had the baby," she said excitedly.

"About time. What'd she have?"

"A girl. They named her Rosie, after my mother. Isn't that cute?" She sniffed as if she were tearing up.

"Very cute. Everyone's doing okay?"

"Yes, but I'd like to head over to the hospital and see them right away. Then I told Chris I'd take over at home so his mom can go see the baby. Mrs. Reynolds is picking Asher up from work and bringing him home, but she has to leave by six. Can you head over to the house as soon as possible?"

"Sure." I had plans with Meg, but I knew she'd understand. And we could see each other later. She could stay over again.

"And do you think you could stay the night there? You're off tomorrow, right? I hate to put you out, but Nina asked if I could stay over to get the older kids off to school in the morning. That way Chris can stay at the hospital. And Asher really shouldn't be left alone so long. I'm worried about another seizure."

I pressed my lips together. My immediate reaction was disappointment tinged with a little resentment—no sex tonight. But as soon as I had the thought, I felt like the biggest asshole on the planet. My brother needed me, and all I could think about was my dick? "No problem. Okay to bring Renzo?"

"Of course."

"Tell Nina I said congratulations."

"I will. Thanks, dear. I'll call you later, when I know what time I'll be home."

"Sounds good." After hanging up, I got in my car and texted Chris.

Me: Congrats, jackass. Eighteen more years of sleepless nights.

Chris: What's sleep?

Me: Maybe try condoms next time. Or keep your fucking paws off my sister, how about that?

Chris: Right now, that seems like an easy task. She is yelling at me to change a messy diaper. Gotta go.

I shook my head and set the phone aside. As Uncle Noah, I'd changed a few messy diapers in my life and it was not an experience I enjoyed much. Give me a dog all day long. Much less messy than a human who lies around in its own pile of turd with a puffy shower curtain strapped to its ass.

But when I got home, I saw that Chris had texted me a photo of him holding his new daughter in his arms, all wrapped up in a little white blanket and wearing a pink stocking cap on her head. Chris looked haggard and sleep-deprived but undeniably happy, and I had to admit the baby was cute. Envy wormed its way beneath my skin. What would it be like to see my child being born? To watch her open her eyes for the first time? To hear her first cries and change her first diaper and be the first male arms to hold her?

Frowning, I told myself to forget about those things and just be happy for my sister and my friend.

After letting Renzo out, I picked up my phone to call Meg.

I hadn't reached out to her yet today, but it wasn't because she wasn't on my mind. Of course she was. Last night had been . . . intense. Sexy and fun in all the usual ways, but different too. It sounds ridiculous, because there aren't *degrees* of nakedness—you're either naked or you're not—but somehow it was the most naked I'd ever felt with anyone.

This morning, I'd felt almost embarrassed by the things I'd told her. I'd never let anyone know how guilty I'd always felt about Asher. How guilty I'd always feel. Men weren't supposed to talk about shit like their feelings, especially those that made them feel bad. Men were supposed to be stoic and resolute. Masculinity, in my mind anyway, meant strength and courage and commanding respect. Your psychological burdens were your own to bear.

But it had felt so good to share mine with her. And she'd accepted that part of me, just like she'd accepted the part of me that needed to get angry. I'd once been a dick to Holly after a bad day like that, and she'd burst into tears and told me I was being emotionally abusive. I wound up comforting her. Meg let me get it out, and then she gave me a blowjob.

(No contest there. Meg wins.)

God, she was perfect. Gorgeous and sexy and funny and smart and kind. Accepting and compassionate. Feisty and sweet. I wanted to make her happy, wanted to be that guy who would fight for her, the one who kept her safe and made her laugh and gave her orgasms every night. The thought of some other asshole touching her made my fists clench and my jaw get tight.

But I couldn't be the one. I just couldn't.

And she didn't want me to be. I was fun on the side, not the real thing. She was all set to go back to DC in a few days, back to her important job and fast-paced life and a city full of guys in fancy suits with law degrees and leather briefcases. It was what she wanted.

As for me, I'd have to be content with that one incredible week we shared before she met the love of her life.

Although he'd never love her better than me. Never.

I swallowed hard as the urge to put my first through a brick wall slammed hard into my gut. I couldn't think like that. I couldn't wonder about the future, the real one *or* the one I refused to let myself imagine. Because it wouldn't do any good.

I had a couple more days with her, and that would be that.

I'd get over her eventually.

I had no choice.

"Hi, handsome."

I smiled and leaned back against the counter. "Is that how you answer all your calls?"

"No. Just yours."

"How was your day?"

"Good. I went shopping and had lunch with April and Sylvia, then I took run. Now I'm about to get in the shower."

I groaned. "Don't say that stuff to me. I get ideas."

She laughed. "Sorry. Are we still on for tonight?"

"Actually, that's what I called about. I'm sorry, but I have to cancel."

"Oh no! I hope everything is okay."

"Everything is fine. My sister had her baby, so my mom—" I had to hold the phone away from my ear because she squealed so loud. "Jesus."

"Sorry," she said breathlessly. "It's just so exciting. A new baby! What did she have?"

"A girl. They named her Rosie." I was proud I remembered that detail.

"So cute! How much did she weigh?"

"Uh . . . I didn't ask."

"Does she have hair?"

I tried to recall if I could tell from the photo, but she'd been wearing a hat. "Didn't ask that either."

Meg sighed. "Men."

"I'll try to get more details from my mom when I see her. I'm staying with Asher tonight so she can help out at Chris and Nina's."

"Of course," she said.

"I'd rather be with you."

"It's okay, Noah. I completely understand, and I'm so happy for Nina and Chris. For all of you."

"I know, but I hate that I won't see you tonight. You're only here a couple more days."

"Don't worry about it." She sounded totally nonchalant, like it didn't matter to her at all. "We can hang out tomorrow. There's something I want to talk to you about."

"Okay," I said. "I'll give you a call in the morning."

"Sounds good. If you talk to your sister, tell her I said congratulations."

"I will. Bye."

"Bye."

We hung up, and for a moment I continued to stare at the phone screen, wondering why it bothered me that she didn't seem to care whether or not she saw me tonight. Or maybe it was that *I* cared so much. What was it going to be like when she left?

I decided it was a good thing that my mother had called. The last thing I needed was to get used to her. If you got used to a person being around all the time, you'd miss them when they left.

And missing someone was the fucking worst.

But later, alone in the bedroom I'd grown up in, I couldn't help picking up my phone. It was almost midnight.

Me: You awake?

Meg: Yes. I'm in bed but not asleep.

Me: Why not?

Meg: I don't know. Just thinking about things.

Me: What kind of things?

Meg: Being home. Family. The wedding. The future.

Me: So not my dick?

Meg: OMG

Me: Sorry couldn't resist

Meg: Well if you MUST know . . .

Me: I must.

Meg: Yes. Your dick has crossed my mind tonight. Several times.

Me: Can you talk?

Meg: Sure. I'll call you.

A few seconds later, my phone vibrated. I answered, keeping my voice low. "Nine-one-one. What's your emergency?"

She giggled softly. "My body's on fire, officer. Can you come over and put it out?"

Just hearing her bedroom voice in the dark was enough to turn me on, let alone the words she said, and I felt myself getting hard. "I'll be right there to make you wet."

"Good. Because it's getting *very* hot in here. I can hardly stand it."

I switched the phone to my left hand as my right slid down my abdomen and took my thickening erection in my hand. "I'm halfway there."

"Tell me what you're going to do when you get here," she pleaded.

"I'm going to lick every fucking inch of your skin."

"*Yes*. I love your mouth on me," she whispered. "I want to feel it."

"Then do exactly as I say." My cock was fully erect as I imagined her naked between the sheets, waiting to do my bidding. "I want you to spread your legs for me. I want your thighs wide open."

Her breathing got louder.

"Now I want you to put two fingers in your mouth and suck them. Get them all wet." I heard a little sucking noise that made my cock even harder. "Now put those fingers on your clit. Rub slowly and softly, the way I lick you at first. The way I stroke it with my tongue."

She moaned softly. "You're so good at this, officer. But I'm afraid it's just making the flames get higher."

"That's because the way you taste makes my cock so hard." I gripped myself tighter, flexing my hips as I thrust through my fist, imagining her taste on my tongue, her thighs cradling my head.

"I wish I was there to suck it," she whispered. "Just like I did last night."

Oh, Jesus. I stifled the groan that threatened as I pictured her red lips sliding down my cock, her big eyes locked on mine. "Are you wet?"

"For you, always."

"*Fuck*," I said, my hand moving faster. "Use your fingers in your pussy. Tell me what it feels like."

"Mmm. Hot. Soft. Drenched. You'd slide in so easily, and I'd take you so deep."

"Put your fingers in your mouth," I demanded. "Suck them." The soft little noises she made drove me wild, and I knew I couldn't hold back much longer. "Good girl. Now put them back between your legs so I can make you come."

"Do it, officer," she breathed. "Fuck me. Yes, just like that. God, I love your cock. Harder, harder, harder . . . Let me feel you come . . ."

Knowing that she was touching herself and thinking about my dick inside her rendered my brain *entirely* useless—I couldn't even think words, let alone speak them. Instead of suave phone-sex police officer, I was reduced to a series of caveman grunts while I frantically jerked myself off listening to her sweet voice telling me she loved my cock and begging me to fuck her harder. It was so hot I came all over myself in under a minute.

I was still lying there, breathing hard with my dick in one hand my phone in the other, when I heard her shy little laugh.

"Oh my God," she whispered. "Did we really just do that?"

"Uh, there's a mess on my stomach that says we did."

"I wish I could have watched you do it."

I stifled a groan. "Sawyer, stop giving me ideas."

Another laugh. "Never."

"Give me a minute, okay?"

"Sure."

I set the phone aside, hurried into the bathroom to clean up, and got back into bed. "You still there?"

"Yes."

"Did you have a good night?"

"It was fine. I just hung out here with family. Played board games, ate popcorn, watched a movie."

"Sounds like fun."

"How was your night with Asher?"

"Good. I got takeout. We ate dinner and took Renzo for a walk, then came back and watched some TV—but *not* Law & Order."

She laughed. "You successfully avoided the torture."

"I did. We had a nice night." I pictured her lying in bed, and felt an ache in my chest. "But I missed you."

"I missed you too. Can I see you tomorrow?"

"Sure. I'm off tomorrow, but I'm not sure yet what the day looks like with Asher and everything."

"No problem. Just let me know. There's . . . something I wanted to ask you."

"You mentioned that earlier." I tried unsuccessfully to fight off a yawn. "What is it you want to talk about?"

"I'll tell you tomorrow," she said quickly. "I know you're exhausted. I am too. Thanks for putting out my fire tonight."

"That's my job, Sawyer."

"You do it well."

I smiled. "Night."

"Night."

I plugged my phone into the charger and lay back in my old bed, thinking that if I could go back in time and tell sixteen-year-old Noah what would happen between him and Meg one day, he probably wouldn't believe it.

I could hardly believe it now. I'd gone from talking to her once every few weeks or even months to feeling as if I was addicted to her. It was a damn good thing she wasn't going to be around much longer.

Addiction was a dangerous disease.

Twenty-Two

Meg

FRIDAY MORNING, I SLEPT IN A LITTLE. BY THE TIME I GOT downstairs, the table was empty and the breakfast dishes were piled in the sink. To help my mom out, I loaded the dishwasher, swept the crumbs from the floor, and wiped off the counters.

Afterward, I sat at the table with my laptop and a cup of coffee. I was sifting through my inbox when Sylvia came in the back door with her kids, all of them carrying shopping bags.

"Hi," I said. "Did you guys hit the mall this morning?"

"We did. The kids needed some things for the rehearsal dinner. I don't know what I was thinking, letting them pack for themselves. Take those bags up to your rooms, you guys," Sylvia directed them. "Keaton, take the shirt out and hang it up. And don't leave the tie all balled up in there either."

The kids obeyed, heading for the stairs while Sylvia put another coffee pod in the Keurig. Her face looked drawn and a little blotchy.

"You okay?" I asked.

"He didn't come." Sylvia stared at the machine as she spoke. "Brett. He didn't get on the plane."

It clicked—her husband had been scheduled to take the red-eye from California last night. "He missed his flight?"

"He claims he was tied up at work." She shook her head. "I think he's lying. He doesn't want to come."

I swallowed, unsure of what to say. "I'm sorry."

"He says he'll get on a flight sometime today or tomorrow morning and be here in time for the wedding." She took her mug from the machine and turned around, leaning back against the counter. "I'll believe it when I see it."

"I'm sure he'll be here," I told her, although I wasn't sure at all. I'd never known Brett all that well.

"We'll see." She sipped her coffee. "What are you up to today? Working?"

"Yeah." I frowned at my laptop and closed it. "But I'm distracted."

"Can't imagine why." Her eyes hinted at a smile. "Have you talked to Noah yet?"

"No." I checked the clock on the kitchen wall. It was just after noon. "He's been with Asher, and I don't want to bother him. But I suppose I should reach out. If I'm going to talk to him today before all the rehearsal stuff starts, it has to be this afternoon. What time do we have to be ready?"

"Mom said five o'clock in the lobby. She's all stressed because the inn is so busy today. All the out of town wedding guests are checking in."

I winced. "I should offer to help, shouldn't I?"

"No. I'll help her. It will keep my mind off my imploding marriage. You go talk to Noah."

"Okay. I'm sorry, Sylvia." I bit my lip. "I want there to be something I can do or say to make you feel better."

"Don't worry about it." She finished her coffee and put the cup in the dishwasher. "Who knows? Maybe he'll show up."

"I hope so." I stood up and stuck my laptop back in its travel case. "I'll see you later."

Upstairs in my room, I texted him.

Me: Hey you. How's your day going?

He didn't reply right away, so I brushed my teeth, threw on some leggings and a tank, and pulled on my running shoes. I was tying them when he finally texted back.

Noah: Hi, beautiful. All good. Took Asher to work and now hanging out with my little nephew while my mom runs errands for Nina and Chris.

I bit my lip. He had his nephew this afternoon, which was sweet but not very conducive to a heart-to-heart talk.

Me: Aww. Uncle Noah. What are you guys up to?

Noah: We're at the park. Want to meet us?

Me: I'd love to. I just got dressed for a run, so that's perfect. I'll meet you there in 20.

After zipping over to the inn, where I found my dad hiding from my mother in his office, I made sure it was okay to borrow his car, grabbed his key, and headed for the park. When I arrived, I saw Noah, his nephew, and Renzo right away. As I walked toward them, I put my hand over my mouth and giggled.

Noah was sitting at the top of the slide, looking huge and uncomfortable, with a grinning tow-headed toddler on his lap. "Ready?" he said. "One, two, three." On three, he pushed off and slid down to the bottom, where Renzo waited with his tail wagging. Fucking adorable.

"Hi, guys," I called.

Noah got to his feet, setting his nephew on his forearm. The little boy promptly put his head on Noah's shoulder as I approached. My heart was a puddle.

"Hey," he said, giving me a quick kiss on the lips.

My stomach fluttered. Even in a cap, faded gray henley and jeans, he was sexy. "You're a little big for that slide, officer," I teased.

"Tell me about it. But he loves it. Don't you, buddy?" Noah poked his nephew in the belly a few times, making him laugh.

I smiled. "What's his name?"

"Ethan."

"Hi, Ethan."

Noah bounced him up and down on his arm. "Say hi."

Ethan smiled shyly and stuck his fingers in his mouth.

"No." Noah swatted them out. "Your hands are dirty. Come on, you want to go on the swing?"

Ethan looked toward the swings and pointed.

"Yep, right over there. One more time, and then it's nap time for you." He started walking toward the swings, Renzo at his heels. "You said you wanted to talk to me about something. What's up?"

I followed him, nerve endings twitching beneath my skin. I hadn't exactly planned out what I would say. How should I even start? "Yes. Um, I wanted to get your thoughts on something."

He set Ethan in the toddler swing and moved behind him, setting the swing in motion. "Can you be more specific, Sawyer?"

I laughed nervously, wringing my hands together at my waist. "Yeah, sorry. So I was thinking about . . . I've been thinking that I'm really glad I came home for the entire week."

"Me too," he said, pushing his nephew higher and giving me a sexy sideways grin. The swing chains moaned.

More nervous laughter from me. "Right. There's that, and then I've also just really enjoyed being around my family and spending time in my hometown. I feel happy here. Happier than I've been in a long time."

"That's . . . good."

But the way he said it, with the tiniest hesitation, put me slightly on edge. Had I imagined it?

"And I haven't really talked about this much, but I have to move out of my apartment in DC. I shared it with Brooks, and the rent is too pricey for me to pay on my own. And I don't really want a roommate."

More hesitation. "DC is a big city. You'll find something."

"Well, I was kind of thinking, since I have to move out of there and I've had such a great time at home, maybe I'd move back here permanently."

Noah didn't say anything. He just kept pushing his nephew. He wasn't smiling, either. What did that mean?

"What about your job?" he finally asked.

My job? My *job*?

"Um, I guess I'd find a new one. Here."

"Not many job openings for political strategists around here."

I stared at him, the butterflies in my stomach turning to stone. "I could also see about keeping my job but working remotely."

Silence. The groan of the swing chains seemed even louder.

"I was thinking I could help you with your campaign for sheriff too," I said.

"I haven't decided to run."

"If you do." I swallowed, and the taste in my mouth was bitter. "Noah, what's the problem? Do you not want me to move here?"

"You can move anywhere you want." His jaw had taken on that hard, stubborn angle.

"Can you look at me, please?" At this point, I was struggling not to cry.

He turned his head toward me, but his face was shadowed by the ball cap. It was impossible to read his expression.

"I thought you might be happy about this," I said, my voice wavering. "We've had so much fun together this week, and if I move here, we could . . . Don't you . . ." I had to stop and swallow against the lump lodged in my throat. "Don't you want this to continue?"

Looking straight ahead again, he kept pushing the swing, even though Ethan had started to fuss. "For how long?"

"What?"

"For how long?" he asked, louder. "I mean, if you move here, how long do you think this can last?"

"I don't know," I said.

"Because we agreed right from the start that this was a temporary thing," he snapped, grabbing the back of the swing to stop it. "It was just for this week. Just for fun."

"I know, but then—"

"I never lied to you, Meg. I never made you any promises." Noah yanked Ethan from the swing and started striding toward the parking lot, Renzo right beside him.

I followed, nearly at a jog, to keep up. "I never said you

did! And I'm not asking for any promises. I just think what we have is too good to cut so short. Why can't we give us a chance?"

"Because," he said angrily. "We don't want the same things."

"But that could change!"

He huffed. "*Women.*"

"What do you mean by that?" I yelled, getting mad now too. He was being stubborn and ridiculous and mean. He wouldn't even stop and listen, he just kept racing away from me!

"I mean, even when a guy is totally up front about what he can and can*not* offer, a woman just hears what she wants to hear." Noah yanked open his rear driver's side door, and once Renzo had jumped in, strapped Ethan into the car seat. "I told you the truth about what I'm capable of and you didn't believe it. That's not my fault."

I put both hands to my head. "It wasn't the truth! It was a bunch of lies you tell yourself because you don't think you deserve to be happy."

He stood up and slammed the door. "Don't fucking tell me what I think. And don't you fucking dare use what I said against me."

But I couldn't stop. I pointed a finger at him. "I know you, Noah McCormick! I know how you think!"

"You don't know anything," he seethed quietly.

"Yes, I do!"

"Because we fucked? After five days, that makes you the expert on me?"

"No, asshole! Because I've known you more than half our lives! I know how much you love your brother—how much your entire family means to you. I know how much you love your job. I know how much you want to protect good people and punish the bad, and how angry you get when you can't. I know you feel guilty about Asher, and it tears you into pieces inside." I lowered my voice, although there was no one around. "And I know what your body wants. I know how it feels on mine. I know how good we are together. And I know from the way you're looking at me right now that you're thinking about it too." I moved closer to him and tried to put my hands on his chest.

He grabbed my wrists. His lips were so close. "Don't."

"Why are you pushing me away?" I asked, tears spilling from my eyes.

Instead of answering, he crushed his mouth to mine, his fingers tight my wrists. But all too quickly, he broke the kiss and gently shoved me back. "Go back to DC, Meg. Leave me alone."

Without another word, he jumped into his SUV, started the engine and drove off, leaving me standing there alone in tears.

Placing both hands over my face, I sank down onto the concrete parking stop and sobbed.

Twenty-Three

Noah

"FUCK. FUCK! *FUCK!*" I BANGED THE STEERING WHEEL with the heel of my hand every time I cursed. In the backseat, Ethan continued to cry. He'd probably repeat the F word when we got home, and babysitting would be yet another thing I'd fucked up today.

And it wasn't even half over.

"God*dammit!*" I yelled. "Why am I such an asshole?"

I knew I'd treated Meg abominably, I'd known it even as I was doing it, but I couldn't fucking help it. She'd started talking about *moving* here, about *staying* here, about *us*, and I'd fucking panicked.

She couldn't live here, for God's sake! I wouldn't be safe if she lived here. I wouldn't be able to handle seeing her all the time, and I wouldn't be able to stay away.

But it couldn't go anywhere, and I couldn't just pretend like we could have a future, not the kind of future she wanted and deserved. What would happen when she realized that? What would happen when she realized that she'd quit her awesome job, moved back to this podunk town she'd been so excited to leave, and given up everything she'd worked so hard to get . . . for *me*? Once she realized that I couldn't be what she wanted me to be, she'd hate me.

Plus, the more time I spent with her, the deeper my feelings got. She had me questioning decisions that I'd already made a lifetime ago.

No. She had to leave. That was the only way.

And now that I'd been such a dick to her, maybe she wouldn't even hesitate. Maybe she'd come to the conclusion that she'd been wrong about me and could do a hell of a lot better. Why would she want a guy like me anyway, who lashed out at her when he got mad or scared or frustrated, who said things he didn't mean, who didn't know how to love her the way he should? I hadn't even been able to say the word.

But God knows I felt it. I fucking felt it hard.

I always would.

My mother invited me to stay for dinner. Asher said he wasn't hungry yet and went to his room to lie down, so it was just her and me at the table. After about ten minutes of me scowling silently into my chili, she knew something was wrong.

Damn women and their Spidey sense. I was so sick of being probed by their know-it-all minds.

"What's with you?" she asked.

"Nothing."

"Doesn't look like nothing. I know that face. Your dad used to make it after a bad day."

"I had a bad day." I picked up the beer bottle I'd opened and took a drink.

She eyeballed me shrewdly. "What's Meg doing tonight?"

"I don't know."

"Rehearsal dinner?"

"Maybe."

"You seeing her later?"

"Doubt it."

She was quiet for a moment, but I felt her judgmental eyes on me. She knew I'd fucked it up somehow.

"What time's the wedding tomorrow?"

"Dunno."

"You're still going, aren't you?"

"Nope."

She set her spoon down with a clunk. "And why not, Noah McCormick?"

"Because she doesn't want me there."

"Oh? How come?"

I took another few swallows of beer before deciding I might as well tell her the truth—or at least part of it. "Because we had a disagreement."

"A disagreement! About what?"

"About whether or not she should move back home."

"Uh huh." Her fury radiated off her in waves. "And which side were you on?"

"There weren't sides, Ma. She asked me if I thought it was a good idea, and I said no."

"And why's that?"

"Because I don't want her quitting her job and moving back here for me."

"And you know for sure it would be for you, is that it?"

I shrugged. "That's pretty much what she said. And

I don't want to be anyone's boyfriend. I told her that from the start."

"Uh huh." She was keeping her temper in check, probably because she was worried Asher might hear. He hated shouting. But after another minute of silently seething, she grabbed her half-full bowl and stood up. On her way to the kitchen, she used her free hand to whack me upside the back of my head so hard my cap flew off and landed on the table.

"Hey!" I yelled.

"That's for being an idiot," she said calmly, exiting the dining room.

I grabbed my hat and angrily shoved it back onto my head. From the front room, Renzo came trotting over to my side. Grateful, I scratched behind his ears. At least someone still loved me.

"Come on, boy. Let's go home."

I left my mother's house without speaking to her and went home, but being there only reminded me of Meg. It was unnerving that I'd lived there for years and been just fine, but now everything I saw, every piece of furniture, was somehow connected to her. The kitchen counter. The couch. The bathroom. My bed.

I cracked open another beer and sat in front of the TV, but before I'd even finished half the bottle, I found myself too restless to sit still. My head was full of questions. What was she doing? Did she hate me? Had she told her family I was an asshole? Was she ever going to speak to me again?

Frowning at the television, I scolded myself for letting it come to this.

Hadn't I known better? Hadn't I warned her? Hadn't I been saying all along—since I was sixfuckingteen—that there were good reasons not to mess with her? I'd been right! Look what had happened! How the hell I ever thought we'd be able to navigate this road once we threw sex into the relationship was beyond me.

My mother was right—I *was* an idiot.

Twenty-Four

Meg

I'M NOT SURE HOW LONG I SAT ON THAT STUPID PARKING STOP bawling my eyes out. Ten minutes? Twenty? An hour?

I just kept hoping he would change his mind and come back. I imagined him pulling up, stopping the engine, and jumping out of the car to take me in his arms and tell me how wrong he'd been. Tell me I wasn't alone. Tell me he loved me.

But it was a fantasy.

Things like that don't happen in real life. Not to girls like me, anyway. Even Sylvia, beautiful, perfect Sylvia, had cried over her broken heart this morning. If she couldn't figure this out, what chance did I have?

Eventually, I dragged myself back to my car and went home, lacking the energy to take the run I'd planned. Thankfully, no one was in the kitchen when I came in, and I was able to make it upstairs without talking to anyone.

In my bedroom, I curled up on my bed and cried some more, replaying the entire week in my mind, wondering how I could have been so wrong about him. After a few minutes, I heard a knock on my door.

"Who is it?" I called, wiping my cheeks.

"It's Sylvia. Can I come in?"

"Yeah." No point in putting this off.

My door opened, and my sister appeared. She wore the khaki pants and green Cloverleigh Farms shirt of an inn employee. Her face had been made up. "Hey. You okay?"

"No." I stayed where I was, curled into a ball. "Did you bring any Twinkies?"

"No, sorry." She shut the door and sat at the foot of my bed. "I take it you talked to Noah?" she asked gently.

"Yes. It didn't go well." Fresh tears filled my eyes, and my nose was running terribly. "Can you get me a tissue please?"

Sylvia looked around, and spying the box on my dresser, went over and pulled out several sheets.

"Just bring the whole box," I told her.

She brought the box over to the bed and set it down on the mattress. "That bad, huh?"

"Worse." Sitting up, I grabbed a tissue and blew my nose. "I'm so stupid."

"No, you're not." She sat down and put a hand on my leg. "You're brave. And beautiful. And brilliant."

"I don't feel any of those things." I started weeping again, feeling helpless against the tide.

"Tell me what happened."

"I went to the park to see him. He was babysitting his nephew Ethan this afternoon, and you should see him with that little boy. He's so good with him. There's no way he doesn't want kids deep down."

"You brought up having kids?" Sylvia asked, her eyes going wide. "I thought you were only going to talk about moving here."

"I was. I did." But now I couldn't recall exactly what I said. "It wasn't like I was pressuring him to get married or anything. All I did was ask him what he thought about me living here."

"And?"

"And he pretty much said he didn't care where I lived." Between fresh bursts of tears, I told Sylvia how we'd argued, how he'd gotten angry with me, how he'd refused to give us a chance.

She rubbed my leg. "I'm really sorry, Meg. I know how you feel about him."

"I'm in love with him, Syl." I flopped back onto my pillow. "And it's hopeless. He doesn't love me back."

"He didn't say that. I think he does love you, Meg. He just doesn't want to lie to you or lead you on."

"So then what good is love anyway?" Angry, I curled up on my side again, wishing I could shut myself away from the world. "My entire life, I've been waiting to fall in love like this, and now that I have, I'm even more alone than I was before."

"But isn't it better to know now?" she asked. "Before you turn your life upside down for him?"

I sniffed, unwilling to see it that way.

"Listen, you know how I told you that Brett is unfaithful?"

"Yeah. Bastard."

"At this point, I wish more than anything he'd just admit it. I can't stand all the lies."

"Would you leave him?"

"I don't know." She wiped away her own tears. "All I'm saying is that even if it's not what you want to hear, you have to be grateful that at least Noah is telling you the truth."

I grabbed another tissue from the box and blew my nose again. Was she right? Should I take my lumps and go home thankful that Noah wasn't telling me lies just to keep screwing me? After all, Noah had always been my protector. Maybe that's what this was—he was trying to keep my heart safe. And maybe I was wrong about him wanting a family deep down . . .

But it hurt. It hurt worse than any breakup I'd ever had. I began to cry again.

"God, I'm sorry, Meg." Sylvia lay down behind me and wrapped an arm around my waist. "I came in here to make sure you were okay and now I made things worse. Some big sister I am."

"It's okay," I sobbed. "I'm sorry for you too. I'm sorry for both of us."

She held me and let me cry it out for a little while and then gave me a squeeze. "Listen. I'm probably dateless this entire weekend too. There's no way Brett is going to show. Want to hang out with me?"

"Sure." I blew my nose into a soggy tissue.

"We'll carry flasks in our purses and ditch our heels for flip flops and when all the romance is too much for us to bear, we'll go up on the roof, smoke cigarettes, and curse."

I had to laugh. "You don't smoke cigarettes."

"No," she admitted, "but I feel like I should take up a bad habit or two. I'm tired of doing everything by the book." She gave me another hug. "Plus I wanted to make you laugh."

"Thanks, Syl. I'm so glad you're here."

"Me too."

Much to Sylvia's surprise, Brett *did* show up that night. He'd gotten on a plane without telling her and showed up at the rehearsal dinner at Abelard Vineyards wearing a wrinkled suit and a five o'clock shadow. He charmed everyone with sincere apologies and remorseful smiles, and took the empty seat next to Sylvia, giving her a kiss on the cheek before putting his arm around the back of her chair. I was directly across from him, and even from there I could tell he smelled like scotch and someone else's perfume.

My sister remained stone-faced, and I suddenly understood her expression in all the family vacation photos.

Between cocktails and dinner, I stole a moment alone out on Abelard's brick patio, which overlooked the neat rows of grapevines planted on the gently rolling hills. I breathed in that autumn smell I loved and vowed not to let the lump in my throat grow any bigger. After a minute, April came out and joined me.

"You okay?" she asked.

"Not really, but I'm trying."

"Sylvia told me what happened."

"That's fine. Saves me from having to tell it again." I wasn't sure I could get through it anyway.

"I'm really sorry, Meg. And totally surprised. I thought for sure he'd—"

"You know, the more I think about it, the less surprised I am. No matter how good it was between us, he never once said anything about the rest of our lives. He never even said anything about next weekend, for that matter. It was always a temporary thing for him."

"Still . . ." She reached over and took my hand. "It hurts. And I'm sorry."

I tipped my head onto her shoulder and pressed my lips

shut to keep the sob from escaping. This wasn't my night, and the last thing I wanted was to draw attention to myself.

When I was sure I could talk without breaking down, I let go of April's hand and cleared my throat. "We better go back in. I think Mack is going to make a toast, and I don't want to miss it."

April rubbed my back as we walked in. "I'm right behind you."

Twenty-Five

Noah

I BARELY SLEPT ON FRIDAY NIGHT. MY SHEETS STILL SMELLED like Meg, and even though I could have easily changed them, I refused. It was torture, but I deserved it.

Saturday morning, I woke up cranky and stiff. I thought maybe a run and some playtime in the park with Renzo would cheer me up and loosen my muscles, but it didn't.

I ate lunch even though I wasn't hungry, and was throwing some laundry in when I got a text from my mother.

Ma: Nina and the baby are home. Go see them.

Still mad at her for smacking me at the dinner table like I was eight years old, I didn't text her back.

But I did shower up and head over to Nina and Chris's. On the way I stopped at a drugstore and bought a card, some candy, a bunch of pink and red flowers, and a box of newborn diapers.

"They're not for me," I snapped at the checkout girl, who looked at me like I was nuts.

"Okay," she said.

"I meant, I don't have a baby. I don't want one."

"Okay."

"Not everyone wants kids. Some people just don't, and that doesn't mean their lives aren't complete. My life is plenty complete."

"Right," she said, glancing around.

I grabbed the bags and got out of there before the poor thing called security on me.

Once I was back in the car, I found a pen and signed the card. At Chris and Nina's, I knocked gently on the door in case the baby or my sister was asleep. Violet opened it. "Hi Uncle Noah." She gave me her toothless grin. "Did you come to see the baby?"

"I came to see you, but if the baby is here, I guess I could take a peek."

"She's here. They got home from the hospital this morning," she lisped, eyeing the bags as Renzo and I entered the house. "Did you bring her a present?"

"I brought everybody a present."

That earned me another grin. "Mommy! Daddy! Uncle Noah's here!" she shouted, shutting the door behind me.

I followed her through the living room and kitchen to the big, open addition they'd put on the back of their house, where the family spent most of their time. My bleary-eyed sister was on the couch holding the baby, and she frowned at Violet. "Hey. Daddy is trying to get Ethan down for his nap. Can you keep it down please?"

Violet shrugged. "I can try."

"Here." I handed her a bag of Swedish fish and a box of Milk Duds. "Share these with Harrison."

"Because sugar will keep them quiet." Nina rolled her eyes. "Where is Harrison anyway? I can't keep track of all these kids."

"Whose fault is that?" I teased, setting the card and

flowers on the coffee table and the box of diapers on the floor.

"He's in the basement," said Violet, taking off toward the stairs with her loot.

"They're probably going to eat it all in one sitting." Nina sighed. "Does that count as lunch?"

"Definitely." I sat next to her and peeked at little Rosie, who was wrapped up burrito-style in a flannel blanket, fast asleep. One hand was by her face, and I couldn't get over how tiny her fingers were. She had my sister's mouth and Chris's blond hair. "She looks like you guys, only she's cute," I said.

"Thanks."

"Can I hold her?"

"If you want to."

I reached for Rosie, who frowned and made a couple noises like she didn't appreciate being moved mid-nap, but settled comfortably in my arms. Watching her sleep, I felt my chest grow a little tight. I'd never have this for myself.

"I forget how little and light they are when they're born," I said.

"They don't feel that way when they're in your belly, believe me."

"Yeah, your belly was much bigger than this one baby. Are you sure there's not another one in there?" I joked.

She slapped my arm.

Chris walked into the room, looking only slightly less exhausted than my sister. "Okay, I think he's asleep."

"I think I am too," Nina said drowsily. "I can't even tell if my eyes are open or closed."

I glanced at her. "Closed."

Chris flopped into a recliner and shut his eyes too. "Where are the other two?"

"In the basement," I said.

"Did I feed them yet?"

"No. But Noah brought candy," said Nina. "They're fine."

"Oh, good."

I looked at my sleep-deprived sister and her husband and shook my head. "I know she's cute and all, but are you guys sure this is worth it?"

"No," answered Chris without opening his eyes.

My sister picked up her head and threw a pillow at him. "She can hear you. Be nice, or she will pay you back when she's a teenager."

He groaned and tucked the pillow behind his head. "I don't want teenage daughters."

"Too late now." My sister rubbed her eyes and stood up. "I need to get some food."

"I'll get it, babe," Chris said, rising to his feet. "You rest."

"Thanks." She looked over at me. "Are you good with her for a few minutes? I'd love to lie in my own bed and close my eyes."

"I'm fine. Go ahead. You look like you could use the beauty sleep anyway."

"You're the best. I mean, you're a total dipshit, but you're the best." She walked like a zombie toward the stairs.

Carefully getting up off the couch, I followed Chris into the kitchen and stood there holding the baby while he rummaged through the fridge. "I think your mom made soup or something—aha, there it is." He pulled a container out, took the top off and smelled it. "Mmm. Real food. Hospital food sucks."

"But everything went okay?" I asked. In my arms, my

newest niece sighed like she was completely content, and it nearly broke my heart.

"Yeah. All good." He poured some soup into a bowl and stuck it in the microwave. "What's new with you?"

"Not much." I didn't really want to talk about myself.

"How are things going with Meg?"

I hesitated, but decided to be honest. I had nothing to hide. I'd done the right thing. "They've . . . cooled off, I guess you could say."

"Oh yeah?" He scratched his head. "Why?"

"She's leaving tomorrow. No point in dragging things out."

"Oh." He dug around in the freezer and pulled out half a baguette in a Ziplock bag. "Think this is still good?"

"Sure, why not? Just stick it in the oven or something."

Chris shrugged, turned the oven on, and placed the baguette inside it. "Don't let me forget that's in there. I'll burn down the house."

The idea of a fire made me think about Meg's sexy 911 call, and I quickly shoved the memory aside. For fuck's sake, I was holding a baby. This was no time to think dirty thoughts. Rosie started to fuss and I began to bounce her a little, twisting back and forth at the waist the way Ethan and Violet had liked.

"I gotta admit, I'm kind of surprised," Chris said, taking a seat at the kitchen island and propping his head in one hand. "Nina and I thought maybe you guys would do a long-distance thing. Or maybe one of you would move."

"Nah." I kept bouncing and twisting, hoping Chris would drop the subject, although now that my mother knew what happened, Nina would know pretty soon too.

"You guys never even discussed it?"

"We did," I said. "And she offered to move here, but I said I didn't think that was a good idea."

Chris yawned. "Really, dude? Why not?"

"I *told* you already. Because there's no point," I said, feeling like I'd said this a hundred times in the last twenty-four hours. Why didn't anyone understand? "I'm doing her a favor by cutting things off now."

"How's that?"

"She wants marriage and kids, and I don't."

"Not ever?"

"Not ever." I was growing agitated, and I think the baby could tell, because she was getting fussy too. I put her up over my shoulder and patted her back. "Look, I know it's hard for all you guys with kids to believe, but not everyone is meant for it."

"I don't know. Looks pretty good on you, brother." Chris gestured toward the baby against my chest.

"Well, I don't want it, okay?" I'd told the lie a thousand times, so often that it had become my truth, but it had never put such an ache in my chest. "I'll have enough to deal with taking care of Asher."

"You don't want kids because of Asher?" Chris looked confused. "Is this about what Holly said?"

"No, goddammit. It's not because of Holly and it's not because of Asher, and everybody needs to stop trying to fucking analyze me."

"Okay, okay. Sorry I brought it up." The microwave went off and Chris got off his stool to go get the soup.

I watched him making lunch for his wife even though he was so tired he could hardly stand up and felt bad. "Look, I'm sorry. I didn't mean to be a dick to you. In a way, yes, it is about Asher. Someday, I'll be all he has. You've got your kids, and I've got him to worry about."

"Not really the same thing, though."

"Yes, it is. Your kids will always need you, and Asher will always need me."

"But what about what *you* need?" Chris opened the oven door and looked at the bread.

"I don't fucking need anybody," I said angrily.

"You know what, dude? I am too damn tired to argue with you." He closed the oven and stood up. "Now where do we keep the spoons?"

I stayed at their house a couple hours before heading home, and even though I had fun with the kids and Nina was grateful for the nap, I was still in a shitty mood. All I could think of was Meg. I fucking missed her, and it was killing me to think that she was still here and I couldn't be with her.

I felt like I needed to keep my hands busy, so I tackled some projects around the house—the slow shower drain upstairs, paint touch-ups on the front and back doors, laundry, the kitchen floor, vacuuming up dog hair. The entire time, I wondered how the wedding was going, what Meg looked like in her dress the color of cinnamon, whether she wore her hair up or down, whether she was having a good time or was miserable like me. Was there an empty chair next to her? Would she get mad every time she saw it? Would anyone ask her to dance?

I felt like punching him, whoever he was.

Around six, I ordered a pizza, and when it arrived, I sat in front of the TV with a beer again. Scrolling through channels, I happened to stumble upon an episode of Law & Order, and I nearly smashed the remote to bits. Instead

I moved on, trying to find something that suited my mood and didn't remind me of Meg.

Eventually I switched the TV off and leaned back on the couch. Renzo got off the floor where he'd been lying, picked up a toy and hopefully came over to nudge my legs, but I didn't feel like playing. "Sorry, buddy. Not now."

I hadn't felt this shitty since my dad died. I felt like I was losing Meg too. Did she hate me? Would she ever forgive me? Was I ever going to see her again? There was only one other time I could remember asking myself that question— right before I left for boot camp. I recalled how she came over with cookies and a letter.

Without thinking, I got off the couch and went upstairs, Renzo on my heels. In my bedroom, I opened the closet door and reached for an old shoebox I kept on the top shelf. It was dusty and beat-up, and the corners had been taped together several times. But inside, the contents remained the same. Some old photos, awards and certificates I'd saved from school, family letters I'd saved from when I was deployed.

I found her letter toward the bottom, still in its plain white envelope. On the front she'd handwritten my name in blue ink, and beneath it in all caps, it said DO NOT READ UNTIL AFTER YOU LEAVE.

I pulled the letter out, sat down on my bed, and unfolded it. Immediately the photo she'd tucked inside fell into my lap. I held it up and looked at it.

Jesus. We were so *young*.

Someone had taken it at her graduation party, and we stood side by side, Meg in a white dress and me in a shirt and tie, because my mother had made me wear one. I look tall and gangly, and my hair, which I wore a little longer back then, had a stupid cowlick that never behaved. I have an arm around Meg, who looks beautiful, and she has both of hers around my waist, her hands clasped above my hip. We are both smiling.

I flipped it over. On the back, she'd written, *So you don't forget what I look like haha.*

Setting the photo aside, I picked up the letter. I probably hadn't read it in fifteen years, but once upon a time I'd practically known it by heart.

Dear Noah,

I can't believe you are leaving tomorrow!! I am going to miss you so much. It will be weird not to be able to hang around with you this summer, or call you when I have a problem I need you to fix haha.

Seriously, you are like the best friend ever, and I don't know what I will do without you. The past two years have been so much fun, and then there is that whole situation where YOU SAVED MY LIFE! I am so thankful you were there that day at the beach. I always will be.

Even though I am sad you are leaving, I understand why you want to go and I am SO proud of you. I will think of you every single day and pray that you do not have to go to Iraq. But even if you do, I know you will be safe because you are the bravest guy I know.

Don't forget me! I love you like a brother, Noah. Thanks for being so sweet to me. You'll always be my hero.

Love,

Meg Sawyer

I read it over several times, and the emotions I'd felt reading it for the first time hit me all over again. My throat tightened up. My chest hurt. I remembered feeling confused, torn between being sad I'd never even tried to kiss her and glad she thought so highly of me.

For a hot second, I'd thought about driving over to her house and kissing her goodbye just in case I never got another chance. I had no idea where in the world I was going to end up—Iraq was a pretty good guess—but even if I didn't get blown up by an IED, I sensed instinctively that she'd have a boyfriend at college pretty quick. She was going to Harvard, for fuck's sake. The guys there were going to be smart enough to see how amazing she was.

But I hadn't gone. I always wanted her to think of me as her hero, and I couldn't risk fucking that up.

Like I'd done this week.

"Christ, I was smarter at eighteen than I am now," I muttered, carefully folding the letter again and tucking it and the photo back inside the envelope.

As I placed the shoebox back on the shelf, I caught my reflection in the full-length mirror on the inside of the closet door. I turned to face myself.

I didn't like what I saw.

I tried squaring my shoulders. Lifting my chin. Sucking in my stomach. But it was no use. The same asshole stared back at me.

Angrily, I slammed the closet door and got ready for bed, even though it wasn't even nine. I just wanted this fucking day to end.

But I couldn't sleep.

I tossed and turned and cursed and fretted and kept checking the time. Nine o'clock. Ten o'clock. Eleven.

Christ almighty, I was exhausted. Why the fuck couldn't I sleep?

Because you owe her an apology, you jackass, said a voice in my head. *You treated her like shit today, and she's going to get on a plane tomorrow and hate you forever if you say nothing.*

But wasn't that better? Why shouldn't she hate me? I hated myself.

You used to be this girl's hero. She thought you were brave. Now you can't even get out of bed and go say you're sorry? Your dad would be ashamed of you.

"Okay, okay. Just shut the fuck up," I grumbled to the voice, throwing the covers off. "I'll get out of bed, I'll go say I'm sorry, I'll try *again* to explain why it's better if she doesn't stay here, but just shut the fuck up."

I glanced at my suit hanging in the closet, the one I'd planned to wear tonight, but ended up throwing on a pair of jeans and an army-green button down shirt. As I rolled up the sleeves, I checked my reflection again and wished I would have shaved today, but it was too late now.

I threw on a cap, grabbed my keys, and headed out. I had one goal—get her to forgive me.

Forgive me and *leave*.

Then I could sleep again.

Twenty-Six

Meg

FRANNIE'S WEDDING WAS BEAUTIFUL.

The entire farm was transformed. In the orchard where the ceremony took place, lanterns hung from the trees and candles lined the aisle. Garlands of autumn leaves were draped along the backs of chairs. The air smelled like hot apple cider and cinnamon.

Frannie had never looked happier as my father walked her down the aisle toward Mack, who struggled to keep his composure when he saw her. *My* composure was a lost cause—I'd held myself together right up until the ceremony, but as soon as the string quartet started, the tears began to flow. Next to me in the second row, Sylvia took my hand and we both blubbered shamelessly as our baby sister glided toward the love of her life. After my dad shook hands with Mack and sat down, April quietly slid onto into chair on my other side.

"Need a tissue?" she whispered. "I brought plenty."

"Thanks," I said. "I'm a mess."

I quieted down during the vows, but when the officiant pronounced them Mr. and Mrs. Declan MacAllister, I burst into tears all over again, clapping and crying at the same time.

In the bathroom, I mopped up my face, reapplied my mascara, and posed for family photos. I could only hope that I didn't look like a red-nosed reindeer in all of them.

At the reception, I sat at a table with my parents, Brett and Sylvia, April, and Henry DeSantis, the winemaker at Cloverleigh. There were two empty chairs—one for Noah, and one for Henry's wife. I'd told my mother that Noah was with his family tonight, since his sister had just had a baby, and she seemed to believe the lie. Henry had said his wife had a migraine.

"I'm sorry Renee isn't feeling well," my mother said to Henry at dinner.

"Thanks. She'll definitely be sorry she missed all this, but she's . . . she hasn't been herself lately." He seemed embarrassed by what he'd said and quickly dropped his attention to his plate of prime rib, and April and I exchanged a look. She shrugged slightly, which told me that she wasn't sure what he meant.

"Well, tell her we missed her." My mother smiled at Henry. "And we need to have the two of you over for dinner again soon. It's been ages, hasn't it?"

Henry, a tall and lanky guy who looked like he might have been a cowboy in an old Hollywood western, reached for his bourbon on the rocks and took a sip. "Actually, Daphne, Renee moved out. She and I are separated."

My mother's jaw fell open, her cheeks coloring, and I knew she was mortified that she'd brought Renee up. "Oh. Oh my goodness, I had no idea. I'm—I'm sorry, Henry."

"It's okay. I didn't say anything because—well, with the wedding and everything, I didn't want to put a damper on anyone's mood." He looked around the table, clearly uncomfortable. "Sorry to break it to you here at your happy family occasion."

"The timing is my fault," my mother said. "No need for you to apologize at all."

After dinner, Sylvia and I went to the ladies room together, and she asked me if I knew what happened.

"No clue," I said, digging though my bag for my lipstick. "But what the heck is in the water these days? Can *no* relationship survive?"

She sighed. "I don't know. I hope so."

"How are things with Brett?" I asked, reapplying the crimson lip color I hoped would brighten up my face.

"Fine, I guess. He's not saying much. Checking his phone a lot." She held up her wrist, where a diamond bracelet glittered. "He gave me this to apologize for being late."

"Pretty."

"Yes. It is." She dropped her arm. "But I'd have been fine with a sincere *I'm sorry* and a hug."

I stuck my lipstick back in my bag. "I wish I had words of wisdom for you, Syl. But I'm barely keeping it together tonight." Our eyes met in the mirror and I struggled to keep mine from misting over.

"No word from him?" she asked.

"Nope." I looked at my bloodshot eyes. "Hard to believe we managed to destroy a nearly twenty-year friendship in just a few days, but we did."

She rubbed my arm. "Maybe once some time goes by, you can repair it."

"Maybe." But my feelings were so hurt, it was hard to imagine I'd ever be able to talk to him again the way we used to. He hadn't even seemed like the same person by the end of our argument.

We went back to our table, where I picked at a piece of cake, drank hot tea with lemon, and watched happy couples on the dance floor. The hours dragged, but I didn't feel like I could cut out early. I had to keep reminding myself that this day was bigger than my disappointment. I still had a great job, good friends in DC, and if Frannie and Chloe could find love, then I could too. I would find a new place to live, stop saying yes to everything, and enjoy my down time more. I'd get back to working out regularly and maybe even pick up a new hobby or find a new cause to support. That always got me fired up.

I'd get that vibrator too.

I checked the time again—almost eleven-thirty. I'd promised myself I'd stay until midnight, which was when the band stopped.

"Meg. Is that Noah?" April nudged me with her elbow.

My stomach flipped. "Where?"

"Over there by the door."

I looked over at the entrance to the barn, and sure enough, it was him. "Oh my God. What's he doing here?"

"Go find out," she whispered.

I rose to my feet and began walking toward him, one hand on my stomach, which felt like it was on spin cycle. My heels suddenly felt two inches higher, and I wobbled on them, feeling completely off balance.

He watched me approach, his expression serious and his hands clenching into fists at his sides. He looked gorgeous and rugged in jeans, boots, and a cuffed-up army-green shirt, his chest straining against the buttons.

You should have been here with me, I thought. *You should be wearing a suit and sitting in that empty chair next to me and refusing to dance every time I ask you. You should be here making me laugh and teasing me for my tears at the ceremony and looking so good I can't keep my hands off you. We should be together.*

But when I finally got close enough to say something, I couldn't find it in my heart to get angry at him—not because he didn't deserve it, but because I was emotionally wrung out.

"What are you doing here?" I asked quietly.

"God, Meg. You look . . ." He struggled for words.

"Upset?" I suggested.

He shook his head. "I was trying to come up with a better word than beautiful. But it's all I can think of when I look at you."

"Thank you," I replied tightly.

"Is there somewhere private we can go to talk?" He glanced over my shoulder at the crowded dance floor.

Did I want to be alone with him? I had to think about it.

"Please," he said, seeing my hesitation. "I need to say something to you, and I can't think with all the noise and people around."

"Fine. Follow me." I led the way, heading past the bar, down a back hallway to a storage room. It was fairly empty since all the tables, linens, and many of the other decorative props we had for weddings were in use. I snapped on the light, and Noah shut the door behind him. The music and conversational hum from the reception softened.

"Thanks," he said.

I crossed my arms. "What do you want to say?"

He swallowed and nodded. Readjusted his cap. Fidgeted. "Meg, I'm sorry," he finally blurted. "I feel like shit about what happened."

"Is that it?"

"Well, yes."

"Apology accepted. Goodnight." I moved for the door and he caught me by the elbow.

"Wait. Please." He took a breath and closed his eyes for a second. "There's more."

I pulled my arm from his grasp and hugged myself. Stood with one foot crossed over the other. "Okay."

"I don't think I explained myself very well yesterday. You caught me off guard when you said you might move back, and what you got was a gut reaction."

"But was it honest?" I asked. "Is that the way you feel?"

"Yes," he admitted, "but—"

"Then I think you explained yourself just fine, Noah. There's no confusion." My eyes filled. "I didn't want to say goodbye, and you did."

"But it's not because I don't care about you." His expression was agonized as he took me by the shoulders. "You have to know that. I've never felt about *anyone* the way I feel about you. No matter where I go or who I'm with or how long we're apart, I never stop thinking about you. I never stop wanting you. I've always loved you."

"Bullshit," I said, unable to stop the sobs from escaping. I shook my head. "If you loved me, you wouldn't have taken my heart and crushed the life out of it yesterday. You would have given us a chance."

He gripped my shoulders harder. "You don't understand. I can't be what you want. I can't give you everything that you deserve. I can't make you happy."

"That's a choice you're making!" I cried. "It's not that you can't, it's that you *won't*."

"It's the same either way. And it's not going to change." His voice lowered to a whisper. "Please don't hate me for it."

"I'll never hate you," I wept helplessly, tears streaming down my face. "I love you too much."

He pulled me into his chest and held me so tight, I could hardly breathe. I clung to him, crying into his shoulder, my tears, lipstick and eye makeup smearing all over his shirt. "I'm sorry," he kept saying, his voice breaking over the words. "I'm sorry. I wish things were different."

It only made me cry harder. I forced myself to break away, wrenching myself from his arms. "So do I, Noah. I'd hoped this would be only the beginning for us. But instead, this is goodbye."

Without giving him a chance to stop me, I turned from him and ran from the room.

Twenty-Seven

Noah

MY GUT INSTINCT WAS TO CHASE HER, BUT I SHUT IT down. Like she'd said, this was my choice, and I had to be willing to watch her walk away.

But it felt like knives being thrown into my heart.

She was so damn beautiful. And that dress—oh my God, I'd nearly dropped to my knees at the sight of her in it. She'd said it was long, but she hadn't mentioned the thigh-high slit in the front. And she'd said it had sleeves, but she'd neglected to tell me the neckline plunged so low. I don't know how I'd have survived sitting next to her all night without wanting to get my mouth on her bare skin.

She'd worn her hair down, too, in soft golden waves that looked like silk. When I took her in my arms, I'd breathed in the scent of it and wanted to stop time.

I was so fucking angry at myself for hurting her. Had I made things worse by showing up here tonight? I'd only wanted to tell her I was sorry, make sure she knew how I felt. I didn't want her going back to DC thinking I was a callous asshole that didn't care. I'd thought that by telling her I loved her, somehow it would absolve me.

But it hadn't. If anything, I'd only made it harder to let her go.

Fury and self-loathing surged through me. "Fuck this," I said, storming out of the room. Spying a back exit, I headed for it, glad I wouldn't have to run into anyone on my way out. Because fuck everyone. Fuck this week, the mistakes I'd made, the friendship I'd ruined, the heart I'd shattered.

Fuck my own heart too.

And fuck love.

Despite the fact that I had to get up for work in about six hours, I drove straight to a dive bar on the outskirts of town, parked myself on a stool, and proceeded to get stinking drunk. I talked to no one, and no one dared talk to me. If I sensed anyone even looking in my direction, I gave them a *piss off* stare. I wanted to be alone with my misery. I wanted to numb this pain and punish myself for what I'd done.

By last call, I was good and fucked up, slurring my words as I ordered one last whiskey.

"Okay. And then I'm gonna call you a cab, deputy." The bartender gave me a no-bullshit look. "No driving for you."

"I can call my own cab," I scoffed, irritated I'd been recognized. Couldn't I even go out and get shitfaced like a regular guy? "I don't fucking need anyone to do anything for me."

The guy poured my whiskey and set it in front of me. "Suit yourself."

I yanked my phone from my pocket and was just about to get myself a ride home when I noticed that fucking bastard I'd interviewed at the hospital standing near the door, drinking a beer and laughing.

Something took over me, and I couldn't stop myself. Fueled by righteous anger and a fuck ton of whiskey, I crossed the floor in three long, angry strides and spun him around by the shoulder.

"This is for your daughter, asshole," I snarled before throwing my fist at his face. A sickening crack told me I'd likely broken his nose, but that didn't stop me from moving in again and delivering a violent jab to his solar plexus, which sent him over backward, gasping for air. I stood over him threateningly. "And *that* was for me."

Someone grabbed me before I could do any more damage, and I was tossed into a back office and told to sit down and stay quiet.

I threw myself into a chair and flopped forward over the desk, wondering if I'd wrecked my friendship with Meg and my career in one day.

Then I passed the fuck out.

A couple hours later, I was handed a cardboard cup of coffee, driven home by another deputy in the sheriff's department, and told to take tomorrow off. Lucky for me, this would all be swept under the rug. The responding officers, friends and co-workers of mine, had told the jerk-off I'd hit to go home and shut up, and assured me the agency would pretend the whole thing had never happened.

But I knew I'd fucked up. And I felt like shit—not for punching the guy, because he'd deserved it, but for losing control.

This was why you couldn't let emotions drive you. They were dangerous. They made you weak.

Exhausted and miserable, I trudged up the stairs and fell into bed, my heart and my head and my hand aching.

Tomorrow was going to suck.

But at least she'd be gone, and I could go back to being who I was before.

No matter how much it hurt.

Twenty-Eight

Meg

APRIL DROVE ME TO THE AIRPORT AFTER THE WEDDING brunch, which I barely touched.

"Did you sleep at all?" she asked, her voice full of sympathy.

I shook my head and took a sip from a travel mug full of hot black coffee, which Sylvia had thrust into my hands on the way out. "Not really. Which is why I'm keeping these sunglasses on all day." My eyes were bloodshot and puffy, with deep purple circles beneath them.

After I'd gone back to our table last night, I'd quickly grabbed my purse and bolted for the door. Luckily, my parents had been elsewhere, and Sylvia's family had already left. Just Henry and April had been left at the table, and April had given some excuse to Henry and followed me back to the house. Up in my bedroom, I'd cried on her shoulder for a solid hour, telling her that Noah showed up to apologize and tell me he loved me, but hadn't changed his mind.

"Mom say anything to you this morning about why you left without saying goodbye last night?"

I sighed. "Yeah, but I just said I was tired. I think she knew something was up though. Just now, she gave me this extra long hug and told me she only wants me to be happy." I sipped again. "As if it were a simple thing."

"I think it is for some people. Look at Mack and Frannie. Chloe and Oliver. Mom and Dad."

"But look at Sylvia and Brett. Henry and Renee. Noah and me."

"I'm trying to cheer you up here, Meg."

"I don't think it's possible today. Sorry."

April glanced at me. "You going to be okay?"

"Eventually. I know you probably think I'm crazy, getting my hopes up so high after just a few days. But I really thought things with Noah were going to work. I thought he was the one."

"I don't think you're crazy. You love him. That's how you're supposed to feel. What's crazy is that he loves you too, but you're still getting on a plane today. That's the part I don't understand."

I bit my lip. Unwilling to betray Noah's confidence, I hadn't told April what Noah had confessed to me about feeling so guilty over Asher's disability that he had to deny himself things he wanted. That it was his way of atoning for a sin he hadn't committed but believed he should suffer for.

I'd only said that he admitted he loved me but didn't want the same future I did. "Sylvia says I'm better off knowing now."

"I guess that's one way to look at it," she said. "But it doesn't make it hurt any less, does it?"

"No. It sure doesn't.

At the departures drop-off, April hugged me tightly and

told me to call her anytime if I needed to talk. I flew home and went back to my lonely apartment, putting myself to bed without eating dinner or even unpacking.

It felt like the same old story.

He loved me, but not enough.

I went back to work and put in long hours to catch up on everything I'd missed. I renewed my gym membership and made sure to run a few miles at least three times a week, and I signed up for a 5K race for a children's charity. I started lifting some weights at the gym too, hoping the added physical strength would translate to my mental and emotional well-being. I allowed myself a Twinkie here and there.

But I still struggled.

I accepted invitations from my girlfriends to go out and be social, but my heart wasn't in it. I turned down a couple dates. There was no one who could compare to Noah.

"Just give yourself time," April said over the phone. "It's only been a couple weeks."

"Has it? God, time goes slowly when you're miserable." I took a breath. "Have you seen him?"

"Once," she said. "At the grocery store."

"How did he look?" I asked.

"Terrible."

I sighed. It didn't even make me feel better to hear it.

"How's the apartment hunt going?" she asked. "Find anything yet?"

"Not yet." Truth be told, I hadn't even hunted all that hard yet. And I needed to, because Brooks had texted that because living expenses in Manhattan were so high, he could really only afford to cover half the rent for this apartment through November.

"You know, you could still move back here," April said. "If you really want to. It doesn't have to be for him—it could be for you."

"I know. But I don't think I could handle it. Seeing him would just be too hard."

"I understand," she said. "Hang in there. Things are bound to get better with time."

I really hoped she was right.

Twenty-Nine

Noah

I T HAD BEEN NEARLY TWO WEEKS SINCE I'D SEEN MEG.

Nothing felt right. Not sleeping in my bed alone, not running in the park, not even my bones beneath my skin. She hadn't called or texted, and I was too ashamed to reach out. I told myself that I'd been half in love with her for sixteen years and it was going to take some time to get over that, but I couldn't see my way clear.

I was messed up over her, and I didn't know how to get out from under it.

It was Asher who offered me a distraction.

The day before the 5K race for veterans in need of service dogs, I took Asher to adaptive swim class and finally got to meet Alicia in the rec center lobby when it was over. She emerged from the ladies' locker room in a motorized wheelchair, and like my brother had said, she had long red hair, which was wet and hanging down to her shoulders in ringlets, and freckles across the bridge of her nose and cheeks. She was in her mid-twenties, and her face lit up when she saw Asher waiting for her.

She reached out to shake my hand after Asher

introduced us using his speech device. "It's nice to meet you," Alicia said.

"You too," I told her. "I've heard a lot about you."

She blushed. "Asher is sweet. He's going to help me edit some videos for my new vlog."

"Really? That's cool." I glanced at Asher, who was staring at Alicia like a kid in a candy shop. It was kind of funny actually. "What's your vlog about?"

"Well, I'm studying to be a forensic scientist, so I want to teach people about the different ways crimes are solved using forensic evidence. And I also want to encourage people, especially kids, with disabilities to go after their dream careers, even if they think it's not possible."

"That's awesome," I told her. "I'm in law enforcement, so let me know if I can be of any help."

"Thanks. We're trying to figure out the best place to work right now," she said. "My house is pretty noisy because I've got four younger siblings. And neither of us drives, so meeting up is a little challenging."

"I can drive Asher anywhere."

"I've told him I can come to his house too." She glanced at my brother, who suddenly took an interest in his shoes. "But I don't know if that would work."

"Uh, I'll check it out," I said, wondering what the hell Asher was thinking. Was he too shy to invite her over? "There's always my house too. I've got a dog, but he's pretty quiet most of the time. And I can take him to the park while you're working."

She smiled. "Well, it was nice to meet you, Noah. I better go see if my ride is here."

"Nice to meet you too, Alicia. Take care." I smiled and watched her turn and head toward the accessible doors, and when I faced Asher again, he'd already tucked his device back into his messenger bag and was walking in the opposite direction, toward the stairs and main door.

"Hey," I said, catching up with him. "Why don't you want to have her over?"

He didn't answer me, and I wasn't sure if I should push it or not. But once we got in the car and I'd started the engine, he took his device out.

"Can I talk to you?" he asked.

"Of course, Ash. You know you can always talk to me." I looked over at him, feeling a sympathetic tug. I knew what it was like to be attracted to someone and wonder if she liked you back. But this girl liked him—I could see it. "Is it about Alicia?"

"It's more about Mom."

"Mom?" Frowning, I signaled and changed lanes. "What about her?"

"She embarrasses me. And she'll do it in front of Alicia."

I grimaced. "Yeah, Mom can be intense."

"I keep trying to ask her about getting my own place, but she won't listen."

My jaw nearly hit my chest. "You want your own place? I didn't know that."

"I didn't used to. But now I do."

I was still processing it when he went on.

"When I tried it before, I was not in a good place. I could not get a job, and I was scared. But I have a good job now, and I have much more confidence. They even offered me more hours. Mom doesn't want me to take more, but I would like to."

"She worries about you getting too tired."

"I know. But I will get tired whether I work more or not. And more hours will mean more money. I will be able to afford something on my own, even if it isn't fancy."

I was still trying to wrap my brain around this. "So have you asked Mom about moving out?"

"I have asked her a couple times. I have been thinking about it for a while, but after Dad died, I didn't want to leave her alone. And she gets upset when I bring it up. Or when I tell her that I don't need help with every little thing. That is why I have not mentioned it to you. I don't like to upset her."

My internal temperature was shooting up. I understood that she was lonely after my dad died, but she couldn't expect Asher to fill that void. If he wanted more independence, he should have it. "God, Ash. I'm sorry. I wish I had known. I just assumed you liked living at home."

"It's not that bad. But I am thirty-three. I am ready to try living on my own, even if she is not ready to let me," he went on.

"Do you have somewhere in mind?"

"I have done some research online, and there are a few places where I could live independently but get support when I need it, which is not as often as Mom thinks."

I nodded.

"I have never even been on a date. I have never been alone with a girl I like, and I want to know what it's like. Can you help me?"

"Yes," I said, proud of him for facing his fears and moved that he was asking for my help. "I can. I have that race tomorrow, but afterward I promise to talk to her."

"Thank you. I wish I could run in that race with you."

"Maybe you could walk it. I'd walk with you."

"I could walk a little way, but I would not be able to finish. And I don't have the right kind of power chair for a race."

My throat closed up as I stopped at a light and watched a man cross the street pushing a jogging stroller, his wife next to him, their dog walking ahead.

Then I had an idea.

"Wait a minute. I think I know how you can do the race with me."

"Really?"

"Yes. Let me do some checking."

I dropped him off, went home, and made phone calls while taking Renzo for an evening walk. It took me a couple hours, but I finally located what I was looking for—an all-terrain, three-wheeled chair in which I could push Asher during the 5K. It would only be on loan from a local medical supply company, but they were happy to lend it for the cause. I'd pick it up at nine A.M, an hour before the race started. Then I contacted the person in charge of the event, making sure it was okay to enter Asher at the last minute. Not only did she say it was fine, she loved the idea of a more inclusive event and promised to work on promoting it that way in the future.

I texted Asher as soon as it was arranged.

Me: You are entered in the race. Do some stretches tonight!

Asher: Are you serious? But I can't run.

Me: Yes. Don't worry about anything. I've got you.

When I went to bed that night, I was the closest thing to happy I'd been in weeks.

But all I wanted to do was share it with Meg, and I couldn't.

The next day, Asher, Renzo and I took part in the race, with my mom, Nina's family, and tons of people in the community cheering us on from the sidelines. I even saw a couple of Meg's sisters in the crowd, and they waved at us enthusiastically. I waved back, but inside, my heart was breaking all over again. I wished more than anything she could have been there running beside us. Her absence felt all wrong.

Later, I took my mom and Asher out for Italian. Watching my mom cut my brother's spaghetti, I said, "Ma, you don't need to do that for him. He can do it."

"I don't mind," she said, and went right on doing it.

Asher said nothing, but he looked at me, and I understood.

"Ma, Ash and I have been talking a little."

"Oh?" She picked up her wine and sipped.

"Yeah." I cleared my throat. "What do you think about looking around for an apartment for him?"

"Don't be silly. He's got a place to live."

"That's *your* place."

"I'm not going anywhere. And I like having him there. Besides, he needs me."

"But it might be good for him to have some—"

Right then Asher accidentally knocked over his water, which wasn't that big a deal and happened occasionally because of his muscle spasms, but the timing was unfortunate.

The conversation was derailed as my mother cleaned up the table and dabbed at Asher's pants, and I didn't feel right bringing it up again at the table. But his defeated expression wrenched my heart.

When we got home, Asher said he was tired and went

to his room. I followed him a minute later, knocking on his closed door. "Ash?"

He opened it.

"Can I come in?"

He shrugged and went to sit on his bed.

"Sorry that didn't go as planned." I leaned back against his computer desk.

He spoke without the use of his device. "It's okay. I haven't had luck either."

I frowned. "No, it's not okay. And I'm going to try again."

"She'll say no." The words were tough to decipher, but I understood.

"She can't say no, Asher. You're a grown man."

He pulled his SGD onto his lap. "She'll say I can't handle it. And she could be right."

"But she doesn't get to just decide that for you," I said angrily. "You get to choose what you want to do with your life. I'm going to talk to her again." Getting off the desk, I went to the door and opened it.

"Noah."

I turned to look at him over my shoulder. "Yeah, bud?"

"Have you talked to Meg?"

"No," I said.

"You should say you're sorry."

I shook my head. "That won't fix it."

"What will fix it?"

"I don't know," I said.

"I think you do."

I stared at him, and he stared back for a full ten seconds, almost like he expected me to argue, but then he plugged his device into the charger.

I walked out, pulling the door shut behind me.

I found my mother making tea in the kitchen. "Is he ready to get undressed?" she asked, stirring in a teaspoon of honey.

"Yes, but let him do it himself. He *is* capable."

"I know, but it takes extra effort, and he's already exhausted." She went to move past me but I blocked the entrance to the hall. "Noah, let me by." She tried to push me aside, but couldn't.

"No, not until we have a serious conversation about what you're doing."

She stuck her hands on her hips. "What am I doing?"

"You're sabotaging Asher's efforts to be more independent."

"What? I am not!"

"Come on. He'll hear us." I went through the kitchen into the front room, half-expecting her to dart back to Asher's room once I was out of her way, but she followed me.

"What's all this about?" she demanded.

"This is about you using Asher as an excuse not to move on with your life," I told her.

"Don't be ridiculous," she huffed.

"It's true, Ma. I love you, and I know how hard this is, but you can't keep Asher here because you need him to need you. It's not fair."

Her face burned with anger. "I don't know what you're talking about."

"Yes, you do. Dad wanted Asher to live on his own, Ma. I remember the conversation. He wanted Asher to have some independence so you could too."

"Your father had unrealistic expectations," she snapped.

"And it doesn't matter anyway, because now he's gone. I've got no need for independence."

"Yes, you do, but even if you put that aside, think of Asher's needs. Put him first."

She reacted as if I'd slapped her. "I have *always* put the needs of my children first. It's how I love them, by taking care of them!"

"If you love him, honor his wish, Ma." I took a breath, reminding myself to stay calm for Asher. "He wants to leave."

"Are you putting that in his head?" She crossed her arms. "He never wanted to leave before."

"No, this was all his idea. He came to me. Getting a job and being good at what he does has boosted his confidence. You should be happy about this."

"But what if something happens?" she cried. "What if he falls or has a seizure or needs help or—or what if people out in the world are just mean to him because they don't understand?"

Moving forward, I took her gently by the shoulders. "He's not a child anymore, Ma. And he doesn't want to be treated like one! And who knows? Maybe he'll hate being on his own and want to move right back home, but the point is—you have to let him make that choice." I let go of her. "If you ask me, you could take a page from his book."

Her arms came undone, and her chest puffed out. "And what's that mean?"

"It means he's choosing to face his fears and get out on his own even though it's going to be hard. And you're choosing to remain here focused on caring for him instead of living your life."

"Well, you're one to talk!"

I frowned. "This isn't about me."

"Oh no?" Her eyes took on a shrewd look. "What really happened with Meg Sawyer, Noah?"

"Stop it."

"And don't give me any nonsense about not wanting to be anyone's boyfriend. You're in love with her, and you know it! And you've been miserable since she left. So why did you push her away?"

"It's none of your business," I snapped.

"My children are always my business," she snapped right back. "And like it or not, I'm your mother. I know you. And I know what you're doing. I've always known."

"What are you talking about?"

She moved closer to me, pointing a finger. "You're afraid to let yourself be happy because you feel so bad about the gifts God gave you. I saw it when you were a kid and I see it now. But it's not right, Noah. You need to stop blaming yourself."

"You don't know what you're talking about." But my heart was pumping hard, and I raised my voice. Her words were a little too close to home. "All I'm doing is trying to help Asher, and trying to honor my promise to Dad. Before he died, he *told* me not to let you run yourself into the ground caring for everyone but yourself. He made me promise I'd see to it that you got on with your life."

"Well, you know what he said about you?"

I said nothing, my chest tight with anger, my breath coming hard and fast.

"He said to me, Carol, don't let that boy suffer all his life. Don't let him punish himself for things that were in God's hands. Tell him he deserves to be happy."

"I am happy!" I roared, although I knew how ridiculous

it sounded. "And I don't need you or Meg or Asher or Nina or Chris or even Dad's ghost breathing down my neck telling me I'm not!"

I turned and headed for the front door. I didn't need to listen to this. Here I was trying to do something for Asher, and somehow she'd turned it around on me. How come every time I tried to do the right thing, it fucking backfired on me?

At home, I took Renzo for a fast-paced walk to work off a little steam. My blood was boiling.

How dare she? I thought to myself with every angry stride. How dare she throw my dad's last words about me in my face? She was the one who needed to change the way she thought, not me! I'd never been so furious in all my life.

I was mad at my parents for knowing me so well, for being able to somehow read my thoughts and feelings. Had I been so transparent?

I was mad at my mom for her incessant nagging about my personal life. Would she ever get off my back and leave me alone?

I was mad at my dad for dying and leaving me to fill his shoes.

I was mad at Nina and Chris, for getting everything so right and making it look so easy.

I was mad at Meg, for making me fall in love with her, making me trust her, and calling me out on my bullshit.

I was mad at myself, for fucking up at every turn, for failing and hurting people I loved, for being unable to find a way out of the mess I'd made.

The only person I wasn't angry with was Asher. I'd let him down tonight, but I wouldn't give up. In my mind I saw his face when I'd left his room earlier tonight, after saying I didn't know what to do to make it right with Meg. The certainty in his eyes as he'd said, *I think you do.*

When I'd looped the block, I stood in my yard, looking up at the dark October sky, and begged the stars for answers.

They were bright and beautiful and infinite.

But they were silent.

Thirty

Noah

THE NEXT NIGHT, I STOPPED BY CHRIS AND NINA'S HOUSE after work. It was a Sunday evening, and they were busy getting the kids ready for bed. Chris had Ethan in the tub in one bathroom, Violet and Harrison were spitting water at each other while brushing their teeth in another, and Nina was holding the baby in one arm and trying to pack school lunches for tomorrow with the other.

"Let me take her," I said, reaching for Rosie.

"She needs to burp," my sister said, gratefully relinquishing the squirming child.

"I can handle it." I put the burp cloth over my shoulder, gently hoisted Rosie up there, and patted her back while I paced the kitchen floor. Renzo hung out by the island, probably hoping Nina would drop a scrap or two. "Did you go to Mom's today after church?"

"Uh huh," she said, spreading almond butter on a slice of bread.

"Did she say anything about yesterday?"

"Uh huh." She moved on to another slice.

"So?"

"So what?"

"So whose side are you on?" I asked impatiently.

She didn't answer right away. She spread grape jelly on a slice of bread and matched it with one covered in almond butter. Then she peeled a banana and began slicing it. "When it comes to Asher, I'm on your side. Chris and I have always thought more independence would be good for him. I was thrilled to hear that he wants to try living on his own. In fact, we spoke with him in his room and told him we fully support him. We told Mom that too."

"Good," I said, feeling vindicated.

She placed banana slices on the remaining piece of almond-buttered bread. "But Mom is right about you."

I clenched my teeth. I'd had a feeling it was coming.

She peeked at me over her shoulder. "Don't you think?"

"I don't know what I think anymore."

"Yes, you do. You're just too stubborn to admit you were wrong."

I glared at her, continuing to pat Rosie's back. "Why is everyone so sure they can read my mind?"

Nina laughed as she stuck some grapes into small Ziploc bags. "You don't have to be a mind reader to know how you feel about Meg. It's obvious. And you don't have to be a math whiz to add things up—you guys finally hooked up, it was amazing, she offered to stay, you freaked out, and now you're miserable and regretting it. Am I missing anything?"

"Yes," I said stubbornly. "The part where I did what I thought was right because she wants to get married and have kids and I don't."

Nina gave me an *oh please* face and gestured to the baby in my arms. "Because you hate kids?"

"No, I love kids. But because—" My brain stumbled

over the next part.

"Because of Asher?" Nina turned around and leaned back against the counter. "Chris told me what you said. About us having our kids to care for and you having Asher. It's bullshit, Noah. And you know it."

"It is not," I insisted. "It's very likely he'll need to live with me someday."

"You're doing the exact same thing Mom is, using Asher as an excuse not to fully live your life. You're just projecting it onto the future, whereas she's doing it right now."

"It's not the same." But my words lacked fight.

"It's exactly the same. Both of you need to get over yourselves. Asher is finally ready to get out on his own and live his life on his own terms. Are you?" she challenged.

While I was thinking about it, Rosie let out an enormous belch.

My sister and I laughed together, and some of the tension diffused. "Impressive," I said. "Takes after her dad. I hope she's a better secret keeper. He wasn't supposed to tell you what I said."

"Don't be mad at him." Nina went to the pantry and pulled out a package of Oreos. "I was torturing him with questions that night and he was sleep-deprived. He just told me to get me to shut up and let him sleep."

I sighed, taking the baby from my shoulder and holding her out in from of me. "Everyone's against me, Rosie. I can't win."

Nina laughed, tucking cookies into tiny plastic containers. "Actually, you can, big brother. Go get her back. You two were meant to be together, and the sooner you stop fighting it, the happier you'll be."

The thought of getting Meg back, of being happy

together, filled my heart with excitement. But was it even possible?

"How?" I asked her, cradling Rosie against my chest. "I don't even know what to do. I was such an asshole about everything. I spent all this energy trying to convince her I couldn't be what she wanted. Now I'm going to turn around and say the opposite? Why should she believe me?"

"I'm not saying it will be easy, but you *know* her," Nina said. "Think about it. Try really hard to remember anything she said that might give you a clue as to what she really needs to hear to trust you again."

I kissed the top of Rosie's sweet-smelling head and rested my lips there for a moment. Maybe I *would* have this someday. Maybe it would be Meg and me making school lunches, in *our* kitchen (with Renzo still looking for scraps). Maybe we'd even have a couple little ones upstairs in bed already, or spitting water at each other, or asking for *just one more story*. I wanted it all, even the sleepless nights. Did she? Would she want it all with me? Could she imagine a life together for us in this small town, surrounded by family and friends? In a home where we went to bed together every night, her body tucked next to mine the way I liked?

The memory of holding her close in my bed, whispering secrets to each other in the dark, sent a spark shooting up my spine.

And just like that, I knew what I had to say.

Thirty-One

Meg

ANOTHER WEEK CRAWLED BY.

I was doing my best to put my body, mind, and spirits in a better place, but it wasn't easy. The one thing I had to look forward to was a surprise visit from April.

She'd called me on Friday afternoon and said she'd decided last-minute to purchase a booth at a wedding trade show in DC next week. The expo was Monday and Tuesday. If she flew in early on Sunday, could I spend the day with her?

I said of course and made sure my schedule was clear. Since I'd returned to DC, I'd been much better about leaving room in my planner for down time.

I offered to pick her up at the airport, but she said it wasn't necessary and asked if I'd meet her at her hotel. From there we could walk around downtown, see the sights, grab drinks and dinner, and catch up. I said that was fine. She was staying at the Mandarin, which seemed oddly pricey for April, but whatever—everyone deserves a splurge now and then.

She texted me Sunday around noon.

April: Hey, I'm here! My flight got in early and it's so beautiful, I can't stay inside. Meet me at the WWII memorial instead? It's walking distance from my hotel!

Great. Did she have to choose the one place in DC that reminded me of Noah?

Me: Okay. I'll be there in 20.

On the cab over to the memorial, I wondered how different things would have been if he had kissed me that day. But no matter how I tried to see our story play out another way, I couldn't. Our timing wasn't the problem. His feelings were.

But I paid the driver, promising myself there would be no tears today. As I walked toward the fountain, I vowed to put Noah McCormick out of my head, even if it was only for twenty-four hours. Stepping onto the stone plaza bordered by granite pillars and book-ended by two victory arches, I took a deep breath and looked around for my sister.

Since it was a weekend, the memorial was fairly crowded. It was a little chilly today, so I tightened my scarf and stuck my hands in my coat pockets to get them out of the wind. Searching the groups of tourists from one end of the memorial to the other, I didn't see anyone resembling April. I was about to pull out my phone and call her when I saw a man about ten feet away who reminded me of Noah. The same short, dark hair. The same broad shoulders. The same solid stance.

My breath caught as the similarities piled up.

The same chiseled jaw covered in scruff.

The same fire in his eyes as he moved toward me.

The same deep voice as he spoke my name.

My jaw dropped. "Noah?"

"God, I almost forgot how beautiful you are." Without

another word, he took my head in his hands, and kissed me full on the lips.

Someone in the crowd whistled.

I pulled back. "What are you *doing* here?" My heart was beating so fast.

"I came to slay a dragon."

"What?"

"I came to fight for you, Meg. I never should have let you go in the first place."

Tears filled my eyes.

His thumbs brushed across my cheekbones as he spoke quietly but forcefully. "Years ago when we stood right here, I wanted to kiss you. I wanted to tell you what you meant to me and take you in my arms. I wanted to tell you to wait for me, that I'd come back for you."

"You said—you said you couldn't be sure you'd even come back. I remember." The tears started to fall.

"I was scared. And stupid. I didn't think you wanted me, and I knew I didn't deserve you."

"Oh, Noah." I shivered, but I wasn't cold anymore. "I did want you."

"Let me tell you what I want." He spoke quietly but forcefully. "I want the chance to make you happy. I want to be the only one you'll ever love. And I will fight like hell every single day of my life to deserve it."

"Really?"

"Really." He pressed his lips to my forehead. "I love you, Meg. I want to be your hero again."

"You were always my hero, Noah." I looked up at him. "And you always will be."

He crushed his mouth to mine as we wrapped our arms around each other, oblivious to the howl of the wind or the hoots of the crowd or the rush of the fountains bedside us.

It was just Noah and me, starting our forever.

Finally.

"I still can't believe you're really here." I was lying next to Noah in his hotel bed, an arm and a leg thrown over his torso, our skin warm and damp.

"I'm here."

"Tell me again how you managed this."

He laughed. "I've told you like ten times."

"I know, but I love the story. And I need to memorize it to tell our grandchildren."

"Christ, I've got grandchildren already?"

I giggled. "Not yet. Relax. And tell me again."

"Well, I didn't manage it all on my own. I had help." He kissed the top of my head.

"From who?"

"April was a key player. I called her and explained the situation, and she was more than happy to help me plot and plan."

"I love April," I said with a sigh. "Although I can't believe she kept the secret from me."

"And then there was Nina. A conversation with her—in which she basically kicked my ass for being a stubborn jerk—prompted me to reach out to April. Also, Nina gave me her number."

"Sisters are the best."

"And Asher. Seeing him assert more control over his life has been amazing. He's the strongest, bravest person I know. I realized I want to be more like him."

"That might be my favorite part. I think we can all learn from Asher."

"Definitely. And what's crazy is that as much as I've tried all my life to protect and defend him, I've done a shitty job of really listening to him. Of treating him like I would any other brother. Which is really what he wants—not to be pitied or babied or so protected that he can't fail. He wants the chance to make mistakes, to fall down sometimes. Who are we to keep that from him?"

I kissed his chest. "And your mom is on board?"

"She has to be. Asher is a grown man capable of making his own decisions. He's conflict-averse, and he needed my help to get the conversation started, but they've been discussing it more. He showed her all the research he did, and apparently there are some new places that have opened up within an hour's drive of where he works. They're going to check them out this week."

"That's awesome."

"I can't say she's excited about it, but I do think she's coming around."

"Has she talked about traveling?"

"Still working on that."

I squeezed him. "Give her time. Things are okay between you and her? Sounds like it was a pretty big fight."

"Oh yeah. We're fine. She and I are a lot alike—we've got a temper, and we can blow up, but we don't hold on to being mad too long. It took us about a week to cool off and see things from one another's point of view, and we needed Nina to sort of mediate things at first, but we hugged it out. She's even watching Renzo for me while I'm here."

"Good."

"It helped that I was coming here to try and win you back. She was beside herself."

I laughed. "Oh yeah?"

"Yeah, I believe her exact words were something like, 'O most gracious Virgin Mary, thank you for not forsaking me.'"

"She prayed to the *Virgin* Mary for this?" I winced, looking down at our nakedness. "Doesn't seem right."

"Whatever. If she sees this as the answer to her prayers, so be it." He rolled on top of me, his hips over mine. "It's definitely the answer to mine."

I grinned, wrapping my arms and legs around him. "Mine too. Think Asher can help *me* find a place to live?"

"I think he'd love that." He lowered his lips to mine. "And you know you can stay with me while you look. Don't feel like you have to have everything perfectly in place before you come home."

"Thanks. I *am* working on trying to loosen my attachment to perfectionism."

"As someone who is definitely far from perfect, I fully support that effort."

"And I do want to move back sooner rather than later." I kissed his jaw, rubbing my lips along his scruffy chin. "I missed you so much."

"I missed you too." He buried his face in my neck and inhaled deeply. "Let's never be apart again."

"Deal. From now on, it's you and me."

"And Renzo."

"And Renzo," I agreed. "And my four sisters. Plus their significant others. And my parents."

"And my mother. And Nina's family. Plus Asher."

I giggled. "We might never get a moment alone."

"Oh no. We'll get plenty of those, no matter what." He rolled to his back, taking me with him so that I lay along the muscular length of his body. "I'll always be a family man. But *our* family will come first."

My heart thumped so hard against my ribs, I thought it might jump from my chest into his. "I love you so much. That means everything to me."

We kissed, our bodies igniting again, and I felt him growing hard and thick between us.

I smiled. "Do you think we'll ever get enough?"

"Hell no," he said, turning me beneath him again and easing inside me. "But I'll never stop trying."

"My hero," I whispered, before he crushed his mouth to mine.

And maybe there's no such thing as perfection, but that moment?

It came pretty damn close.

Epilogue

Noah

"YOU READY, BUD?" I SCRATCHED BEHIND RENZO'S ears. "This is a big day."

Renzo panted and wagged his tail, his tongue hanging out of his mouth. Pretty much exactly the way I got watching Meg get ready for bed at night.

We'd been living together for six months now—she'd moved back to Michigan right around Thanksgiving and stayed with me while she looked for an apartment or condo, but by Christmas I'd convinced her to give up the hunt. *You belong here with me*, I'd told her. *Stay.*

And she had.

"Come on, boy. Let's go. She's waiting for us." I grabbed Renzo's leash and we went out the back door. Meg was already at the event getting last-minute entrants registered for the 5K race she'd helped organize—a fundraiser benefitting the organization that provided service dogs for veterans. But what made this particular event really special was that Meg had worked tirelessly to make sure the race was totally inclusive. She solicited donations for racing push chairs for both kids and adults with special needs who wanted to participate, using her connections in Washington and her new job as a lawyer and advocate for a regional branch of the American Association for People with Disabilities.

A job Asher had helped her get, by the way.

He saw the posting on the website, sent it her way, and Meg got the position. She loved what she did, and felt like it was the perfect balance of legal work and fighting for justice. Did she make the salary she'd made in DC? Not even close. But she said she didn't care, because she got something more valuable than money out of the job.

She was still trying to get me to agree to run for sheriff, but I was content to enjoy life as it was for now. I hadn't written it off, but there had been a lot of changes in the past six months, and we all needed time to adjust.

Asher was living on his own in an adaptive home he'd found that offered 24/7 support if it was needed but encouraged as much independence as possible. He was working Monday through Friday, had gotten a raise, and saw Alicia at least a couple times a week. It wasn't romantic between them yet, he told me, but he was working up the nerve to kiss her.

"Just don't wait as long as I did," I told him. "It took me seventeen years to kiss Meg."

"Don't worry," he said. "I am much smarter than you."

He'd participate in the race today, as well as Alicia with one of her sisters, Nina and Chris, Meg's parents, Mack and Frannie, all three of Mack's girls, April and Chloe Sawyer, Chloe's fiancé Oliver, and Henry DeSantis, the winemaker at Cloverleigh. My mom was watching my nieces and nephews, but she planned to bring them to the event to cheer everyone on.

And to witness what would happen at the finish line.

Smiling, I patted the zip pocket of my running shorts once more before getting in the car.

The ring was still there.

Of course it was, I'd just zipped it in there less than five minutes ago. But I wouldn't feel a hundred percent at ease until it was on her finger.

"Okay, buddy," I said to Renzo as I started the engine. "Let's do this."

Meg

It was one of those spring Saturdays that felt like a gift. Temperatures in the sixties, bright blue sky, a few puffy clouds, and plenty of sunshine. The weather had been the one element of today that was not in my control, so all I'd been able to do was hope for the best.

And by some miracle, I got it.

Everyone's mood was sunny too. I'd never seen so many smiles at the starting line of a race. It was a little chaotic getting everyone all lined up since there were multiple start times and tons of strollers and push chairs and gait walkers, not to mention all the dogs. But we hadn't turned anyone down—and if it made the event a little more hectic to organize and get going, so be it.

I ran too, alongside Noah and Asher, who held Renzo's leash. We waved to family on the sidelines, encouraged those whose energy flagged, shared a kiss at the finish line and gave out high-fives as participants crossed it. I felt proud and happy and exhilarated. But by the time every entrant had completed the course, I'd lost Noah in all the celebration.

I searched for him in the crowd, but he was nowhere to be found. Spotting Asher talking to his friend Alicia, I jogged over to them. "Hey Ash, do you know where Noah is? I can't find him."

"No," he said, without the use of his device. I'd noticed him growing more confident with his own voice lately. "Maybe he's with my mom?"

"I'll check, thanks." I smiled at them before shading my hand with my eyes and scanning the area again.

Just then, I spotted Renzo trotting toward me. It was totally unusual for Noah to let Renzo loose in a crowd, so I got worried for a moment. "Hey, you." I knelt down to pet the dog, who sat obediently. "Where's your dad, huh?"

That's when I noticed the black bow tie Renzo was wearing.

I laughed. "You're so fancy," I told him. "Were you wearing this the whole time? How did I not see it?"

I looked closer at it—then I gasped. The bow tie had a tiny attachment with a snap hook at the end . . . and hooked to it was a diamond ring.

"Sometimes we don't see something right away." Noah's voice came from behind me. "Even if it's been there all along."

I jumped to my feet and spun around to see him standing right there. I covered my mouth with my hands.

"Come here, boy." Noah motioned for Renzo to come to him, and the dog obeyed. Removing the ring from the hook, Noah went down on one knee, and my stomach turned cartwheels. Was this a dream?

"I know it hasn't been that long, but then again, I waited seventeen years to put this in motion, and I promised myself I'd never waste that kind of time again."

"Oh my God," I said, my voice trembling and muffled behind my hands. A hush had fallen over the crowd.

"I didn't think I was the type to get down on one knee and ask somebody to spend the rest of her life with me, but dammit, Sawyer—you've got a way with me. And I can't live without it."

Happy tears filled my eyes.

He grinned at me. "You gonna give me that hand, or do I have to come get it?"

Laughing, I held out my left hand. "It's yours."

He slipped the beautiful, classic solitaire on my finger and kept my hand in his. "What do you say, Sawyer? Want to change your name to mine?"

"Meg McCormick," I said softly, wanting to weep and shout for joy at the same time. "I like it."

"Does that mean you'll marry me?"

"Yes," I said, unable to stop laughing even as the tears fell. "Yes!"

He stood up and embraced me, and people around us cheered. But we only kissed for one blissful moment before our families accosted us with hugs and tears and jubilant congratulations.

"Did you guys know?" I asked my sisters, all four of us wiping our eyes.

"I had a feeling," April said, "but I didn't know for sure."

"I was clueless!" Frannie exclaimed.

"I was clueless too," added Chloe. "But it was the best surprise ever!"

"It was," I agreed.

"Another wedding to plan." Frannie poked April's shoulder. "You up for it?"

"Of course." April beamed at me. "Just don't ask me to get you a cake made out of Twinkies."

I gasped. "That is an awesome idea!"

Noah came over and was accosted by my sisters, who all wanted to hug and kiss him. Then his family came over, with tears in their eyes and huge smiles and heartfelt congratulations. I was thrilled they were all here to share this day with us, but I was also dying to get him alone.

When it finally happened, back at home in our kitchen, he put his arms around me and held me tight.

"I'm so proud of you," he said. "I hope you know that."

"I do. Thank you for everything. Today was a dream come true." I held out my hand behind his shoulder and peeked at the ring he'd given me. "I can't believe I'm going to be your wife."

"Me neither. Can I still call you Sawyer, even after you change your name?"

I laughed. "Call me any name you want. Just call me yours."

"I will." He hugged me so close I felt his heart beat against my chest. "Now. And always."

THE END

Also by
Melanie Harlow

Acknowledgments

It would have been impossible to write this story without the help of K-9 officer David W. Cole, who so graciously and patiently answered all of my questions and shared stories about being on the job with his first dog, Renzo (for whom the dog in this story is named), and his current K-9, Merlin. Thanks as well to Joan Scribner for making the introduction. You can follow Merlin on Instagram at www.instagram.com/k9_merlin!

I would also like to thank Becky Brown for thorough and thoughtful answers to all my questions about cerebral palsy and so generously sharing her daughter's story with me. Many thanks also to Kelly Beckstrom for reading early and helping me ensure a realistic and respectful portrayal of CP, which looks so different in everyone. My gratitude as well to Mindi Adams for taking an early peek with law enforcement eyes. Any inaccuracies relating to police work are solely my fault—sometimes I needed things to go a certain way for the romance, even though it's unlikely a cop would actually leave his back door unlocked at night…

As always, my love and gratitude to the following people for their talent, support, wisdom, friendship, and encouragement…

Melissa Gaston, Brandi Zelenka, Jenn Watson, Hang Le, Devyn Jensen, Kayti McGee, Laurelin Paige, Sierra Simone, Lauren Blakely, Corinne Michaels, Sarah Ferguson and the entire Social Butterfly team, Anthony Colletti, Rebecca Friedman, Flavia Viotti & Meire Dias at Bookcase Literary, Nancy Smay at Evident Ink, proofreaders Michele Ficht, Shannon Mummey, and Alison Evans-Maxwell, Stacey Blake at Champagne Book Design, Andi Arndt & Katie Robinson at Lyric Audiobooks, narrators Stephen Dexter and Savannah Peachwood, the Shop Talkers, the Harlots and the Harlot ARC Team, bloggers and event organizers, my Queens, my betas, my proofers, my readers all over the world…

And especially to my family, for your endless patience, your smiles, your hugs, your unconditional love. You're everything to me.

About the Author

Melanie Harlow likes her heels high, her martini dry, and her history with the naughty bits left in. In addition to *Insatiable*, she's the author of over a dozen additional contemporary romances and a historical duet.

She writes from her home outside of Detroit, where she lives with her husband and two daughters. When she's not writing, she's probably got a cocktail in hand. And sometimes when she is.

Find her at www.melanieharlow.com.

(If she's not there, try The Sugar House.)

Made in the USA
Monee, IL
05 August 2021

75062591R00184